Lesbian
Travels

Lesbian Travels

A Literary Companion

~

EDITED BY
Lucy Jane Bledsoe

WHEREABOUTS PRESS   SAN FRANCISCO

Published in the United States by
Whereabouts Press
2219 Clement Street, Suite 18
· San Francisco, California 94121
www.whereaboutspress.com

Distributed to the trade by
Consortium Book Sales & Distribution

Library of Congress Cataloging-in-Publication Data

Lesbian travels : a literary companion / edited by Lucy Jane Bledsoe.
p.   cm.
ISBN 1-883513-07-3 (alk. paper)
1. Lesbians—Travel—Literary collections.
2. Americans—Travel—Foreign Countries—Literary collections.
3. Voyages and travels—Literary collections.
4. American prose literature—Women authors.
5. American prose literature—20th century.
6. Lesbians' writings, American.
I. Bledsoe, Lucy Jane.
PS648.L47L465   1998
810.8'0355—dc21   98–37807
CIP

10 9 8 7 6 5 4 3 2 1

Contents

"I am an American," wrote Gertrude Stein. In her vocabulary and the rhythms of her sentences, in her belief in the continuity of the present, and her optimism, she was very American. But she was also an American who did not entirely belong to her country.

"I have lived half my life in Paris," she continued, "not the half that made me, but the half in which I made what I made." The half that made her, the first half, made her a daughter, a sister, a coed. But it also made her a girl who did not graduate from Johns Hopkins, a girl who fell in love with another girl and didn't know what to do about it.

What she did was flee to Europe to rejoin her strange and similar and beloved brother. There, in Paris, safely away from the land of her birth and from the place where she had fallen in love, Stein wrote *Q.E.D.*, a novella based on the triangular relationship she'd had with May Bookstaver and her lover, Mabel Haynes.

Q.E.D. is the story of three women who have a painful entanglement while traveling across the Atlanic on steamer. The naive Adele, based on Stein, tells the more experienced Helen, "As for passion, you see I don't understand much about that." *Q.E.D.* was Stein's first full-length work. Written in 1903, it was composed in a kind of earnest realism Stein would put behind her as she reinvented American literature. It was also written from a kind of emotional anguish she would put behind her when she met the love of her life.

In 1907 Stein met Alice B. Toklas, another odd young woman

who was getting away from the expectations of American womanhood by traveling to Europe. They spent the following summer in Italy and when they returned to Paris, set up house. They lived together for the next forty years, until Stein's death in 1946. They only returned to America once, for a lecture tour, in 1934.

"Writers have to have two countries," Stein wrote in *Paris, France*, "the one where they belong and the one in which they live really." She could have written the same thing about lesbians. We have one country, one set of behaviors, one tradition in which we are raised and to which, for a time, we belong. This is the country of being daughters, of being young, dependent, pre-sexual innocents, of believing that our parents, our roles in our society, our jobs as girls are still correct.

But we as lesbians have another country, too, the one in which we "live really." This is the country we discover on our own, or with the guidance of another woman who teaches us the customs. This is the country we explore to discover an important part of ourselves, where we learn how to speak a language new to us, but that we understand immediately. It is a country where what our parents regard as strange and dangerous is familiar, welcoming, desirous to us. It is a country where we recognize our kind.

In 1974, my last year of high school, I was an exchange student. Under the auspices of an organization whose mission was to foster international goodwill, I spent a year in Europe. Usually we lived with families, but I was part of a new, experimental program and was placed in a boarding school. Most of the teachers in the school were unmarried women. They were smart and severe and did not wear makeup. Some of them, in fact, wore suits. Some of them lived with one another. It was an all-girls boarding school, and I was seventeen.

Something happened that first year away from home, and when I went back to the States after it, I was changed.

Maybe the change had to do with my age. I'd never had sex before that year. Maybe it had to do with the women I met. I'd never met so many women like them. But I also believe it had to do with the place. It had to do with not being in my native land, with being foreign. None of the people there had known who I was before. They didn't know who my parents were or the daughter I had been. I felt free to act like I hadn't before.

Like Stein, Toklas, and other women who have traveled away from home, it took leaving my native land to realize I was a lesbian. I had to leave the country that made me to begin to make myself.

The writers whose stories fill this collection begin their journeys knowing they are lesbians. They are fully aware that though they are sexual outsiders, they are also members of an international clan of self-made women. They have access to secret and glorious lesbian subcultures invisible to other travelers. These stories remind us that we are resilient, amazing women. We are able, though always foreigners, to create ourselves, to find one another, to make the world our home.

Rebecca Brown
JUNE 1998

When I was twenty years old, I traveled by boat across the Strait of Gibraltar, from the southern tip of Europe to the northern tip of Africa, where I planned to meet up with my girlfriend who was making a film in Tangier. Having traveled on my own for several months, my loneliness caused my bad judgment in accepting the companionship of an American soldier who bragged that he was transporting drugs in the soles of his sneakers. We sat side by side on the wooden third-class passenger bench throughout the long night at sea. He chatted amiably as if we were the best of friends, describing what he would do with his profits. I couldn't move away from him because there was nowhere else to sit in this small cabin reserved for third-class passengers. So I stayed with my drug-trafficking soldier, rocking miserably during that rough crossing, seasick and cold, imagining the insides of Spanish or Moroccan prisons.

I was out of my element. Way out. A lesbian traveling with a straight man, a civil disobedience-trained peacenik traveling with a soldier, both of us at sea traveling between two foreign continents. It was a scary night, but I don't regret a minute of that journey with my American soldier. As a traveler, what I want most is to get out of my cultural and geographical cage, or at least to get a view of it from a different angle.

Being a lesbian, a sexual border-crosser, allows me this outsider's perspective within my own country, which, in turn, opens me up to unique insights when I travel across other borders. As a devoted fan of travel literature, I have long wanted to read stories from my own lesbian perspective, writing that addresses the intersection of sexual identity and geographical exploration. In this first collection of lesbian travel writing, I have selected pieces in which the authors are not so much focused on their sexual identity as they are in using this identity as a lens through which to observe themselves and others. Here you will find pieces from all over the globe. Sonja Franeta travels some three thousand miles on the Trans-Siberian railroad with lesbian friends from Russia, Mariana Roma-Carmona returns home to Chile after an absence of thirty years, Nisa Donnelly finds herself in the midst of the Chiapas uprising, Sarah Jacobus comes out as a Jew among Palestinian activists in Gaza, Donna Allegra studies dance in Guinea, Marianne Dresser explores butch-femme roles in a Japanese lesbian bar, and in Alaska Susan Fox Rogers and her father discuss lesbian sex, to name just a few of the adventures found in these pages.

I received many more wonderful travel stories than I was able to include in this volume. Besides choosing diverse voices and travel destinations, I indulged my strong preference for nonfiction narrative—writing that tells a story. I looked for pieces in which the author is out as a lesbian and also learns something new about herself as a result of her travels. Finally, I included writing that explores the deeper meaning of boundaries—not just geographical, but cultural, sexual, intellectual, and even temporal.

Literature, like travel, is about crossing borders. The most exciting thing about borders is that by stepping over them, they cease to be barriers and become gateways. A border that can be crossed is a border that is no longer successful at containment and separation. Therefore, each new book read, each new geographical territory explored, expands the reader's and traveler's horizons. May your world grow a little bigger by traveling with these authors.

I am grateful to the many people who contributed to this

project, including all the authors who shared their stories with me. For taking an early, and crucial, interest in this project, a big thank you to Mary Bisbee-Beek. Susan Fox Rogers was especially generous with ideas (and even mailing lists) for soliciting work. For phone numbers, addresses, and guidance, I thank Brian Bouldrey, Michael Bronski, Katherine Forrest, Richard Labonte, Sarah Schulman, Jerry Thompson, and Barbara Wilson. A heartfelt thank you goes to David Peattie and Ellen Towell of Whereabouts Press for their hard work in helping to bring this project from proposal to book. Most of all, thank you to Patricia Mullan, my favorite traveling companion, for perennial consultation.

Lucy Jane Bledsoe
JUNE 1998

Barbara Wilson

Invisible

The shoes were two-toned, mahogany brown and dark navy, of pleasingly supple leather, with a rounded toe and a soft wide tongue over which the laces crossed with casual elegance. The soles were flexible yet strong, giving the foot a sense of ease and bounce along with support. The shoes made you feel you could do things you hadn't done for years, or had never done, like starring in a musical comedy or leaping over a river or a tall building. They were English shoes, too, which gave them even more mystery and desirability.

I'd told my partner Tere that we should buy her shoes when we were in England. I remembered from my many stays there that English footwear seemed to be generally wider than in the States. And Tere's feet are wide. "Hobbit feet," other kids called them in junior high. They still look like that—broad, chunky, with long toes—prehensile feet that seem made for gripping branches or vines in the jungle. Many of the women in Tere's family have these feet. When Tere and her sister Sparky met their long-lost half sister Linda, the first thing they did was ask her to take off her shoes. Linda obliged and the rejoicing was great.

Now we sat surrounded by eager saleswomen in a shop in Brighton on the south coast of England. It was the morning of a warm summer day. My old lover Kath, whom we'd been visiting in the country, had dropped us at the station so we could take the train to London. But we were lingering. London seemed too overwhelming, just as Paris had been: two enormous cities in the August heat. How pleasant it was just to sit and have kindly middle-aged women in serge skirts and low pumps bring us shoes to try on. In Paris Tere had bought a pair of sandals from a young man who had cast a shocked look at her hairy ankles before summoning a lowly assistant to fit her. Tere wore the sandals out of the shop, and two blocks later we were looking for French Band-Aids.

"You should get them," I urged her now. "Get a couple of pairs." Then I added, "I think I might get a pair too." To keep Tere company and not because I needed more shoes, I had tried on the same pair, though in other colors, including an extravagant red.

"Get the red pair," said Tere.

"I actually like the two-toned best."

"But I'm getting the two-toned."

"Well, I want them too," I said, my resolve now hardening.

"But then we'll have the *same* shoes," Tere said. She was the middle child with a sister only thirteen months younger, and she knew the necessity of keeping things separate. I was the older child in my family, with competition only from a younger brother.

"No," I said calmly, surveying my beautiful new feet. "I like *these.*"

"How will we be able to tell our shoes apart?"

"It's simple. Yours say '40' on the bottom, and mine say '39.'"

"We're merging," she joked gloomily.

But I thought that unlikely. It had been a common complaint among my women lovers that I didn't merge *enough.* I was always insisting on my boundaries and my separateness. On going my own way. Before Tere and I met up in Paris, I had spent a month traveling by myself in Scandinavia and northern Europe. It had been, truth to tell, a little hard to adjust to having her around again, even though back home, in our house, I was used to seeing her every day.

I had never been ambivalent about whether traveling alone

was better than traveling with a friend or lover, and I had defended my position many times. Traveling alone opened up possibilities for adventure and emotion that were not available when you had to decide what to do and where to go with another person, when you had to take her feelings into account, when you had to be available to her.

Earlier this trip I had visited my friend Ida in Bergen, then taken the coastal steamer up to Ålesund. It was the very same ship I'd worked on as a dishwasher over twenty years before, the *Kong Olav*, now one of the smaller vessels on the route and destined to be retired soon. I had taken, extravagantly, a cabin for the overnight trip, and just as extravagantly I had spread the contents of my bag over both bunks and the floor. I wanted to claim it entirely, though I'd hardly spent any time there—I'd been so excited about walking the decks and watching the spectacular coastline. I'd stayed up past midnight, gotten up at six, eaten an ice cream cone for dinner and pickled herring for breakfast, made drawings in my sketchbooks and written in my journal. And the whole time I never had to say a word to anyone, or explain how I felt, or do anything I didn't want to do.

But most of all, I had been anonymous and had felt invisible, and there is little I like better than to be on my own as an observer. To look at the world but not be seen myself. To not be *recognized*. I love to walk, unnoticed and a stranger, through a new landscape or town, or even in the streets of some vast city that I know well. Among the crowds I could be anyone—or no one. I can achieve this at home in Seattle, especially if I go to parts of the city where no one I know lives. Still, there is the chance of running into someone I'm acquainted with, of being seen and recognized. In foreign countries this possibility invariably drops to almost nothing.

This invisibility is only a fiction, of course. There are some places where I do fit in, where I look like the native population;

my grandmother was Swedish, and I have her coloring and eyes. When I'm in Scandinavia, especially Sweden, I look around and see my face. But in many other places, my clothes, my skin color, my accent or lack of language, my uneasy or too-free habits mark me as a tourist, an outsider. I am observed and pegged even at the moment when I feel myself most unseen. When I was younger, I was even less invisible, especially to men. They followed me down streets, demanding to know my name, where I was going, what my business was, and whether they could intervene in it. Now that I am middle-aged, that attention is mostly gone, though occasionally I find myself the focus of well-meaning people who wish to help me or take my money in some way.

What is important is not the reality but the *pretense* that I am invisible, that I am a ghost flitting by, that the substance of my body has disappeared so as to become more thoroughly concentrated in my eyes, ears, and nose, the better to take in the new world around me. This pretense offers the way to a loss of self, with all the baggage that entails. Roaming in foreignness, I find myself lighter, freer. Waked up. I lose my self-consciousness about what I look like and become what I see. Travel is a delight to me because of the very vividness of my sensations. Travel restores to me the childhood sense of marvel. Everything is new, is radiant, is shocking, is old, is stinky, is threatening, is glorious. This childhood delight in color and in smell is combined with a maturer sense of history, an aesthetic formed by culture. In an old district of Budapest, a faded ocher wall, still spattered with bullet holes, is beautiful in itself—but also because it makes me think about Veronica, a friend I had in college, whose family left Hungary for Peru in 1956. It makes me think about European history and its sadness. In the same way, the swell of the deep Atlantic off the Irish coast is breathtaking, but I can't stand there in the wind without thinking melancholy thoughts about all the Irish who had to emigrate.

The imaginative, associative, highly romantic part of travel (the pleasure of feeling sad—from a distance) has always livened up and made tolerable the other parts: the loneliness, the homesickness, the tedium, as well as the many fears travel stirs up—of getting on the wrong bus, going down the wrong road, making the wrong choice of who to trust. Romance, fear, heightened senses—all these go together with being on my own in some foreign place. Foreignness may now have lost some of its shocking unfamiliarity, since over the years I have been to some countries many times to live and work, and I have friends there with whom I stay or dine. Still, whenever I'm alone on the road, there are periods when I lose all sense of myself, when I am awake like a poem. Aware and alive, in some larger sense.

All this changes when I travel with someone else. When I travel with a lover. When I travel as a lesbian.

The day after we arrived in London from Brighton, I set off by myself in my new shoes, leaving Tere to her own devices. We agreed to meet up later at the hotel to go to a Proms concert at the Royal Albert Hall. It was a long day, a hot day, and by the time I returned to the hotel at five, my feet were killing me. I kicked off my new shoes (so much for being light and flexible) and went to take a shower. Returning to the room, I borrowed one of Tere's French Band-Aids and took a nap. When I woke up Tere was back, dressed to go out.

"Aren't you going to wear your new shoes?" she asked as I got ready.

"No, I need to switch," I said. "They gave me a blister today."

"Oh, good," Tere said, looking down with pleasure at her beautiful two-toned feet. "As long as we don't wear them at the same time, it will probably be all right. . . ."

But on the long walk from the South Kensington tube station to the Royal Albert Hall, she complained, "These aren't as comfortable as I thought they'd be."

"I know," I said. "I think it's partly the heat."

When we found our seats, high up in the hall, Tere began to take off her shoes.

"What are you *doing?*" I whispered urgently. In Paris, she had embarrassed me greatly in a courtyard restaurant by removing her too-tight sandals and resting her bare feet on the tile. But this was the Royal Albert Hall, we were surrounded by well-dressed people, and the performance was about to begin.

Tere was holding up a shoe as the lights dimmed.

"Well, no wonder my feet are killing me," she said in disgust. "These are 39s. They're *your* shoes."

Until the age of ten I was a little girl who liked very much to be looked at. I had an energetic and self-confident personality that adored attention. As the first child, as the daughter of a mother who encouraged my creativity and of a father who believed I was smarter than his community college students, and as the sister of a brother who could be convinced that I knew everything worth knowing, I was fairly certain that I was as interesting to everyone as to my family and myself. But when I was ten my mother's face became disfigured. I have written elsewhere of our Christian Science beliefs and of the religious crisis that led her to try to kill herself by drinking liquid Drāno, a suicide attempt that ravaged the lower part of her face. For the next two and a half years, until my mother died of cancer, I lived in fear of being looked at. And that childhood horror of people staring and whispering or averting their eyes in a desperate, last-minute attempt not to be caught staring has stayed with me all my life.

It has given me a dislike of being photographed and of being on television and a paralyzing stage fright. I have avoided, as much as possible, situations where I have to talk publicly. Any ease I have now at giving readings or speeches is hard won and the result of practice. And when asked to give a toast at a party or called on with my hand in the air, I can still freeze up unexpectedly. Eloquence rarely comes; I sometimes, in fact, lose the power of speech altogether or blurt out something incoherent.

I recall my flamboyant friend Ginny once telling me, laughing, that when she entered a room, everybody noticed; when I entered a room, it was as if I were invisible. Vaguely resentful, I had to acknowledge that this was true and that in some way I had caused it to be true. Over the years, beginning when I was young, I seem to have reduced my aura so that it attracts little attention, to have rearranged my features so that they are almost instantly forgettable. Few people who have met me once or twice remember me later, and it takes me aback when they do. Sometimes I still love attention, and I surprise myself occasionally when, in the midst of giving a reading, I suddenly become a dramatic actress or stand-up comic, but for the most part I am content to pass as unnoticed as I can through the world.

Half Magic, a children's book by Edward Eager, remains one of my favorite novels. In it four children find a magic coin that gives them only half of what they ask for. In order to get the whole adventure, they have to wish twice, or double, for what they want. Sometimes, in a rage, one of them forgets and bursts out with a wish that is fulfilled by half: "I wish I belonged to a different family" and "I wish I wasn't here!" It's the youngest, Martha, who makes this wish one hot afternoon at the movies when her pushy older brother and sisters have squeezed her underneath the seat to make her stop fidgeting. Of course Martha, mistakenly clutching the coin, doesn't get her full wish. She becomes half visible, a ghost who runs through the movie theater and the streets of the town, frightening everyone.

I have often thought this form of half magic is the writer's and the traveler's special art. We are here, very much so, in our physical bodies, eager to eavesdrop, to sniff, and to stare. But we don't all want to be noticed doing so. We want to be half visible, perhaps.

Yet as soon as I write this, I think, no, it's not that way for all writers. Some of us are wildly, vividly visible, used to being recognized and delighting in it. Am I only rationalizing my fear of being stared at by saying, It's because I am a writer and a traveler? And how does being a lesbian, a marginalized woman, fit into this? If I fear being stared at in public, if disliking attention has become so much a part of my personality, how much more do I fear that the person I am with will be stared at? Or that the two of us will be seen as being *together?*

It was an August night and stifling up there in the top rows of the Royal Albert. The program was long and interesting: a Shostakovich symphony followed by the London premiere of a piece by a young Chinese composer now living in New York, and finally the world premiere of another piece by the same man. The program, which we read in the intermission, gave information about the instruments the Scottish National Orchestra would use to simulate Chinese musical sounds, as well as detailed instructions about the humming vowel sounds that we, the audience split into three sections, would make loudly when asked.

I read the program intently while people filed past us out to cooler air and the refreshments. Tere stayed where she was, interested once again in her feet. She had already removed her shoes and now she did the unthinkable: she took off her socks and examined her soft, fresh blisters with close attention.

My girlfriend is not a lady. She grew up in a highly physical family in sunny Santa Barbara, California. As a child she biked, swam, and hiked. She rarely wore shoes and almost never a jacket. Her mother was very young (seventeen when she married) and seemed born without a sense of danger. She scuba dived, sailed, and ocean kayaked, in addition to working full time, taking college classes for a B.A., playing the recorder, sewing her children's clothes, and writing poetry. Tere and her sister are both lesbians. Sparky became a car mechanic and then a manager at an oil refinery, specializing in dangerous emergency procedures. Tere became a union carpenter. She is happy wearing a tool belt and big boots. She has no fear of high places.

Now she briefly rested one bare foot on the top of the vacant seat in front of her, sighing, "My feet feel like they're on fire." Someone looked over at her and smiled.

Naturally, I fled.

I fled to the safety of one of the anonymous anterooms where no one knew me and where I knew no one.

I have traveled with other women before Tere, women with loud voices who talked of intimate matters on elevators and in otherwise silent cafés; women who got into quarrels with ushers or airline officials; women who wanted to discuss our problems while interested bystanders looked on. Even my English lover Kath, usually a model of British rectitude, would occasionally lapse. Once when we were on the tube together in London (a rare occasion, since she usually drove), I began telling her about the self-defense class I had started taking at the Drill Hall and how much I liked it.

"Oh, you just like jumping on top of women," she joked loudly, just as the car came to a halt at the station and a chilled silence enveloped the passengers.

Once I found myself in a train compartment passing through a European country with a lover who was irritated about something that had happened with friends of mine the day before. They had hurt her feelings and she wanted to discuss it, even when it was clear I would have preferred not to, even when it was clear that the previously pleasant, open face of the Australian man beside her was turning purple with embarrassment as he realized that not only were the women she was discussing a couple but that *we were too.*

I told myself later that it would have been the same if my lover had been a man, or if I'd been a man, or if we'd been friends and not lovers. I told myself it was not just about being lesbians or being lovers. It was about being overly personal in public, about being looked at, about being involuntarily seen as making a fuss.

But that wasn't true. It was very much about being a lesbian in public.

Internalized homophobia makes us want to be invisible, makes us want to pass. Don't draw attention to yourself; look as if you're just two women traveling together; look as if you have money and education; look as if you know what you're doing; look as if you belong.

Don't look crazy. Don't look like a dyke. Don't look poor, uncultured, or ill at ease.

Don't do anything wrong.

I've never been in the closet. I come out regularly, even tediously, because I have to and because I don't want to hide. But I have never been enthusiastic about it, only morally impelled. And coming out by choice is not the same as feeling observed and judged.

I've told myself that I like to be invisible because I like to watch and to make up stories, and because I don't like being stared at, and because I was once stared at too often. But the truth is partly that I don't fully feel I have the right to exist and take my place in the world. That I don't belong and never will belong. My religious upbringing as a Christian Scientist gave me the expectation that I would always be marginal and a minority, but my experience with a mentally ill, disfigured mother gave me the fear of calling attention to myself and the person I am with.

My lover was angry that day in the train and she did embarrass me in front of the Australian man. But when I look back I also feel admiration for an indignation that could be made public. She felt she had a right to be who she was; she believed she had a place in the world, as a dyke who looked like a dyke and had a right to live her life openly and talk about what she wanted when she wanted. I preferred to pass, to delude myself that I was unseen. Forgetting, or not understanding, that when you travel with another lesbian, a lover, you can never be invisible.

Your relationship is the visible thing between you.

After the interval, the Scottish National Orchestra started in on the first piece by the Chinese composer, and then came the second, for which we'd been briefed on our vowel sounds. But just before the conductor could raise his baton, there came a flickering of lights, then darkness, then more flickering, and then a low mechanical humming, which was the generator going on.

The power had gone off, and we had twenty minutes to leave the concert hall before the lights went out altogether. As we made our way through the packed corridors and dim stairways, we heard rumors that the power outage had knocked out a large section of the city. People began to panic, to thrust themselves forward down the stairs and out to the taxi queues. Others made a rush for the buses that came by. All the street and building lights were out in our vicinity; would the tubes be running?

"It must be at least three miles, probably five, back to Bloomsbury," I said.

"My feet!" said Tere.

We began walking along the road back to the South Kensington station, just to see if it was open. With each step Tere groaned.

"We never should have bought the same shoes!" she said.

"They're *my* shoes," I said. "With every step you take you're stretching them out!"

"I can't believe you said that! When I'm suffering!"

The night was warm and dark, with that friendly feeling created by a sense that technology falls short and leaves us under the stars with our own resources. The crowd surged along, and as it surged the mood grew more relaxed.

Tere and I were laughing now. We had always gotten along well, from the moment we met some years before. Our wrangling had been partly in jest and was soon behind us. We walked slowly and talked, remembering how lovely Brighton had been on yesterday's summer morning and what an adventure we'd had there. We'd bought the shoes and then had midmorning tea. We'd visited the Pavilion and gawked at the dragon chandeliers and red silk walls; we'd had fish and chips for lunch on the pier and walked along the stony beach, admiring the amusement rides. Brighton had given both of us a sense of home; we'd both grown up at seaside resorts in California, and the smell of cotton candy and suntan oil mixed with saltwater and frying things was familiar and welcome.

And as we talked about Brighton and remembered the visit with Kath and the week in Paris, I realized how much I'd missed Tere when I'd been traveling alone a few weeks earlier. I thought of the nights when I hadn't been able to sleep well and of the times when I'd longed for someone to share a laugh with over the irritations that came up. I thought of the meals I'd had that had tasted flat and the evenings that I'd spent walking up and down the same streets vainly trying to feel inspired and instead just feeling lonely. For every adventure like taking the *Kong Olav* up the Norwegian coast, there had been two dull days when I would have loved to share with her what I was doing and seeing. When it would have been wonderful to hear a friendly voice and see the face of my lover lighting up to see me. *To see me.* To really see me with loving eyes. Yes, I'd had many anonymous strolls in foreign cities and done my old pretending on trains and boats that I was a romantic traveler without attachments. I had carried a notebook in my bag to record my sense of life's impermanence and history's melancholy, and I had sat in plenty of cafés writing and being the writer. But I had not had Tere by my side saying, "Isn't it too bad we never got to hear the world premiere? Think how that poor composer must be feeling," and "It was really wonderful, what we did manage to hear," and "I think, yes, it looks like the tube station is open. It has its lights on."

When my mother changed from being beautiful into being damaged, the fabric of our relationship was torn as well. Part of what I lost was the sense of being looked at with eyes of love. When I became invisible to my mother, I began to be invisible to myself and to the world. It has been this relationship with Tere that has restored to me the sense of being seen the way I want to be seen, with eyes of love.

That warm summer's evening in London we strolled in the large, dark, breathing crowd down the street to the lighted underground station and held each other's hand. Tere limped and I thought, I hope she doesn't stretch those shoes out *too* much. The crowd was full of lovers, friends, and solitary travelers, and we had a place there and belonged.

Marianne Dresser

A Queer Night in Tokyo

"I'll see you in Roppongi at 11:00," Ulrike said and hung up the phone. I hurriedly wrote down the specific instructions—which corner of the train station, which exit: north or south, the nearest architectural landmark, and what commercial logo to look for on which neon billboard—all necessary reference points for successfully arranging a rendezvous in the vast urban chaos that is Tokyo. After two and a half months in Japan, I was at last going to sample some of its hidden *rezubian* subculture.

Well, perhaps "subculture" is too grand a term, implying a more obvious presence, a recognizable community. There *are* lesbians in Japan, but unlike the flaming gay boys who throng the streets of Shinjuku, Tokyo's oddly antiseptic "sleazy" quarter, they are hidden to the point of invisibility. Hardly surprising, given the patriarchal cast of Japanese society with its feudal cultural and gender codes still firmly in place underneath an outward appearance of cutting-edge modernity.

So I was delighted that my intrepid friend, a Dutch lesbian photographer on a year-long student exchange program, had managed not only to find a real Japanese *rezubian* bar but had also acquired the personal contact there that would allow us access. Without a preliminary introduction, a *gaijin,* or foreigner, would never get past the elaborate politeness that masks the iron-clad impenetrability of Japanese society.

After another typically confusing day at my job serving as the token *gaijin* in a small, hip architectural firm, I negotiated the clockwork commute from midtown Tokyo to the tiny, pristine apartment in a northern suburb that I shared with my girlfriend. Janet had been here for over a year, engaging in a well-paid but ultimately futile attempt to teach English to Japanese teenagers at a private school. Following my fervent but terribly misguided heart, I had relocated to Tokyo to be with her. Although neither of us was willing to admit it, we were enacting an expat queer version of a "Can this marriage be saved?" scenario.

Worried that she might lose her job, Janet was emphatically *not* out; we played our public role as two Western women "friends" living abroad. But no foreigner in Japan has any real privacy, and every shopkeeper within a mile knew exactly where the two strange American women lived. Although I was too obedient to ever say so, I thought our precautions were ridiculous. We were incontrovertibly *gaijin*, and secretly I was beginning to enjoy my newfound capacity to elicit squeals of fright from small children or whiplash-inducing headspins from blue-suited *sararimen*. We were already seen as particularly interesting specimens of alien creatures, freaks of nature, so I didn't see how any other "queerness" on our part could possibly matter. In the end, Janet's paranoia and her mastery of passive-aggressive control tactics won the day, and so we carried on with the transparent pretense, fooling no one but ourselves.

But after-hours and away from the incessant curiosity of her students, Janet was as eager as I to check out the *rezubian* bar. So, after our evening rice and miso, we began the important work of planning our respective costumes for the night's outing. After some deliberation, we both ended up in the little-boy drag that was the current unisex fashion rage for trendy Tokyoites. Maintaining the conventions of heterosexual femininity to which she would eventually revert, Janet tipped the scales of her gender-bent image with eye shadow and lipstick. Bravely we ventured out in our baggy black Comme des Garçons suits, down-scaled men's shoes, and short slicked-back hair. The subway ride was no more nor less alienating and hilarious than usual. We received the requisite ambiguous stares and were correctly identified by two kids shouting *"Gaijin-san!"* (roughly translatable as "Mister Foreigner"). Thankfully, no one attempted to practice their English on us.

Our Dutch friend met us at the designated place, her solid northern European body stretching the contours of a dark-blue Japanese schoolboy uniform. With Ulrike in our midst, looking like a Eurodyke version of an obsessed Mishima character, any notions of blending in with the crowd were discarded. We three unlikely pilgrims set off on the convoluted back-alley route to a nondescript bar tucked between a *yakitori-ya* and a karaoke place emitting a thin stream of heartfelt (if off-key) wailing.

Ulrike knocked on the door and conducted the elaborate display of baroque pleasantries, roundabout introductions, and name-dropping that allowed us entry. We were ushered into a narrow room veiled in cigarette smoke. A long, dark wood bar paralleled the left side of the room. Leaning against it were five or six gray- and blue-suited businessmen carrying on with one another in the characteristically gruff, casual speech reserved for Japanese males. A few women clad in frilly pastel dresses were seated demurely at the tables in the no-man's-land between the bar and the entryway. The exaggerated birdlike tones of *onna-kotoba*, "women's speech," floated toward us from their conspiratorial conversations.

I was seriously confused, certain that there had been a mistake. This was just another typical Tokyo dive filled with *sararimen* and bar "hostesses" whose job was to make sure their male customers' glasses were never empty and provide inane, ego-stroking conversation at their whim. Our arrival had caused a noticeable ripple among the inhabitants; we were being thoroughly scrutinized with dozens of brief, oblique glances from every set of eyes in the room. But no one approached us, and we made our way to a deserted corner table. Ulrike went off to the bar for drinks, for once amazingly preempting the instantaneous service that is standard in Japanese public places. Janet and I gazed at the scene and each other and laughed incredulously.

When Ulrike returned with our drinks, I accosted her immediately: "I thought you said this was a lesbian bar. What are all these guys doing here?"

"It took a long time to find this place. Let's just stay for a while. *Kampai!*" she toasted, and drank.

We drank, looked at each other and at the other patrons, while they appraised us with intense sidelong glances. I sensed an imminent approach; the knot of excited voices at the bar signaled that someone was screwing up the courage to cross the great cultural divide to actually *talk* with the strange trio holed up in the corner. After about fifteen minutes of mutual inspection, two self-appointed emissaries swaggered over nervously. They wore the uniform of the thousands of corporate drudges and petty bureaucrats who elbowed me in the subway every morning: dark suits, stiff white shirts, perfect replicas of British club ties. It was only when they began to speak to us in their heavily accented English that I realized these garden-variety businessmen were in fact women. Despite the flawlessly executed, typically male manner in speech, stance, and gesture, their voices heard up close, pitched higher by nervousness and coerced bravado, revealed an elaborate gender ruse in progress.

Our new friends exchanged a few rapid-fire salvos with their compatriots at the bar and we were soon faced by a phalanx of extremely curious, extremely "male-identified" Japanese *rezubians*. Summoned by their dates, a few of the flashy femmes joined us, plying us with bottomless glasses of *sake* and *shochu* while their masculine counterparts proceeded to grill us about Western lesbian habits. Our bizarre conversation, conducted in a mixture of broken English and equally maimed Japanese, ran the gamut from what kind of underwear we wore to whether our wives were pretty.

Our wives? In her serviceable Japanese augmented by a few crude gestures, Janet explained that she and I were "together." This was met with utter incredulity. None of our eager inter-rogators would be caught dead going out with their "wives." The other women in the bar were either their "mistresses" or a queer variant of the bar hostesses I had imagined them to be. Like typ-ical Japanese married ladies, the wives waited patiently at home, kept dinner warm, and would, on their return at 2 or 3 A.M., get up immediately to prepare a meal or a hot bath for their "hus-bands." Didn't we have wives too? How could we two "boys" be together?

By now an alcoholic haze was descending, and the verbal ex-change was reduced to monosyllabic grunts and headshaking incomprehension at our mutual strangeness. Janet, Ulrike, and I managed to extricate ourselves from our hosts' inexhaustible hospitality and stumbled out. We walked back to the train sta-tion sharing our bemusement, smug in our notions of cultural superiority. In a twisted parallel to the youth culture obsessions currently sweeping Tokyo—James Dean, rockabilly rebel pos-turing, and completely unattainable *Route 66* road-trip fan-tasies—Japanese lesbians seemed to be living in a slightly twisted version of a fifties butch/femme universe. We Western dykes were *far* beyond that. We weren't internalizing our homophobia, participating in our own oppression, or reenacting the patriar-chal heterosexist model. We didn't have "wives," we had part-ners, colleagues, sisters in the struggle, fellow radical lesbian feminist separatists. Right on!

And yet, all the way back to our tiny closet in Takinogawa, I kept thinking about the *rezubian* bar and the women we had met there. Those passing Japanese androgynes, with their "wives" and "mistresses," were negotiating a particularly virulent form of *samurai* patriarchy. In a society that gave its women up for lost if they weren't married by age twenty-three, a few lesbians had found a way to be together. The "businessmen" in the bar spent every day of their lives conforming to the corporate monolith in order to support themselves and the women who depended on them and who loved them. Some part of me recoiled from the oppressive gender-coded social mimicry in which they lived. But even though it made me uneasy to admit it, I found these women oddly beautiful and brave. And the more I thought about the fallacious equality of my relationship with Janet, the more I envied the clarity and brutal simplicity of their tyrannical coupling. While we Americans hashed about in mushy realms of "compromise" and "process," those *rezubians* knew who wore the pants and who steamed the rice.

I never made it back to the *rezubian* bar, and after a few months I left Tokyo to pick up the shreds of my abandoned life in San Francisco. It took another year and a couple of long-overdue affairs, but eventually I left Janet as well.

Sarah Jacobus

Some New Ideas

Maha and Nadia were waiting in rattan chairs in the cool tile lobby of the YMCA in Gaza City when I arrived from Jerusalem. They wore ankle-length skirts, the *hijab*—the traditional Muslim woman's head covering—and sullen expressions.

A glimmer of recognition ignited briefly in Nadia's eyes as we shook hands, then vanished. Maha nodded but didn't speak. They were accompanied by a journalist named Naji, whom I'd met before. A man of seemingly inexhaustible good cheer, he spoke fluent English from the years he'd lived in Detroit and projected the self-assurance of someone who had tasted life beyond barbed wire.

While Naji and I talked about the current situation in Gaza, the two women sat in silence. I kept looking toward them, trying to include them in the conversation. I addressed them in clumsy Arabic, asking about the work of the Palestinian women's committee of which I knew they were a part. They stared at me with vacant faces. Naji repeated my question, which Maha answered in animated Arabic addressed to Naji, not once making eye contact with me.

I expressed my interest in meeting women activists. Maha and Nadia nodded in understanding. I'd met Nadia on previous visits, when I'd come alone or with delegations of American women peace activists to learn about women's organizing efforts in Gaza.

Naji drove us to a busy street corner nearby and dropped us off, apologizing that he had to attend to other matters. Maha hailed a taxi and gestured for me to squeeze between her and

Nadia in the backseat. I knew that they'd seated me there so that I'd be less visible from outside. Foreigners were an increasingly rare sight in Gaza, especially in these last months of escalating violence and closure of the occupied territories.

The driver maneuvered through snarls of city traffic onto the coast road. The Mediterranean, pale turquoise and glassy in the midday sun, lapped at a picture-postcard stretch of white sand beach. On the other side of the road, military watchtowers hovered over fields of rubble and stones.

Maha swiveled toward me. "Where do you want to stay tonight?" she asked in confident English. "With Nadia or with me?"

Caught off guard, I was slow to respond. "I don't know," I answered in Arabic.

"Nadia lives in a big house with a beautiful garden," Maha said, "in the town of Khan Yunis, but I live in a poor house in the camp," meaning the refugee camp that adjoined the town.

There was no decision. Of course I would stay in the camp. Did she really think I would choose comfort over solidarity?

Nadia rolled her eyes and giggled. "She does *not* live in the camp," she said, also trying out her English for the first time, "she lives in town in a little bit smaller house but also with a beautiful garden."

Maha studied me to see how I was taking her joke. "All right, all right, but Sarah, where do you want to stay tonight, with me or Nadia?"

It was still early in the day. The initial tension between us had only now begun to ease. The women were at least talking to me. I had no desire to offend either of them. I answered in Arabic, confessing that this was a difficult question I was not yet prepared to answer.

They both laughed. A test had just occurred, and I had apparently passed.

At the intersection where the road turned toward Khan Yunis were barricades of concrete and razor wire. Two Israeli soldiers waved each car heading toward us to a stop. There was no checkpoint in the direction we were traveling, but my stomach tightened, and I looked straight ahead as we passed the soldiers and made the turn.

"Do you feel safe here, Sarah?" Maha asked. "I mean, because you're Jewish."

A flicker of understanding passed between us—so she knew. I wondered what answer she might be expecting, if this were another test.

"It's important to me . . . to be here," I said, tasting each word for truthfulness. "I wouldn't stay away out of fear. I trust who I'm with and that nothing bad will happen to . . ."

"Oh, no, of course not," Maha said, "nothing bad will happen to you," as if I'd somehow accused her.

An awkward pause. Nadia was leaning on the front seat, giving the driver directions.

"Are you married, Sarah?" Maha said.

"No, I'm not."

"Why not?"

"Oh, I like my life the way it is," I said, my customary answer when I wished to skirt the issue of coming out. Maha nodded, as if this reasoning made sense to her, and didn't press further.

"Are you married, Maha?"

"No, I don't want to marry."

"And why don't *you?*" I said, teasing.

She hesitated before answering. "I don't want to bring children into this life here in Gaza. The best thing for this life is that it should be over quickly."

Maha and Nadia hurried me up several flights of stairs in a dim, musty apartment building on one of the main streets of Khan

Yunis. As we climbed, Maha told me that we were going to see the mother of one of the men from Hamas, the Islamic resistance movement, who'd been expelled from Gaza by the Israeli government and remained stranded in Marj az-Zahour, a mountainous strip of no-man's-land in southern Lebanon. The woman preferred that we not come to her home but would speak with us in the kindergarten where she worked.

I'd barely had time to consider this information when a door opened and we were swept across a room full of noisy children, murmuring hellos and shaking hands with women as we passed by, and then ushered into a small side room. Two women emerged from the blur of faces, entered the room behind us, and closed the door.

Maha introduced me to the older woman, Um-Awad. Her son was one of those expelled to Lebanon. She was a tall, round woman dressed in a long black skirt and white blouse. Her dark eyes were shadowed and tired, cheeks flushed with heat from the warm room. She had let her *hijab* fall to her shoulders. Waves of long gray hair were pressed to her head, a few wisps loose around her face and damp with perspiration. Her look was mild, not at all forbidding.

The other woman, Mufida, who I was told was the fiancée of the deportee, had a dark, earnest face that stood out sharply against the white *hijab* tucked around her head and pinned under her chin. She wore a long, rust-colored gabardine skirt and a billowy white satin shirt, giving her a matronly appearance that contrasted with her youthful face and unlined hands. The sleeves of her shirt were rolled halfway up her forearms, which in this context suggested a peculiar informality.

Rather than waiting for Maha to begin, I introduced myself, surprised at the efficiency of my Arabic. I explained that I'd come to learn more about the difficult conditions that faced the Palestinian people under occupation and would share the information with other Americans when I returned to the United States. Um-Awad gazed at me with kind eyes, nodding encouragement as she might to one of her kindergarten charges.

With the help of Maha's translation, Um-Awad told me the story of her son Wafiq's expulsion.

Mufida spoke up. "We were to be married," she said. "Now I don't know when I will see him again. They say he is a terrorist, but he is not, he is just struggling to be free in our land."

The poignant details swelled like rising bread into the two women's declarations about the evils of occupation and the need for an independent Palestinian state.

"And where would this state be?" I asked.

"The West Bank and Gaza," Um-Awad said, "just give us the West Bank and Gaza and we can live in peace."

Emboldened by the relative tameness of her rhetoric, I said in a tone bland as soap, "Some people think that Hamas wants to kill the Jews. What would you say to someone who believed this was true?" Was this a ridiculous question, or did I simply want to be convinced that this unassuming woman was not my enemy?

Maha's translation to Um-Awad rushed by too quickly for me to catch its specifics, but I was sure there was nothing there about killing Jews. Whatever it was Maha had said, Um-Awad, whose Arabic I was better able to understand, responded by expounding on the similarities among the basic values of the three major religions: Islam, Christianity, and Judaism.

"All the religions believe that people should be kind to each other," she said. "For example, you . . . you are Muslim, Christian?"

It didn't occur to me to hesitate. "*Ana Yehudiyeh.*" I'm Jewish.

Maha drew a quick breath through her teeth and dug her elbow into my ribs. Um-Awad's face froze. Mufida straightened in her seat like a marionette pulled from above by invisible strings. Nadia plunged into the silence, hastening to assure the two women that I was an *American* Jew, not Israeli, that I was against the expulsions, against the occupation, against Israeli government policies.

"Yes, yes," I said, "and there are many American Jews who have the same views I do." I prattled on in passable Arabic about progressive organizations and Women in Black vigils and Jewish-Palestinian dialogue. I realized that I was more concerned about assuaging Maha and Nadia's discomfort than I was about justifying myself to Um-Awad.

She quickly regained her composure and returned to her previous theme of the similar belief systems of the three religions. The tension dissipated. We parted with good wishes and blessings.

When we were outside again, Maha and Nadia unleashed a furious torrent of words between them, speaking low through gritted teeth. They dashed into the street toward an approaching taxi, leaving me to run to keep up. I couldn't understand a word they were saying, but I knew exactly what they were talking about. They practically pushed me into the taxi.

Maha turned to me. I braced myself for a scolding.

"Sarah, it's really not a very good idea to go around telling people that you're Jewish," she said. "*I* don't have a problem with it myself, but some of these people, you know, they might want to hurt you."

"I respect your opinion, Maha," I said, aware that I was inching out on a tightrope, "and I know that you and Nadia are taking a risk just by going around with me. But I wasn't going to lie to Um-Awad and tell her I was Christian."

She didn't respond.

"But I trust your judgment about who to tell or not tell. I won't bring it up again."

She seemed satisfied and relayed what I'd said to Nadia in Arabic, who flashed me a relieved smile, as if to suggest that she knew she could count on me to cooperate.

I sat in grumpy silence as the taxi bounced through the pitted streets of Khan Yunis and entered the refugee camp. I knew that Maha and Nadia's reaction had more to do with their own security than with mine. There *were* serious safety issues for the two women. In Gaza, where Israeli intelligence routinely charaded as journalists and foreign visitors, the lines distinguishing foreigner, Jew, and Israeli were blurred. Still, masking who I was—Jew and lesbian—left me feeling hollow and unsteady.

We stopped in a broad thoroughfare that bisected mazes of narrow alleyways and dwellings. Children crowded around us as we disembarked from the taxi. Nadia shooed them away while Maha paid the driver. They then hustled me down one of the alleys. I walked quickly, eyes on my feet. Sand glazed my sandals and collected between my toes. I straddled shallow ditches of sewage coursing down the center of the pathway, catching my breath at its stench. I'd practiced this walk many times, trying to perfect body language—a stance, an expression—that projected consideration and respect. Would anyone in this sagging village of crumbling cinder block decipher it, or even care to?

A large woman loomed out of nowhere, waved us through a door in the wall into an interior room, then was gone. There were stacks of household objects, furniture, and bedding, telltale signs of transition that meant someone had had to move from a demolished house. Maha, Nadia, and I squeezed onto a reed mat on the floor at one end of the room, the only place to sit.

The woman was Um-Muhammad, Maha and Nadia told me. Her home had been destroyed because her son was a wanted man, and she'd come to live with another son. She was a powerful woman in the camp, a hero, known for her stubborn resistance to the Israeli army.

Um-Muhammad returned. I heard her shouting at the children who had followed us and were now clamoring at the outside door. She bolted the door and lumbered, breathing heavily, into the room where we waited. She removed three cans of cola from the nest of her apron, popped the tops and handed them to us, then lowered herself onto the floor beside us, mopping her brow with the end of her head scarf.

Um-Muhammad motioned for me to drink my soda. I daubed the grit from the sweating can with the edge of my sleeve, trying to be inconspicuous, then noticed Nadia pluck a yellow Kleenex from her bag and daintily wipe around the top of her can before she took a sip.

Nadia gave Um-Muhammad what had become the standard introduction about my peace work and taking information back to the States. Um-Muhammad looked skeptical.

"What do you want people in the U.S. to know about your situation here in Gaza?" I asked her.

"What do you care about our situation here?" she said. "You just think we are terrorists, because that is what your government tells you. Do your American people know about the soldiers who destroyed my home and put my son in prison, the men who lost their jobs with this closure, families selling their furniture to buy food?"

Um-Muhammad's gesticulating hand just missed my nose. Maha looked as if she were trying to determine how I was holding up under this blast of anger.

"Your government will do whatever Israel tells them to do, they will do nothing good for us!" Um-Muhammad said, just as there was a loud pounding on the door. Someone outside was shouting her name. Her hand gripping my shoulder, she slowly rose to her feet and picked her way over us and out of the room.

"Do you think there's a problem?" I asked Maha.

"There's always a problem," she said.

In Um-Muhammad's absence, I asked Maha and Nadia

more about their lives. I remembered that Nadia worked at one of the kindergartens run by the Union of Palestinian Women's Committees in Khan Yunis.

"It's very hard now, since the closure," she said. "The pay is only half of what it was last year, there are more children, and the hours are longer. I still love working with children, but I would like to find another job. Of course, this is impossible now."

Maha had been job hunting unsuccessfully for two years. She was now studying computers at the open university in Gaza City, but what she really wanted to talk about was video.

"An Indian filmmaker came and gave a video course for women here," Maha said. "It was so great, Sarah! We each made films for our class projects. She talked about how important it is for us to document our own experiences, especially as women. Foreign journalists come here, and filmmakers, but they cannot go where we can go."

"Are there women here in Gaza doing the kind of documentation you're talking about?"

"No, and you know, Sarah, this is something I want very much to do, to freelance. I have my own video camera. But how could I possibly make a living this way here in the Gaza Strip?"

"What about the restrictions of the culture? Would anyone try to stop you as a woman doing a nontraditional job?"

"Maybe the men would say that a woman should not be doing this work, that we should not be in the street like this. That's why we have to have our rights as women and be independent so that no one can stop us from doing what we want, living the way we want."

Buoyed by this evidence of like-mindedness, I began to relax into the conversation. There was something insistently familiar about Maha—her lively intelligence, her humor, a quality of immediacy that melted away the distance between us, between our worlds. If I had been sitting with this woman over coffee in Los Angeles, it would not have felt much different than this.

I chanced asking Maha and Nadia their ages. Maha wanted me to guess. Nadia clicked her tongue between her teeth, pretending scorn.

"She's twenty-four," Nadia said.

"And you?"

"Oh, I'm old." She paused. "I'm thirty."

"Sarah, I want to be straight with you," Maha said abruptly, turning to me. "I would never to talk to the Jewish, whether they were for us or against us. I refused. This morning, when Naji told us that the woman who was coming was Jewish . . . well, I felt stuck and wanted to get out of it. But I decided that I wanted to go with you."

"What made you change your mind?" I asked.

"I listened to the way you talked with Naji and thought that maybe I will hear some new ideas."

"And?"

"Yes, it's true."

I was touched by Maha's admission. She too felt the bond.

When Um-Muhammad returned, she seemed impatient with our presence. As soon as we rose to go, she became congenial again. "You tell your Clinton about us," she said, fingering my sleeve, "tell him that we just want to live like any other people in the world."

On the way out, Maha grabbed a curved blade with a wooden handle from a box of kitchen things. She brandished the blade in my direction and leered at me with mock ferocity.

"And I thought I was safe in Gaza!" I tossed back at her, amused. The other women laughed, too, but I knew that only Maha could make sense of what I'd said.

Nadia was right, the garden at Maha's house was beautiful, flowering in colorful profusion in a walled courtyard in front of the old stone structure on a quiet side street in the town of Khan Yunis. Maha and an older sister, Aysha, accompanied me as I strolled through the beds of carnations, snapdragons, and kalanchoes, patiently responding to my requests to know the Arabic names of everything.

Maha's father, a short stately man in a tan djellaba, bent over a rosebush with shears in hand, snipping flowers and picking bugs off the leaves.

I was ushered inside to a chair in the front parlor while a procession of Maha's women relatives came to greet me. "*Ahlan wa sahlan*," welcome, they murmured, shaking my hand, then took seats across the room where they stared at me with expressions ranging from shy curiosity to amused contempt.

I couldn't decide which of two older women was Maha's mother. One wore a shapeless gray dress and a gray kerchief that swallowed her head. Her face was speckled with liver spots. One of her eyes was a clear brown, the other milky and clouded, perhaps sightless. The other woman had a smooth, rosy face and was dressed in bright green, her black hair uncovered.

Maha's father, settled now in what was apparently his official chair, looked gentle and scholarly with his bristly white hair, coffee-colored skin, and horn-rimmed glasses. Perhaps from having seen the attention he'd lavished on his roses, I expected that he'd be friendly with me. Instead, he initiated the conversational practice I found most annoying: directing questions about me to a third party—in this case, Maha.

The women joined in. Who is she? Where is she from? Why has she come to Gaza? Look at her earrings.

I squirmed at the center of this oblique attention, preparing to jump into the exchange on my own behalf, when Maha's father blurted out in clear English, "I don't believe she speaks any Arabic at all!"

I replied in Arabic that yes, I did, but then couldn't think of another thing to say to substantiate my claim. Maha's father walled himself off behind a newspaper.

I couldn't tell if they expected me to stay the night or not.

The clatter of dishes and smells of cooking from the kitchen alerted me to the preparation of food. But it was only 5:30, early for the evening meal. Several of the women drifted into the kitchen to help, trailing Nadia behind them. Maha jumped up to leave the room.

"Maha," I said in a low voice, my hand on her arm, "I'd like to stay here at your house for the night. I want to continue our conversation. There are many things I want to ask you."

"But Nadia wants you to come to her house. It will be very nice there, because her parents are gone. They're in Mecca for the hajj, the pilgrimage."

I tried not to let my disappointment show but could feel my face droop into a sulk.

"Sarah, I am coming with you to Nadia's," she said, as if I should have known this. I looked at her, confused.

"Nadia is my cousin. My parents will allow me to spend the night at her house. Now let me get ready." She rushed off.

The food arrived. Maha's sister-in-law—at least I thought she was Maha's sister-in-law—set a metal tray down on the table in front of me and unloaded a large bowl of steaming saffron rice and another in which islands of meat rose from a tomato sauce with peas and chopped onion. Maha's sister Aysha and the other women gathered around, crouching on low stools alongside the table, but the meal seemed intended only for Maha, Nadia, and me. Nadia dumped a portion of rice in my bowl larger than I could possibly eat. I spooned sauce onto the rice, hoping that no one would notice I'd taken no meat.

The woman in gray lighted on the arm of a chair in order to have a first-rate view of the feeding. She trained her brown eye, piercing as a hawk's, on me, and of course saw that there was no meat in my bowl.

"Nadia, give her meat!" she said. Before I could stop her, Nadia dumped one of the brown chunks in my bowl.

I explained that I was *nabatiyeh,* a vegetarian, and that the rice and sauce were quite delicious and more than enough food, thank you. This revelation caused a small stir. The women tittered among themselves, as Nadia removed the meat from the bowl. The woman in gray did not take the news well. She rose and started back into the kitchen, announcing that she'd prepare eggs for me. I was able to dissuade her, but she looked doubtful as she came to roost again on the arm of the chair. I spooned rice into my mouth and scooped up bites with pita.

Maha and Nadia finished eating. I put down my spoon and sat back to signal that I too was done. But the gray hawk would not hear of it. *"Kulli! Kulli!"* Eat, eat! She did not desist until I'd picked up the spoon and begun to stuff bite after painful bite of rice into my mouth.

Aysha and the woman in green who I'd decided was her mother cleared the dishes until only my bowl remained on the table. "You eat so slow, Sarah," Maha said, and everyone agreed. "We all eat very fast, like machines."

I paused again for breath.

"If you don't finish your rice, Sarah," Maha warned, smiling, "I'll kill you."

"I can see it now," I said, "on my tombstone: 'She died because she couldn't finish her rice.'"

"No," said Maha, "she died for being a Jew in Gaza."

That again. Though I still chalked up this fixation to youthful acting out, Maha's comment provided a last straw in the standoff over food. I would not eat another bite of this damn rice!

Aysha must have taken pity on me, for she removed my bowl before anyone could see that I hadn't finished. A huge platter of fruit materialized in its place, a graceful still life of sliced watermelon and honeydew, loquats and apples beaded with water. I nibbled on some watermelon, which seemed to mollify the woman in gray.

But it was not until Nadia's family arrived to pick us up that the older woman's attention was diverted from me. Nadia's brother Ibrahim and his wife Nisreen balanced on one of the straight-backed benches that lined the walls. Neither of them looked at or spoke to me. Nisreen was stunning, with a flawless complexion and sensual brown eyes whose lids seemed weighted down by thick dark lashes. Her pregnant belly ballooned gently under a tailored gray coatdress. A few locks of dark hair had escaped from under her white scarf. She held a toddler on her lap, a girl named Halla. A young nephew Mahmoud ("His father is with Hamas," Nadia whispered to me) hung on the arm of the bench near Ibrahim. Maha's family fussed over them. I marveled to see that their polite refusals of food were honored.

The edges of the sky were softening into twilight when we reached Nadia's. Little more than an hour remained before curfew. Khan Yunis had withdrawn behind closed doors. Behind a wall on a wide, deserted boulevard, Nadia's palatial L-shaped house sat like two enormous shoe boxes on pillars, with a broad terrace surrounded by a garden in full riotous bloom—geraniums, lacy white jasmine that cascaded over the outside walls, a crown of thorns, bushy and taller than any I had seen before, its red flowers electric even in the fading light.

Nadia herself seemed to bloom in this garden. The shyness that I had tended to mistake for displeasure vanished. She was suddenly vivacious and welcoming, wanted to show me everything, seemed gratified by my delight in the garden. She led me up the flight of steps leading to the front door and into the house.

I had never seen such splendor in Gaza, so much living space and material comfort. I felt worlds away from the squalor and danger of the refugee camps in this oasis of fragrant flowers, plush furniture, and gleaming kitchen appliances. It offered an unsettling sense of insulation.

The evening air was mild, so after dropping our bags, Nadia, Maha, and I settled outdoors on the top steps near the front door. Soon, Nisreen called Nadia to come inside. Maha and I, now alone, sat in silence for a few minutes. I'd been waiting hours for this moment.

"You said earlier at Um-Muhammad's," I began, "that you thought it was important for women to be independent. Do you see yourself as independent?"

Maha took a deep drag on her cigarette. "Well, first thing is I need to be independent financially. How can I do what I want if my parents still support me? I can't find a job. Two years I've been looking."

"Have you gone to college?"

"I started at the Islamic University, but I was kicked out the second week."

"Why?"

"There were too many rules—you have to memorize the Koran, you have to wear the *hijab*, you cannot talk to men. I couldn't take it."

"You know, Maha, my life is very untraditional," I said carefully. "It looks different from that of women I grew up with and many other women around me. Sometimes I wonder, why me? What has made me choose to be different? Do you ever think about your life that way?" I knew I was fishing—what did I think she'd tell me?

Maha flicked ash into a pot of cactus with buttery blooms. "Sarah, this is something I am thinking about very much. . . ."

A shadow fell over us. Ibrahim stood in the lighted doorway, pointing to his watch. "It's eight o'clock," he said. Curfew. As we got up and brushed the dust from our seats, I told Maha I looked forward to continuing our conversation later.

"We'll see," she said.

As soon as we entered the house, Nisreen locked the door behind us. She'd changed into a dress-length T-shirt with a cartoon drawing of Mickey Mouse and the Eiffel Tower. "Mickey in Paris," it said.

Everyone dispersed. I stationed myself on a sofa in the den with my journal and scribbled some notes from the day, waiting to see what happened next. Maha headed for the bathroom, and I soon heard the shower running. Nisreen was rattling around in the kitchen. Mahmoud was the first to reappear. He sat next to me, watching me write.

Ibrahim breezed into the room, switched on the television, and sank into a chair. The program appeared to be a soap opera, but there were wavy lines on the screen and the actors had green faces. Ibrahim's attempts to adjust the picture were futile, but Nisreen insisted that the television be left on. She was following the story and wanted to check in every now and then.

And here was Nadia, now dressed in navy blue shorts and a yellow T-shirt and barefoot. She pulled family photo albums from a cabinet and sat down to show me. Maha emerged from the shower in a cloud of soapy steam, rubbing her wet hair with a towel. She was wearing a short-sleeved cotton nightshirt and flip-flops.

No one looked the way they did before except me. Nadia asked if I had more comfortable clothes with me, but I hesitated. I'd brought a T-shirt and tights to sleep in, but this garb didn't seem appropriate for lounging around with the whole family. Seeing everyone looking so refreshed, the shirt and skirt I was wearing felt dingier by the second. I would have loved to shower but was too shy to ask.

"Sarah, you know what the biggest mistake is you have made today?" Maha asked, almost shouting. I sensed that the window of communication, open for a brief moment, had closed, that this banter was all she would now allow between us. I played my part.

"No, Maha, but I'm sure you'll tell me."

"Your biggest mistake is that you have not brought any alcohol with you for us to drink." This time, I was tongue-tied.

The scene here was constantly shifting. Nadia and Ibrahim disappeared again into the kitchen. A while later, Maha complained of a headache and took two aspirin. "I'm so angry," she said, pacing back and forth. "I feel like smashing something."

I volunteered that a friend of mine had recently hurled her telephone against a wall, which she reported had given her great satisfaction. "No," Maha said, "I want to see blood."

The next morning, I sat at the kitchen table, eating toast and cheese. Nisreen was preparing breakfast for Halla, who was perched in her high chair, banging her hands against the tray. Nadia would have only coffee and aspirin. She and Maha had stayed up until 5:30.

"We never get to do this," she said. "It's something special." She was dressed in her street clothes, the long skirt and long-sleeved blouse, with her head scarf draped around her neck in readiness. There were dark circles under her eyes.

Maha dragged in and poured herself coffee. Halla picked up a knife from the table and waved it in the air. I reached to take the knife away from her, but Maha got there first. Halla, possessive of her new toy, struggled to hold onto it.

"No, Halla, this knife is not to kill me," Maha said in English, "this knife is to kill Sarah."

"It's too early in the morning, Maha. I'm not ready to die," I said weakly, tired of the game.

She grinned, but I felt myself shrinking in my chair until I was as small as Halla.

When we met up with Naji later in Gaza City, Maha ignored me and spoke no English. I wondered if she didn't want Naji to see that there was any rapport between us. But I didn't want to leave Gaza without some sort of closure with her. I wouldn't let her get away with brushing me off as an unpalatable day's assignment.

Before taking me back to the taxi stop to wait for a ride to Jerusalem, we stopped at the Women's Resource Center, a comfortable apartment full of colorful posters and bustling women. Maha immediately disappeared. On the pretense of using the rest room, I searched for her and found her alone in the kitchen making coffee.

"Maha, before I leave, I want to thank you for spending this time with me. I've learned a lot."

"You say thank you too much, Sarah, you know that?"

"I feel like we started a conversation, Maha, and never got a chance to finish."

She sighed deeply. "You know, Sarah, it was not so easy for me, talking to a Jew for the first time. There are things I . . . well . . ."

We were interrupted by one of the women on the staff. "Naji says there isn't much time," she said. On her way out of the room, she stopped and stared at me. "She looks Palestinian," she said in Arabic in a friendly voice, and then to me in English, "Are you from an Arabic family?"

"*La'.*" No. I waited a beat, then met the gaze Maha leveled at me. "*Ana Yehudiyeh.*"

Audre Lorde

Zami

Eudora. Mexico. Color and light and Cuernavaca and Eudora.

At the compound, Easter Saturday, she was just coming out of a week's drinking binge that started with the firing of Robert Oppenheimer, the atomic scientist, in the states. I was full of the Good Friday festivities in Mexico City, which I had attended with Frieda and Tammy the day before. They had gone to Tepotzlán. I was sunning myself on my front lawn.

"Hello, down there! Aren't you overdoing it?" I looked up at the woman whom I had noticed observing me from an upper window in the two-story dwelling at the edge of the compound. She was the only woman I'd seen wearing pants in Mexico except at the pool.

I was pleased that she had spoken. The two women who lived separately in the double house at that end of the compound never appeared at tables in the Plaza. They never spoke as they passed my house on their way to the cars or the pool. I knew one of them had a shop in town called La Señora, which had the most interesting clothes on the Square.

"Haven't you heard, only mad dogs and englishmen go out in the noonday sun?" I shaded my eyes so I could see her better. I was more curious than I had realized.

"I don't burn that easily," I called back. She was framed in the large casement window, a crooked smile on her half-shaded face. Her voice was strong and pleasant, but with a crack in it that sounded like a cold, or too many cigarettes.

"I'm just going to have some coffee. Would you like some?"

I stood, picked up the blanket upon which I'd been lying, and accepted her invitation.

She was waiting in her doorway. I recognized her as the tall gray-haired woman called La Periodista.

"My name's Eudora," she said, extending her hand and holding mine firmly for a moment. "And they call you La Chica, you're here from New York, and you go to the new university."

"Where did you find all that out?" I asked, taken aback. We stepped inside.

"It's my business to find out what goes on," she laughed easily. "That's what reporters do. Legitimate gossip."

Eudora's bright spacious room was comfortable and disheveled. A large easy chair faced the bed upon which she now perched cross-legged, in shorts and polo shirt, smoking, and surrounded by books and newspapers.

Maybe it was her direct manner. Maybe it was the openness with which she appraised me as she motioned me toward the chair. Maybe it was the pants, or the informed freedom and authority with which she moved. But from the moment I walked into her house, I knew Eudora was gay, and that was an unexpected and welcome surprise. It made me feel much more at home and relaxed, even though I was still feeling sore and guilty from my fiasco with Bea, but it was refreshing to know I wasn't alone.

"I've been drinking for a week," she said, "and I'm still a little hungover, so you'll have to excuse the mess."

I didn't know what to say.

Eudora wanted to know what I was doing in Mexico, young, Black, and with an eye for the ladies, as she put it. That was the second surprise. We shared a good laugh over the elusive cues for mutual recognition among lesbians. Eudora was the first woman I'd met who spoke about herself as a lesbian rather than as "gay," which was a word she hated. Eudora said it was a north american east-coast term that didn't mean anything to her, and what's more most of the lesbians she had known were anything but gay.

When I went to the market that afternoon, I brought back milk and eggs and fruit for her. I invited her to dinner, but she wasn't feeling much like eating, she said, so I fixed my dinner and brought it over and ate with her. Eudora was an insomniac, and we sat talking late late into the night.

She was the most fascinating woman I had ever met.

Born in Texas forty-eight years before, Eudora was the youngest child in an oil worker's family. She had seven older brothers. Polio as a child had kept her in bed for three years, "so I had a lot of catchin' up to do, and I never knew when to stop."

In 1925, she became the first woman to attend the University of Texas, integrating it by camping out on the university grounds for four years in a tent with her rifle and a dog. Her brothers had studied there, and she was determined to also. "They said they didn't have living accommodations for women," Eudora said, "and I couldn't afford a place in town."

She'd worked in news all her life, both print and radio, and had followed her lover, Franz, to Chicago, where they both worked for the same paper. "She and I were quite a team, all right. Had a lot of high times together, did a lot of foolishness, believed a lot of things.

"Then Franz married a foreign correspondent in Istanbul," Eudora continued dryly, "and I lost my job over a byline on the Scottsboro case." She worked for a while in Texas for a Mexican paper, then moved into Mexico City for them.

When she and Karen, who owned La Señora, were lovers, they had started a bookstore together in Cuernavaca in the more liberal forties. For a while it was a rallying place for disaffected americans. This was how she knew Frieda.

"It was where people came to find out what was really going on in the states. Everybody passed through." She paused. "But it got to be a little too radical for Karen's tastes," Eudora said carefully. "The dress shop suits her better. But that's a whole other mess, and she still owes me money."

"What happened to the bookstore?" I asked, not wanting to pry but fascinated by her story.

"Oh, lots of things, in very short order. I've always been a hard drinker, and she never liked that. Then when I had to speak my mind in the column about the whole Sobell business, and the newspaper started getting itchy, Karen thought I was going to lose that job. I didn't, but my immigration status was changed, which meant I could still work in Mexico, but after all these years I could no longer own property. That's the one way of getting uppity americans to keep their mouths shut. Don't rock big brother's boat, and we'll let you stay. That was right up Karen's alley. She bought me out and opened the dress shop."

"Is that why you broke up?"

Eudora laughed. "That sounds like New York talk." She was silent for a minute, busying herself with the overflowing ashtray.

"Actually, no," she said finally. "I had an operation, and it was pretty rough for both of us. Radical surgery, for cancer. I lost a breast." Eudora's head was bent over the ashtray, hair falling forward, and I could not see her face. I reached out and touched her hand.

"I'm so sorry," I said.

"Yeah, so am I," she said matter-of-factly, placing the polished ashtray carefully back on the table beside her bed. She looked up, smiled, and pushed the hair back from her face with the heels of her hands. "There's never enough time to begin with, and still so damn much I want to do."

"How are you feeling now, Eudora?" I remembered my nights on the female surgery floor at Beth David. "Did you have radiation?"

"Yes I did. It's almost two years since the last one, and I'm fine now. The scars are hard to take, though. Not dashing or romantic. I don't much like to look at them myself." She got up, took down her guitar from the wall, and started to tune it. "What folksongs are they teaching you in that fine new university up the mountain?"

Eudora had translated a number of texts on the history and ethnology of Mexico, one of which was a textbook assigned for my history class. She was witty and funny and sharp and insightful, and knew a lot about an enormous number of things. She had written poetry when she was younger, and Walt Whitman was her favorite poet. She showed me some clippings of articles she had written for a memorial-documentary of Whitman. One sentence in particular caught my eye.

> I met a man who'd spent his life in thinking, and could
> understand me no matter what I said. And I followed him
> to Harleigh in the snow.

The next week was Easter holidays, and I spent part of each afternoon or evening at Eudora's house, reading poetry, learning to play the guitar, talking. I told her about Ginger, and about Bea, and she talked about her and Franz's life together. We even had a game of dirty-word Scrabble, and although I warned her I was a declared champion, Eudora won, thereby increasing my vocabulary no end. She showed me the column she was finishing about the Olmec stone heads, and we talked about the research she was planning to do on African and Asian influences in Mexican art. Her eyes twinkled and her long graceful hands flashed as she talked, and by midweek, when we were not together, I could feel the curves of her cheekbone under my lips as

I gave her a quick good-bye kiss. I thought about making love to her, and ruined a whole pot of curry in my confusion. This was not what I had come to Mexico to do.

There was an air about Eudora when she moved that was both delicate and sturdy, fragile and tough, like the snapdragon she resembled when she stood up, flung back her head, and brushed her hair back with the palms of her hands. I was besotted.

Eudora often made fun of what she called my prudishness, and there was nothing she wouldn't talk about. But there was a reserve about her own person, a force field around her that I did not know how to pass, a sadness surrounding her that I could not breach. And besides, a woman of her years and experience— how presumptuous of me!

We sat talking in her house later and later, over endless cups of coffee, half my mind on our conversation and half of it hunting for some opening, some graceful, safe way of getting closer to this woman whose smell made my earlobes burn. Who, despite her openness about everything else, turned away from me when she changed her shirt.

On Thursday night we rehung some of her bark paintings from Tehuantepec. The overhead fan hummed faintly; there was a little pool of sweat sitting in one wing of her collarbone. I almost reached over to kiss it.

"Goddammit!" Eudora had narrowly missed her finger with the hammer.

"You're very beautiful," I said suddenly, embarrassed at my own daring. There was a moment of silence as Eudora put down her hammer.

"So are you, Chica," she said quietly, "more beautiful than you know." Her eyes held mine for a minute so I could not turn away.

No one had ever said that to me before.

It was after 2:00 A.M. when I left Eudora's house, walking across the grass to my place in the clear moonlight. Once inside I could not sleep. I tried to read. Visions of Eudora's dear one-sided grin kept coming between me and the page. I wanted to be with her, to be close to her, laughing.

I sat on the edge of my bed, wanting to put my arms around Eudora, to let the tenderness and love I felt burn away the sad casing around her and speak to her need through the touch of my hands and my mouth and my body that defined my own.

"It's getting late," she had said. "You look tired. Do you want to stretch out?" She gestured to the bed beside her. I came out of my chair like a shot.

"Oh, no, that's all right," I stammered. All I could think of was that I had not had a bath since morning. "I—I need to take a shower, anyway."

Eudora had already picked up a book. "Good night, Chica," she said without looking up.

I jumped up from the edge of my bed and put a light under the water heater. I was going back.

"What is it, Chica? I thought you were going to bed." Eudora was reclining exactly as I had left her an hour before, propped up on a pillow against the wall, the half-filled ashtray next to her hand and books littering the rest of the three-quarter studio bed. A bright towel hung around her neck against the loose, short-sleeved beige nightshirt.

My hair was still damp from the shower, and my bare feet itched from the dew-wet grass between our houses. I was suddenly aware that it was 3:30 in the morning.

"Would you like some more coffee?" I offered.

She regarded me at length, unsmiling, almost wearily.

"Is that what you came back for, more coffee?"

All through waiting for the *calendador* to heat, all through showering and washing my hair and brushing my teeth, until that very moment, I had thought of nothing but wanting to hold Eudora in my arms, so much that I didn't care that I was also terrified. Somehow, if I could manage to get myself back up those steps in the moonlight, and if Eudora was not already asleep, then I would have done my utmost. That would be my piece of the bargain, and then what I wanted would somehow magically fall into my lap.

Eudora's gray head moved against the bright serape-covered wall behind her, still regarding me as I stood over her. Her eyes wrinkled and she slowly smiled her lopsided smile, and I could feel the warm night air between us collapse as if to draw us together.

I knew then that she had been hoping I would return. Out of wisdom or fear, Eudora waited for me to speak.

Night after night we had talked until dawn in this room about language and poetry and love and the good conduct of living. Yet we were strangers. As I stood there looking at Eudora, the impossible became easier, almost simple. Desire gave me courage, where it had once made me speechless. With almost no thought I heard myself saying, "I want to sleep with you."

Eudora straightened slowly, pushed the books from her bed with a sweep of her arm, and held out her hand to me.

"Come."

I sat down on the edge of the bed, facing her, our thighs touching. Our eyes were on a level now, looking deeply into each other. I could feel my heart pounding in my ears, and the high steady sound of the crickets.

"Do you know what you're saying?" Eudora asked softly, searching my face. I could smell her like the sharp breath of wildflowers.

"I know," I said, not understanding her question. Did she think I was a child?

"I don't know if I can," she said, still softly, touching the sunken place on her nightshirt where her left breast should have been. "And you don't mind this?"

I had wondered so often how it would feel under my hands, my lips, this different part of her. Mind? I felt my love spread like a shower of light surrounding me and this woman before me. I reached over and touched Eudora's face with my hands.

"Are you sure?" Her eyes were still on my face.

"Yes, Eudora." My breath caught in my throat as if I'd been running. "I'm very sure." If I did not put my mouth upon hers and inhale the spicy smell of her breath my lungs would burst.

As I spoke the words, I felt them touch and give life to a new reality within me, some half-known self come of age, moving out to meet her.

I stood, and in two quick movements slid out of my dress and underclothes. I held my hand down to Eudora. Delight. Anticipation. A slow smile mirroring my own softened her face. Eudora reached over and passed the back of her hand along my thigh. Gooseflesh followed in the path of her fingers.

"How beautiful and brown you are."

She rose slowly. I unbuttoned her shirt and she shrugged it off her shoulders till it lay heaped at our feet. In the circle of lamplight I looked from her round firm breast with its rosy nipple erect to her scarred chest. The pale keloids of radiation burn lay in the hollow under her shoulder and arm down across her ribs. I raised my eyes and found hers again, speaking a tenderness my mouth had no words yet for. She took my hand and placed it there, squarely, lightly, upon her chest. Our hands fell. I bent and kissed her softly upon the scar where our hands had rested. I felt her heart strong and fast against my lips. We fell back together upon her bed. My lungs expanded and my breath deepened with the touch of her warm dry skin. My mouth finally against hers, quick-breathed, fragrant, searching, her hand entwined in my hair. My body took charge from her flesh. Shifting slightly, Eudora reached past my head toward the lamp above us. I caught her wrist. Her bones felt like velvet and quick-silver between my tingling fingers.

"No," I whispered against the hollow of her ear. "In the light."

Sun poured through the jacarandas outside Eudora's window. I heard the faint and rhythmical whirr-whoosh of Tomás's scythe as he cut back the wild banana bushes from the walk down by the pool.

I came fully awake with a start, seeing the impossible. The junebug I had squashed with a newspaper at twilight, so long before, seemed to be moving slowly up the white-painted wall. It would move a few feet up from the floor, fall back, and then start up again. I grabbed for my glasses from the floor where I had dropped them the night before. With my glasses on, I could see that there was a feather-thin line of ants descending from the adobe ceiling down the wall to the floor where the junebug was lying. The ants, in concert, were trying to hoist the carcass straight up the vertical wall on their backs, up to their hole on the ceiling. I watched in fascination as the tiny ants lifted their huge load, moved, lost it, then lifted again.

I half-turned and reached over to touch Eudora lying against my back, one arm curved over our shared pillow. The pleasure of our night flushed over me like sun on the walls of the light-washed colorful room. Her light brown eyes opened, studying me as she came slowly out of sleep, her sculptured lips smiling, a little bit open, revealing the gap beside her front teeth. I traced her mouth with my finger. For a moment I felt exposed, unsure,

suddenly wanting reassurance that I had not been found wanting. The morning air was still dew-damp, and the smell of our
loving lay upon us.

As if reading my thoughts, Eudora's arm came down around
my shoulders, drawing me around and to her, tightly, and we lay
holding each other in the Mexican morning sunlight that
flooded through her uncovered casement windows. Tomás, the
caretaker, sang in soft Spanish, keeping time with his scythe, and
the sounds drifted in to us from the compound below.

"What an ungodly hour," Eudora laughed, kissing the top of
my head and jumping over me with a long stride. "Aren't you
hungry?" With her towel around her neck, Eudora made *huevos,*
scrambled eggs Mexican-style, and real *café con leche* for our
breakfast. We ate at the gaily painted orange table between the
tiny kitchen and her bedroom, smiling and talking and feeding
each other from our common plate.

There was room for only one of us at the square shallow sink
in the kitchen. As I washed dishes to ensure an ant-free afternoon, Eudora leaned on the doorpost, smoking lazily. Her hip-
bones flared like wings over her long legs. I could feel her quick
breath on the side of my neck as she watched me. She dried the
dishes, and hung the towel over a tin mask on the kitchen
cabinet.

"Now let's go back to bed," she muttered, reaching for me
through the Mexican shirt I had borrowed to throw over myself.
"There's more."

By this time the sun was passing overhead. The room was
full of reflected light and the heat from the flat adobe over us,
but the wide windows and the lazy ceiling fan above kept the
sweet air moving. We sat in bed sipping iced coffee from a
pewter mug.

When I told Eudora I didn't like to be made love to, she
raised her eyebrows. "How do you know?" she said, and smiled

as she reached out and put down our coffee cup. "That's probably because no one has ever really made love to you before," she said softly, her eyes wrinkling at the corners, intense, desiring.

Eudora knew many things about loving women that I had not yet learned. Day into dusk. A brief shower. Freshness. The comfort and delight of her body against mine. The ways my body came to life in the curve of her arms, her tender mouth, her sure body—gentle, persistent, complete.

We run up the steep outside steps to her roof, and the almost full moon flickers in the dark center wells of her eyes. Kneeling, I pass my hands over her body, along the now-familiar place below her left shoulder, down along her ribs. A part of her. The mark of the Amazon. For a woman who seems spare, almost lean, in her clothing, her body is ripe and smooth to the touch. Beloved. Warm to my coolness, cool to my heat. I bend, moving my lips over her flat gentle stomach to the firm rising mound beneath.

On Monday, I went back to school. In the next month, Eudora and I spent many afternoons together, but her life held complications about which she would say little.

Eudora had been all over Mexico. She regaled me with tales of her adventures. She seemed always to have lived her life as if it were a story, a little grander than ordinary. Her love of Mexico, her adopted land, was deep and compelling, like an answer to my grade-school fantasies. She knew a great deal about the folkways and beliefs of the different peoples who had swept across the country in waves long ago, leaving their languages and a small group of descendants to carry on the old ways.

We went for long rides through the mountains in her Hudson convertible. We went to the Brincas, the traditional Moorish dances in Tepotzlán. She told me about the Olmec stone heads of

African people that were being found in Tabasco, and the ancient contacts between Mexico and Africa and Asia that were just now coming to light. We talked about the legend of the China Poblana, the Asian-looking patron saint of Puebla. Eudora could savor what was Zapotec, Toltec, Mixtec, Aztec in the culture, and how much had been so terribly destroyed by Europeans.

"That genocide rivals the Holocaust of World War II," she asserted.

She talked about the nomadic Lacandonian Indians, who were slowly disappearing from the land near Comitán in Chiapas, because the forests were going. She told me how the women in San Cristóbal de las Casas give the names of catholic saints to their goddesses, so that they and their daughters can pray and make offerings in peace at the forest shrines without offending the catholic church.

She helped me plan a trip south, to Oaxaca and beyond, through San Cristóbal to Guatemala, and gave me the names of people with whom I could stay right through to the border. I planned to leave when school was over, and secretly, more and more, hoped she could come with me.

Despite all the sightseeing I had done, and all the museums and ruins I had visited, and the books I had read, it was Eudora who opened those doors for me leading to the heart of this country and its people. It was Eudora who showed me the way to the Mexico I had come looking for, that nourishing land of light and color where I was somehow at home.

"I'd like to come back here and work for a while," I said, as Eudora and I watched women dying wool in great vats around the market. "If I can get papers."

"Chica, you can't run away to this country or it will never let you go. It's too beautiful. That's what the *café con leche* crowd can never admit to themselves. I thought it'd be easier here, myself, to live like I wanted to, say what I wanted to say, but it isn't.

It's just easier not to, that's all. Sometimes I think I should have stayed and fought it out in Chicago. But the winters were too damned cold. And gin was too damned expensive." She laughed and pushed back her hair.

As we got back into the car to drive home, Eudora was unusually quiet. Finally, as we came over the tip of Morelos, she said, as if we'd continued our earlier conversation, "But it would be good if you came back here to work. Just don't plan on staying too long."

Eudora and I only went to the Plaza once together. Although she knew the people who hung out there, she disliked most of them. She said it was because they had sided with Karen. "Frieda's all right," she said, "but the rest of them don't deserve a pit to piss in."

We sat at a small table for two, and Jeroméo ambled over with his birdcages to show his wares to the newcomers. The ever-present *chamaquitos* came to beg *centavos* and errands. Even the strolling mariachi players passed by to see if we were a likely prospect for serenading. But only Tammy, irrepressible and preadolescent, bounded over to our table and leaned possessively against it, eager for conversation.

"Are you coming shopping with me tomorrow?" she inquired. We were going to buy a turtle to keep her duck company.

I told her yes, hugged her, and then patted her fanny. "See you tomorrow," I said.

"Now the tongues can wag again," Eudora said bitterly. I looked at her questioningly.

"Nobody knows anything about us," I said lightly. "And besides, everybody minds their own business around here."

Eudora looked at me for a moment as if she was wondering who I was.

The sun went down and Jeroméo covered his birds. The lights on the bandstand came on, and Maria went around, lighting candles on the tables. Eudora and I paid our bill and left, walking around the closed market and down Guerrero hill toward Humboldt No. 24. The air was heavy with the smell of flowers and woodfire, and the crackle of frying grasshoppers from the vendors' carts lining Guerrero hill.

The next afternoon when Tammy and I came from the market, we joined Frieda and her friends at their table. Ellen was there, with her cat, and Agnes with her young husband Sam, who was always having to go to the border for something or other.

"Did we interrupt something?" I asked, since they had stopped talking.

"No, dear, just old gossip," Frieda said dryly.

"I see you're getting to know everybody in town," Agnes said brightly, sitting forward with a preliminary smile. I looked up to see Frieda frowning at her.

"We were just saying how much better Eudora looks these days," Frieda said, with finality, and changed the subject. "Do you kids want *café* or *helado*?"

It bothered me that Frieda sometimes treated me like her peer and confidante, and at other times like Tammy's contemporary.

Later, I walked Frieda and Tammy home, and just before I turned off, Frieda said offhandedly, "Don't let them razz you about Eudora; she's a good woman. But she can be trouble."

I pondered her words all the way up to the compound.

That spring, McCarthy was censured. The Supreme Court decision on the desegregation of schools was announced in the english newspaper, and for a while all of us seemed to go crazy with hope for another kind of america. Some of the *café con leche* crowd even talked about going home.

SUPREME COURT OF U.S. DECIDES AGAINST SEPARATE EDUCATION FOR NEGROES. I clutched the Saturday paper and read again. It wasn't even a headline. Just a box on the lower front page.

I hurried down the hill toward the compound. It all felt monumental and confusing. The Rosenbergs were dead. But this case, which I had only been dimly aware of through the NAACP's *Crisis,* could alter the whole racial climate in the states. The supreme court had spoken. For me. It had spoken in the last century, and I had learned its "separate but equal" decision in school. Now something had actually changed, might actually change. Eating ice cream in Washington, D.C., was not the point; kids in the south being able to go to school was.

Could there possibly, after all, be some real and fruitful relationship between me and that malevolent force to the north of this place?

The court decision in the paper in my hand felt like a private promise, some message of vindication particular to me. Yet everybody in the Plaza this morning had also been talking about it, and the change this could make in american life.

For me, walking hurriedly back to my own little house in this land of color and dark people who said *negro* and meant something beautiful, who noticed me as I moved among them—this decision felt like a promise of some kind that I half-believed in, in spite of myself, a possible validation.

Hope. It was not that I expected it to alter radically the nature of my living, but rather that it put me actively into a context that felt like progress, and seemed part and parcel of the wakening that I called *Mexico.*

It was in Mexico that I stopped feeling invisible. In the streets, in the buses, in the markets, in the Plaza, in the particular attention within Eudora's eyes. Sometimes, half-smiling, she would scan my face without speaking. It made me feel like she was the first person who had ever looked at me, ever seen who I was. And not only did she see me, she loved me, thought me beautiful. This was no accidental collision.

I never saw Eudora actually drinking, and it was easy for me to forget that she was an alcoholic. The word itself meant very little to me besides derelicts on the Bowery. I had never known anyone with a drinking problem before. We never discussed it, and for weeks she would be fine while we went exploring together.

Then something, I never knew what, would set her off. Sometimes she'd disappear for a few days, and the carport would be empty when I came from school.

I hung around the compound in those afternoons, waiting to see her car drive in the back gate. Once I asked her afterward where she'd been.

"In every *cantina* in Tepotzlán," she said matter-of-factly. "They know me." Her eyes narrowed as she waited for me to speak.

I did not dare to question her further.

She would be sad and quiet for a few days. And then we would make love.

Wildly. Beautifully. But it only happened three times.

Classes at the university ended. I made my plans to go south— Guatemala. I soon realized that Eudora was not coming with me. She had developed bursitis and was often in a lot of pain. Sometimes in the early morning I heard furious voices coming through Eudora's open windows. Hers and La Señora's.

I gave up my little house with its simple, cheerful long-windowed room, and stored my typewriter and extra suitcase at Frieda's house. I was going to spend my last evening with Eudora, then take the second-class bus at dawn south to Oaxaca. It was a fifteen-hour trip.

Tomás's burro at the gate. Loud voices beneath the birdsong

in the compound. La Señora almost knocking me over as she swept past me down Eudora's steps. Tomás standing in Eudora's entryway. On the orange table an unopened bottle of pale liquor with no label.

"Eudora! What happened?" I cried. She ignored me, speaking to Tomás in spanish, "And don't give La Señora anything of mine again, understand? Here!" She handed him two pesos from the wallet on the table.

"*Con su permiso,*" he said with relief, and left quickly.

"Eudora, what's wrong?" I moved toward her, and she caught me at arm's length.

"Go home, Chica. Don't get involved in this."

"Involved in what? What's going on?" I shrugged off her hands.

"She thinks she can steal my bookstore, ruin my life, and still have me around whenever she wants me. But she's not going to get away with it anymore. I'm going to get my money!" Eudora hugged me tightly for a moment, then pushed me away. There was a strange acrid smell upon her.

"Good-bye, Chica. Go on back to Frieda's house. This doesn't concern you. And have a good trip. When you come back next time we'll go to Jalisco, to Guadalajara, or maybe up to Yucatán. They're starting a new dig there I'm going to cover . . ."

"Eudora, I can't leave you like this. Please. Let me stay!" If only I could hold her. I reached out to touch her again, and Eudora whirled away, almost tripping over the table.

"No, I said." Her voice was nasty, harsh, like gravel. "Get out! What makes you think you can come into someone's life on a visa and expect . . ."

I flinched in horror at her tone. Then I recognized the smell as tequila, and I realized she had been drinking already. Maybe it was the look on my face that stopped her. Eudora's voice changed. Slowly, carefully—almost gently—she said, "You can't handle this, Chica. I'll be all right. But I want you to leave, right now, because it's going to get worse, and I do not want you around to see it. Please. Go."

It was as clear and as direct as anything Eudora had ever said to me. There was anger and sadness beneath the surface of her words that I still did not understand. She picked up the bottle from the table and flopped into the armchair heavily, her back to me. I had been dismissed.

I wanted to burst into tears. Instead, I picked up my suitcase. I stood there, feeling like I'd been kicked in the stomach, feeling afraid, feeling useless.

Almost as if I'd spoken, Eudora's voice came muffled through the back of the armchair.

"I said I'll be all right. Now go."

I moved forward and kissed the top of her tousled head, her spice-flower smells now mixed with the acrid smell of tequila.

"All right, Eudora, I'm going. Good-bye. But I'm coming back. In three weeks, I'll be back."

It was not only a cry of pain, but a new determination to finish something I had begun, to stick with—what? A commitment my body had made? or with the tenderness that flooded through me at the curve of her head over the back of the chair?

To stick with something that had passed between us, and not lose myself. And not lose myself.

Eudora had not ignored me. Eudora had not made me invisible. Eudora had acted directly toward me.

She had sent me away.

I was hurt, but not lost. And in that moment, as in the first night when I held her, I felt myself pass beyond childhood, a woman connecting with other women in an intricate, complex, and ever-widening network of exchanging strengths.

"Good-bye, Eudora."

When I arrived back in Cuernavaca just before the rains—tired, dirty, and exhilarated—I headed for Frieda's house and my clean clothes. She and Tammy had just come in from the farm in Tepotzlán.

"How's Eudora?" I asked Frieda, as Tammy fetched us cool drinks from the kitchen.

"She's left town, moved up to the District, finally. I hear she's reporting for a new daily up there."

Gone. "Where's she living?" I asked dully.

"Nobody has her address," Frieda said quickly. "I understand there was one hell of a brawl up at the compound between her and La Señora. But evidently they must have gotten their business settled, because Eudora left soon afterward. It all happened right after you left." Frieda sipped her *fresca* slowly. Glancing at me, she took some change from her pocket and sent Tammy to the market for bread.

I carefully kept what I hoped was an impassive expression on my face as I toyed with my fruit drink, screaming inside. But Frieda put her drink down, leaned forward, and patted me on the arm reassuringly.

"Now don't worry about her," she said kindly. "That was the best thing in the world Eudora could have done for herself, getting out of this fishbowl. If I wasn't afraid of losing Tammy to her father in the states, I think I'd leave tomorrow." She settled back in her chair, and fixed me with her level, open gaze.

"Anyway, you're going back home next week, aren't you?"

"Yes," I said, knowing what she was saying and that she was quite right.

"But I hope to come back someday." I thought of the ruins at Chichén Itzá, of the Olmec heads in Tabasco, and Eudora's excited running commentaries.

"I'm sure you will, then," Frieda said encouragingly.

I returned to New York on the night of July 4th. The humid heat was oppressive after the dry hot climate of Mexico. As I got out of the taxi on Seventh Street, the sound of firecrackers was everywhere. They sounded thinner and higher than the fireworks in Mexico.

Judith Barrington

Beds

"Do you have a room for two available?" I asked in my best French. We could have been anywhere, but we were, in fact, in Cahors. We were driving south to Spain.

The gray-haired woman behind the desk looked at me over half-glasses, assessed me for a moment. I watched in silence as she lost interest in me and moved ahead into the usual ritual. It was always the same—very ordinary, at least for most guests. But not for me. I knew the dreaded Question was about to emerge from the woman's immaculately painted French lips—the question that was so simple, so complicated, so well designed to make me feel wrong from head to toe. And it's easy to feel that way in France, even without the Question.

To hide my anxiety, I turned away. There was a flower arrangement at the end of the counter, elegant as only things in France can be. I stared at the russet-colored stripes that marked the pathway into the dark throat of a yellow orchid. Nature's runway for whatever insect it was that ventured in there to pollinate the flower. A simple guide to something necessary and natural. Just what I needed now, as the Question moved through the woman's mouth, passed between her even teeth, and landed between us in the air above the counter.

"A room with two single beds or a double, madame?" (Only in French, she called the double bed *un matrimonial*.)

It wasn't long after this—I had failed to muster the courage to ask for the matrimonial—that I refused to be the hotel negotiator any longer. I was the driver, I said. You—meaning my undeniably female lover—must be the one to go in and ask for the bed that's made for those who are matrimonially related or who can pass as such. We, of course, cannot. From now on, I continued, I will be the big surprise who walks in after the deal is done.

I preferred this role. I could pretend I didn't have anything to do with choosing the bed. I could pretend I didn't even know it had been chosen. For all I knew, it was the only room left, the only bed available for hundreds of miles. I could heave the baggage up seven flights of stairs with goodwill (even though I wasn't a matrimonial person), and my dignity, at the top of the stairs, would always remain intact.

This worked very well in Figueras, Barcelona, Valencia, and several small villages in Andalusia. Was it still the same Question here in Spain, I was wondering all down the coast, as Ruth disappeared into hotels while I sat in the car studying the map. Finally, I asked her. Oh yes, said Ruth. Only here in Spain it's called *un matrimonio.* I was curious about how she dealt with the Question but didn't ask her, since talking about her requesting the double bed was almost as bad as having to do it myself. Maybe she had resorted to the comparative-pricing method— one I had used myself quite often before I resigned. This involved asking carefully, when the Question was posed, which was the cheaper option—singles or a double. Inevitably, the double was the cheapest, allowing a budget-minded traveler to sacrifice herself and her traveling companion in the interests of economy.

I had discovered this method about fifteen years earlier, on my very first vacation with a woman lover. Back then, we had both been in such denial about what we did in the matrimonio that we couldn't even look the hotel receptionist in the eye. But from some deep, stubborn core—perhaps the same one that had propelled me into the relationship in the first place—I dredged up a determination not to pay extra for two beds that slid apart in the middle of the night. Back then, I wouldn't have dreamed of handing over the job—not just because Jean didn't speak French or Spanish, but because it was my responsibility. I drove the car, made the arrangements, and took care of her. If we hadn't been in such denial and if we had known anything at all about lesbians, which we didn't, we might have said I was being butch.

But fifteen years later, I was no longer wedded (in the metaphorical, not the matrimonial, sense) to being butch. I was happy to sit and doze, or to search for a parking space, while Ruth did whatever it was she did to get us what we wanted.

Somewhere in the middle of Spain, as we headed north to Madrid, we stopped, very tired, at a small inn on the highway outside an old fortress town. It was dark and had turned very cold. We couldn't wait to fall into bed. Eagerly we went in together and found an old, toothless woman sitting in front of a small television, knitting. Ruth asked for the room, but with her minimal Spanish was not understood. Since I was fairly fluent in the language, I guessed I would have to participate. "*Tiene usted una habitación, por favor?*' I beseeched. The old woman glanced briefly from the television.

"Two singles?" she said in Spanish.

"Uh-oh," I said to Ruth, who knew immediately what was happening. She placed a hand on my arm calmingly. "Tell her I have to have a double bed to do my back exercises on," she said.

I looked at her in disbelief. Was this what she had been telling hotel managers, receptionists, maids, and night porters up and down the length of Spain? Back exercises?

"I can't do that," I said. "She'll think we're really weird."

"Then tell her we want a double bed because we're lovers and we do unspeakable things together in bed. She'll think we're even weirder."

Stumbling, I tried to explain about the *ejercicios* for the *dolorosa* back, but the old lady had picked up her knitting and was

absorbed in the movie again. Interrupting my blushing expla-
nation, she yelled in that piercing voice possessed by most
Spanish women: *"Jesús! Venga, Jesús!"* For a moment I thought
she was invoking Christ to save her from these foreigners who
were either crazy (the exercises) or immoral (the conversation,
which she might have understood). A wizened man shuffled in
and picked up the lightest of our bags, leading the way upstairs
to a freezing cold room at the end of the corridor. Jesús. The
porter.

Exhaustion and cold proved too much for Ruth, who shiv-
ered all night, in spite of my three forays downstairs for extra
blankets. The third time, handing me two more blankets, Jesús
muttered something about *ejercicios* keeping a person warm, so
I knew we had been discussed.

Our last night in Spain was at Puerto de la Selva on the
Catalan coast. We wanted to celebrate at this little fishing village
I had known years before, since we would be heading back into
France the next day. We checked into the pretty hotel right on
the quay. Its outdoor tables were bright with red-checked table-
cloths. Ruth had dealt with the Question, but unfortunately, we
had ended up with two singles anyway, perhaps because that
was all that was left. Unpacking our bags in the small room with
a magnificent view over the green sea, I pulled out the little table
from between the beds and put it to one side. Then we pushed
the beds together, committed to a night of avoiding the central
chasm.

We swam off the rocks, wandered through the town, and
bought a few last-minute treasures before sitting outside by the
harbor wall and eating a delicious paella. The great bed
Question loomed low now in our assessment of the trip that was
coming to an end, and we felt sad to be leaving Spain. Lingering
over a bottle of champagne, we discussed our return journey
through France, determined to eke out our few remaining

francs by avoiding hotels altogether and using the tent we had stashed in the trunk. The only thing that worried us was the cold: the nights were growing shorter and chillier and our sleeping bags were old and skimpy.

The noise from the bar went on till very late, but we slept through most of it and woke early to pack. Then we went into the dining room and sat down at a table near the open doors. We ordered coffee and stared out at the sailboats and speedboats rocking at their moorings as the sun appeared over the rocky Cabo Creus and began to light up the bay. Just then, a large man dressed in black with a white apron—the man who had carried our bags the night before—walked up to our table with a strange leer on his face. He hovered for a minute, not speaking, yet not going away either, grinning as if he were possessed of some unspeakable secret. Just as I was about to ask what he wanted or summon a waiter to send him away, he wheeled on us, lifted both arms in the air with his fists clenched, and spat.

He was gone before either of us fully registered what had happened. Gone so fast and so completely that it was hard to believe he had ever been there. The coffee and croissants arrived. Peach jam and four squares of butter. I looked outside, trying to feel something. Trying to know what to feel. The sun was higher, the yachts' masts glinting and the wrought-iron lampposts on the quay casting shadows. We poured the coffee and finally began to discuss what had happened. It was the beds, of course. A maid had talked to someone, who talked to someone else. The porter was in on the gossip. Even though it was always hard for me to overcome my reflexive shame about being a lesbian, I had come far enough in the past fifteen years to react with righteous indignation when Ruth burst out with her own anger. I no longer believed—though, God help me, I once had—that lesbians deserved to be spat upon at breakfast. It was a fine thing to be angry.

We settled our bill and went upstairs, where we found the beds made up and back in their unmatrimonial positions. Grabbing our cases, we left the room and slammed the door shut behind us. As we crossed the dark, tiled hallway with its old couches and dark green plants, we noticed a pile of blankets lying on a table with some needle and thread lying beside them. A maid had been darning them, working her way through the huge pile in the light of the floor lamp that glowed weakly in the corner. We stopped and looked at each other. Neither of us said a word as I leaned down and took the top blanket, folded it into a small square, and slipped it between the two sleeping bags I was carrying. We stalked out of the hotel, revved up the car, and still without saying a word, bumped over the cobblestones and headed north.

And that should have been the end of it—except that all the way to the border, breathtaking coves on our right and olive groves to our left, I shook alternately with anger and fear. Righteous anger was one thing; theft as petty revenge another. With my eyes glued to the rearview mirror, I watched for pursuers. Approaching the frontier, I expected to be seized and dragged from the car. No one calls the police for an old, much-darned blanket, Ruth told me. And of course I knew it was true. It was just that I expected to be punished some more—if not for simply being a lesbian and demanding a bed appropriate to that condition, then for fighting back in a small way when spat upon.

As soon as we sped away from the border into France, my fears dissipated. I was not irrational enough to believe that Interpol would get involved with a stolen blanket. So all the way back to England, we slept in our tent under the blanket with its neat repairs. And very matrimonial it was, too.

Margaret Erhart

Marriage

The convent is on the side of a mountain at the edge of the sea. We work every day with the sisters, shelling pigeon peas. In the afternoon I go down into the jungle at the foot of the road and shake nutmeg out of trees. Or watch the men with machetes cutting bananas and plantains. Or the children stripping bark from the cinnamon tree, or picking mangoes, papayas, cocoa, cashew fruit. In the early morning a donkey brays in the nearby village of La Digue.

We have our room and meals for sixteen American dollars a day. Nothing is required of us. Abby and I are here for the last few days of our vacation in Grenada. It is the end of the dry season; the tourists are gone. The Council of Bishops arrives next week to fill the halls of the retreat center adjacent to the convent, but now we are the only two guests. Our room is close to the sisters' quarters. In the early afternoon, the steamy heat of the day, when we rest, I can hear canned laughter from a television, and somebody coughing, somebody singing. I can hear a young boy's pleading voice, and Sister Philomena's measured no, followed by the boy again. I can hear the soft swish of a mop in the hallway, and the hollow sound of a bucket, and the sound of the bathroom door opening, a heavy door. When the day cools in the evening, sometimes we walk the path that leads from the convent out to the edge of the cliff. Half a mile below, the sea breaks on reefs stretching to the horizon.

The path is lined with royal palms, a dozen on a side, a fearsome corridor of trunks a hundred and fifty feet tall and straight with faraway heads flapping like wild green birds in a snare.

Several times during the night I wake up to the clatter of a dry weight falling from a great height onto a stone path: this is royalty shedding. In the morning I watch the gardener from the window of our room, an old, handsome man, very black, tugging what looks like a cross between a feather and a toboggan across the brittle brown grass to the burn pile.

A woman named Cecilia comes up from the village every day to cook. Her face is covered with numerous large wens, and at first I fear she is a leper. She wears a dark blue pleated skirt, a white sailor cap, and a light blue T-shirt that says DONNER WOMEN on the front and QUALITY NOT QUANTITY on the back. I can only think of the Donner Expedition and their infamous meal. It is somewhat perplexing. The sisters instruct us to compliment her at the end of every meal, which we do, though she reacts erratically, sometimes smiling widely, sometimes indifferent. Later we learn she is deaf. The convent kitchen is new and Cecilia sits alone in it most of the morning, head down over her paring knife, peeling sweet potatoes and marmy apples, or making fish pies or cashew fruit cocktail, her jaw set against her stainless steel surroundings and her shoulder-length stainless steel hair falling forward beneath her sailor cap to half mask her discontent. She squeezes soursop into juice and brings it to the table at the midday meal we share with the sisters. It looks like gray, thick milk and is sweet and sour at the same time.

In Sister Philomena's garden, the flowers of Ireland struggle on beside the flourishing flowers of Grenada. Thirsty roses, cosmos, bright lights, lush bougainvillea, hibiscus, zinnias. Lavender monkey flowers spill over the low rock wall surrounding the garden. Impatiens and tropical marigolds spring up between the stones of every path. The last week in April and still no rain. It is coming, it is coming, says Sister Alouicius. She is the oldest sister, in semiretirement, and seems at all times to be in a rapturous state. She laughs and kisses us on the lips and goes to her room to rest and watch her videos of Thomas Keating, an American Trappist monk from Snowmass, Colorado, who looks like Timothy Leary and lectures on how to date and marry God successfully. *Lectio divina* as courtship ritual. The sisters love him. He is tall and gangly. His ears are large and almost round.

Sister Philomena has had trouble with her heart and is plagued this week with indigestion. Dry toast for breakfast, unflavored pudding at noon. One evening she takes to her bed and does not join us for supper, but the next morning she is out in the garden hovering over her roses, feeding them manure tea, washing their leaves with the hem of her veil. She is a short woman, with a few teeth missing on the upper left side of her mouth, thick glasses, a beautiful, clear singing voice. Her favorite expression is "It blows my mind." She has been to Disney World. She has been in two car accidents in which the roof ended up beneath her feet. One morning she leads us in prayer for the West Indian cricket team in a match against their archrival, England. It is all anyone can talk about. Cecilia brings a radio into the kitchen and bends her ear to the static between stations. She is smiling all day, as is Sister Alouicius who breaks the news at vespers: "It is a rout!"

We go with Sister Philomena to the hospital in Saint George's where she is having a procedure for the bile in her belly. Or for the trouble in her heart. It is unclear. The waiting room is crowded but few people are sitting down. Nothing looks clean. There are many eye diseases. Afterward, on our way back to the car, she laughs at herself and waves her hands in the air and says in her Irish brogue, "That barium must have gone to my head! What am I thinking! Here we are about to go home and we haven't even visited the sick!" So we scurry along after her. She is four feet ten inches tall with the stride of a broad jumper. A few hours later, when we say good-bye to her on our way to the airport, I have a feeling I will not see her again, that her heart will explode in her sleep.

I have come to this place with a heavy heart. I do not know it until I'm here, but then in the quiet and in the simplicity of the tasks and in the regularity of the prayer, I feel it—I feel the weight of my heart. I am on the verge of marriage, six weeks away from it, and I am not ready. We have worked so hard to prepare others, to gain the acceptance of Abby's Quaker Meeting where we will say our vows. Now after months of talk and silence, the Friends no longer see our wish to marry as an act of aggression. They are ready. But I am not. I don't know this. Even as we leave I don't know it. Only four weeks later will I know it.

The evening before our departure Sister Maria, the young sister from Trinidad, wants to pray over us. Her mother is East Indian and her father is black African and Italian. She has a high forehead covered with little pimples, and full lips, buck teeth. She is the sallow color of a medieval candle. Her fingers are long. We stand in the chapel. Sister Alouicius has gone to bed after finding a tarantula on the wall and killing it with her shoe. Sister Maria places her hands on my head, a skullcap of knuckle and bone. She prays for God to show himself to me, while Sister Philomena stands nearby singing a dissonant melody, spooky and enchanted. Afterward I sit in the garden and watch the night rise. I believe I hear the roses exhale. My notion of happiness has changed, is changing. I sit and feel the sharp outlines of the mountains, feel them as if they have pierced me.

Amazon Sisters on the Trans-Siberian Railroad

A lifelong dream of mine was to travel across Russia on the Trans-Siberian Railroad. My sense of romance, my Slavic heritage, my studies in Russian literature, my Left leanings—all pointed me in that direction. I yearned to cross one of the most enigmatic countries in the world and experience its expanse firsthand.

In the summer of 1991, I was lucky to have been a delegate at the Lesbian and Gay Symposium and Film Festival in Moscow and Saint Petersburg, a first for Russia. I came back to San Francisco with many phone numbers and invitations to return to Russia for another visit.

I wrote about my Trans-Siberia idea to Asya and Lena, whom I had met in Moscow at the festival. Traversing half the country, all the way from Novosibirsk in central Siberia, they and several other Siberians were stars at the symposium, which had turned into a coming-out event. Being from another city, they felt more comfortable speaking to the press and posing for photographers at the kiss-in. Back home they continued giving interviews to the press, and they set up a post office box for queers wanting to correspond with each other. They were enthusiastic about their fledgling activism.

I called Asya and Lena before I left San Francisco. I had decided to fly to Khabarovsk and start at the eastern end of enormous Russia, make a stop in Novosibirsk, then continue on to Moscow. Lena's mother answered the phone in Novosibirsk and told me her daughter was not home, adding, "The girls (*de-*

vushki) are planning to meet you in Khabarovsk and travel back here with you." I was stunned.

"No, no, it's a journey of over three thousand miles from Novosibirsk," I protested, "that's really not necessary." Imagine going from San Francisco to New York to meet someone in order to accompany them back to San Francisco! I could take care of myself, I thought. But the American independent spirit was not something the Russians were familiar with.

"No, no, don't worry," Lena's mother assured me. "They're already planning on it, it's not a problem."

Lena and Asya, both in their early twenties, stood in line at the *vokzal* (railroad station) and bought an entire compartment with four berths to Novosibirsk on a regular passenger train, not the express. First class was not available on this particular train. First class is two-berth ("soft class" in Russian), second class was the one we were in, the common, or *kupe*, with four berths. Then there is third class (*platskart*), which are open berths, no closed compartment. Fourth class is bare benches.

Foreigners often arrange trips on the Trans-Siberian through travel agencies in the United States and are separated into special first-class cars for foreigners. Non-Russians pay much more than Russian citizens for hotels and travel. I didn't have to show my passport on boarding the train and got away with buying my ticket in rubles, which is much cheaper. In May of 1992, we paid 350 rubles each, which was about three dollars—for the entire trip to Novosibirsk (5,200 kilometers, ninety-seven hours on the train).

The Trans-Siberian Railroad is the longest continuous track in the world. Our starting point, Khabarovsk, built on the banks of the Amur River, is more than a century old. This eastern Siberian city is the main air junction for Russia's Far East. From Khabarovsk, one can go south to Nakhodka and

Vladivostok or west to Lake Baikal, Novosibirsk, or Moscow by train. After Czar Alexander III authorized it in 1886, it took thirty years to build the railway. In 1916, the year before the October Revolution, it became possible to cross the entire two continents (Europe and Asia) from the English Channel to the Pacific Ocean by train.

I rocked to the clicking sounds and gave myself over to the movement. Lena and Asya sat opposite me on the maroon fake-leather berth. We smiled and looked out the window. They were a beautiful couple—Asya with her dark brown short hair and dark eyes and Lena in permed blond hair with hazel eyes. They were always touching or hugging each other. I enjoyed their intimacy.

Ice was thawing and the green marsh filtered the running rivulets rushing to join a river. Siberia has fifty-three thousand rivers; the main three—the Ob, the Yenisey, and the Lena—flow north into the Arctic Ocean. The Amur River, which we were crossing, flows into the Pacific. I thought of how water could carve land, widening rivers, creating lakes, mud, and marsh. I had left San Francisco in the midst of a drought.

Green meadows sparkled in the spring sun. It was downright warm in May, yet Americans have an image of Siberia as a land of permanent ice and snow. *Taiga*—dense forests of spruce, birch, and pinelike ribbons—curved across the flat and sometimes rolling landscape. The tundra was farther north and dominated by permafrost or frozen mud. I had heard about the Kamchatka Peninsula—I imagined it to be similar to the California coast but barren, with active volcanoes and miles of majestic coastal views.

As soon as the train had found its rhythm, Lena set to work arranging our little *kupe*. She found a rag, wet it, and cleaned all the areas we would be contacting—the cheap vinyl headrests above our berths, the table, the doorknobs. "This train is a lot cleaner than the one we took to get here," she said, shaking her head. We struggled to set my luggage under the bunks after I took out the things I would need—my book, toiletries, a sweater, some snacks.

The conductor (*provodnitsa*), a large woman in a navy blue uniform with dyed dark red hair and thick eyebrows, suddenly appeared at our doorway with a bored look on her face holding a pile of clean linens and muttering something. Lena paid her and then began making up our bunks, as if she were at work at the hospital. She was a nurse by profession.

To get out of Lena's way, Asya and I stood in the corridor. Lena pointed us to the other end of the car. Tea was supposedly available, but the *provodnitsa* would decide when. The massive samovar in each car was heated by coal and had to be tended by each car's *provodnitsa*—she or he didn't always feel like it. Later that year on another trip, when I became frustrated waiting for service, I crossed into the next car. A young woman looked me up and down suspiciously and said, "And which car do you belong in?" as if I had crossed some forbidden border. "The next one." I pushed past her to get my water and left before she could complain more. That was after I had learned how to be rude.

Men in army uniforms passed Asya and me closely in the corridor. "We may be the only women in the entire car," Asya remarked, checking my reaction. I told her I had taken self-defense classes before leaving San Francisco. She laughed. Asya had a certain confident elegance about her. She had recently given up a clerical job at the conservatory of music, where her mother was a piano teacher. Such jobs conferred intelligentsia status, whereas in Russia nursing is not as prestigious a profession.

We settled in—I took the lower right berth, Lena the lower left, and Asya the upper left. We all sat on the lower ones for now, arranging our things. Asya took out of her backpack a glass bottle, an empty plastic orange soda bottle, a McDonald's Styrofoam cup, two blue metal cups, and some small pieces of paper that I realized were napkins. She set the table. I took out my Walkman and the latest Ferron and Jane Siberry tapes and some queer magazines. Lena and Asya, looking hungrily at the magazines, smiled as I handed the treasures to them.

Before they could get into them, a man opened our compartment door and, without a word, handed us a folder of eight-by-eleven American photos of male body builders and female fashion models. He apparently wanted us to buy them. We shook our heads no. The man had opened our door as if it were his compartment, no knocking, no "excuse me."

I was also surprised by the *provodnitsa's* power. She even chose when and how loudly to turn on the radio. We could turn down the sound of Russian rap in our compartment but not in the corridors. The train was not the only place during my travels through Russia that I noticed this controlling air of the person in charge and the submissiveness of the passengers, an unwillingness to challenge the status quo.

The toilets on the train were unbelievably disgusting. I later learned that this also depended on the *provodnik* (male) or *provodnitsa* (female) and on the age of the train. At first the smell and filth of the toilet was so overpowering I couldn't stay in there for long. There was no toilet paper or soap, you had to bring your own most of the time. The rocking of the train made it difficult not to touch the dirty toilet seat; I had to hang on to the bar attached to the wall to prevent contact. Of course, there were no showers. Every other day I would take a washcloth bath, which was very refreshing in the pervasive iron and grime atmosphere.

In our *kupe* I took naps, lulled by the swaying train and smell of clean sheets. There was something very comforting about sleeping whenever you wanted to. The "girls" poured over the magazines—*Deneuve*, the *Advocate*, *Outlook*. Like children with new toys, they shared my Walkman and occasionally one got impatient and snatched it away from the other, who of course resisted. At such times their youthfulness really showed.

In one of the back issues of *Outlook*, an old-fashioned, light-hearted drawing depicted a 1950s Doris Day–ish woman point-ing her bottom toward a butch with a whip. Lena kept flipping back to that page. "Which one would you like to be?" I asked Lena. She pointed to the "bottom." I looked at Asya, "And you?" "I don't like that," she paused and then, "but if I had to choose, it would be the other one." I said I couldn't decide. We all laughed.

The train made twenty-four stops from Khabarovsk to Novosibirsk. The total distance from Khabarovsk to Moscow is eight thousand five hundred miles and the total travel time on the train is seven days and six nights. Even though the scenery was so similar—flat steppes and tufts of forest punctuated by lit-tle settlements of wooden houses with lacelike shutters—I never felt bored. People worked in fields, occasionally a truck drove along the road beside the train track, but there were no cars, only tractors or trucks. The steppes were bare, as I had imagined they would be.

In our homey little *kupe,* Asya called Lena "*koshka,*" which means cat, and Lena called Asya "*zayets,*" rabbit. Often they used these endearments in front of other train travelers. When-ever I remarked on their public affection, they laughed, "Oh, we're sisters. Amazons." (The word for sisters in Russian can also mean cousins.) Their romance made them glow. Their slurpy kisses echoed from the upper berth. We talked into the night, as though we were at camp—Asya's lips reddening as she laughed, dimples deepening, and Lena's heart-shaped lips and animated face appearing as she lifted her head from Asya's lap to speak.

I asked each of them to tell me how they knew they were les-bians. Lena was eager to begin, her gray eyes wide open, hands gesturing with abandon. I turned on my tape recorder and began my first real interviews in Russia.

At college I became attracted to a girl named Olga. I had a serious crush on her. She wasn't the first girl I felt this way about. I would call her. She thought it was all some kind of joke. I started kissing her, hugging her. By the way, at that time I didn't really know that I was a lesbian. I had heard of such people but I thought very, very few of them existed, that they were strange. Sometimes friends would say something bad about them. I would agree with these statements, but inside I wanted terribly to meet some of these lesbians. Where are they? How can I meet them?

One day a girlfriend of mine came up to me and said, "I was in the café today and there were some gay men there."

I said, "Really? What were they doing?"

"They sat around a table calling each other Masha and Natasha and other girl's names."

"Oh, how awful," I said. "How gross! Foo! Disgusting!" At the same time I was thinking—how I'd love to see them myself! There was something about them that reflected me, my own outlook.

Lena spoke about her attempts to be straight like the other girls. She thought of marrying Olga's brother to be closer to her.

After school she worked as a nurse in Erfurt, East Germany, in an army hospital. But she continued to feel attracted to other women. She met and fell in love with Tanya, who was thirty-one, much older than she.

Tanya was very good to me. She always invited me on walks; she liked to talk with me. I never was open with her about my attraction to her. I was afraid. We talked

about men and other things. I also felt attracted to
Lena, our supervisor, who was about twenty-nine; I was
twenty-one. Tanya and Lena were very different—while
Tanya was slender and sweet, Lena was a large woman,
but I really liked her . . .

We would all get together, the men and the women,
on October 3, to celebrate the reunification of Germany.
We drank and partied. There was a woman who lived
with us at the dormitory. I wasn't attracted to her, but
she had that quality, that lesbian look. After the party
she was with me. She drew me toward her and began to
kiss me. We fell on the bed and she continued to kiss
me. I got so scared after a while, I ran to my room. My
mind was racing—what was all that about? How did it
happen? And the next day I was so worried that she
would tell someone. Well, she's from Belorussia, kind
of naive, blabs about everything. Everyone was sitting
around in the common room and she suddenly blurts
out: "Lenka, remember how we were kissing yesterday?"
I sat there stunned, thinking, Why is she saying this in
front of everyone?

When Lena began describing how wonderful it was for her
to see her first lesbian erotic film, *Emanuella,* my mind wandered to how I felt when I first saw the film. I was still married
to my husband. I thought how amazing it was that Lena and I—
of such different ages and times and countries—could have such
similar experiences and feelings about coming out.

"What did you feel when you first met Asya?" I asked her,
when Asya had gone off to wash our "dinner dishes" in the bathroom.

The twenty-third of March was supposed to be my
wedding day, but it was actually the day I met Asya, and

all the others [the ones who ended up going to the conference]. It turned out to be such an incredibly happy day!

What did I feel then? I was like a bird. I couldn't believe what was happening, yet I felt like I was doing something I've wanted to do all my life. How could I go to bed with a woman? What would I do? How is this possible? For a long time I didn't know anything about sex, making love. It was forbidden.

I remember the first night with Asya, how scared I was. I even said to her, "I guess we need to make up another bed for you." "Of course not," she said. I was afraid of her. Then I realized she too was inexperienced. I realized I had been walking around all my life under a shell. This, my natural self, my intuition, my love led me to this place.

I have now been with Asya over a year. I love her; she loves me. I think our relationship will be long. What surprises me is, at the same time that I love her immensely and deeply, this doesn't stop me from being interested in, getting excited about, and even wanting other women. I don't think there's anything wrong with it. I think it even helps one in life.

There was no law against lesbian sex in Soviet Russia, but it was "forbidden," as Lena said. I felt I had to explain that there was much homophobia in the United States. In Russia I heard stories of women being institutionalized in psychiatric hospitals and being urged by psychiatrists either to change sexes or force themselves to date men.

I told Asya and Lena that the United States was not the mythic land of freedom they thought it was. I had a friend who suffered electroshock treatments in her youth for her lesbian feelings. Gay bashing occurred in the gay capital, San Francisco. They listened to me but didn't seem to believe me.

Asya was not as willing as Lena to talk; perhaps it was just difficult for her to open up. She thought very deeply, but she was also quite moody. I had to catch her when the time was right on our four-day journey to Novosibirsk. I liked watching her shop for food at the train stations—she seemed to enjoy it. I usually went with her out of curiosity, but she was quite fast and I sometimes lost her in the crowds.

Trains and train stations are the lifeblood of Russia. Everything happens there. From love affairs to murders, from buying and selling to simply sitting and watching, the train station is the place to be in Russia. I also heard that Russian gay men traditionally meet each other there, especially at the public toilets.

In large green canopied stands, peasant women sold homemade potatoes, piroshki, pickles. Some rolled their products around in baby carriages. I grew fond of kefir, a kind of yogurt milk, and *bulochki,* a sweet bread, sometimes filled with jam. People from town would buy cigarettes and vodka from train personnel. Lots of yelling and bargaining, then cursing and pleading and women crying. It was as if every train that arrived was the biggest event in town, and everyone wanted to participate in some way.

Only a few times did we eat in the dining car. The hours were unpredictable and the food was about the worst I have ever eaten—greasy, tasteless, and extremely limited. But the dining car had its own peculiar life. I liked going in there just to watch the supervisor smoking and drinking at a table by herself, her hair piled on her head and her lips smeared with red lipstick. The waiter sashayed down the aisle with his collar turned up, looking very important. "Do you think he's gay?" I asked Lena one day. "*Nyet*," she said with certainty, lowering her eyebrows. He would stand at people's tables shaking his head every time someone pointed to something on the menu, finally admitting in a monotone, "We only have fatty pork and vermicelli today."

One day when Lena was sleeping, Asya and I stood in the corridor, leaning on the curtain bar at the window, staring out at the Siberian landscape. Two sailors stood at a window further down, one behind the other leaning against each other affectionately. It was startling for me to see this kind of relaxed intimacy among military men. But it was not the first time. I had also seen other pairs of men with their arms around each other's waists or on each other's hips. I later noticed that young women were even more affectionate with each other, often kissing and nuzzling each other in public, as well as holding hands. That's why no one seemed particularly perturbed when Asya and Lena hugged each other sensually in the corridor!

I told Asya how strange it was for me to see men being affectionate. She smiled. I explained, "If an American came across people of the same sex being so affectionate, he or she would immediately think they were being sexual. I feel sorry for straight women who may want to be affectionate with each other. They're too afraid of being identified as lesbian."

Asya frowned, "Who knows—maybe that will eventually happen here!"

"When did you first identify as a lesbian?" I ventured, hoping she would at last want to tell. She kept staring out the window and spoke softly in her sexy, deep voice.

As young as eighteen. But you know, it wasn't that serious. I could never put myself in some kind of a box and say—this is what you are, this is where you belong and that's it. No. I very calmly took on that name, lesbian. I was twenty-one when I wrote that first letter. Even though I had had no experience whatsoever with lesbians, had never even talked with one, I was very clear and just wrote, "The fact of the matter is I am a lesbian."

I wondered if she was attracted to her girlfriends?

Yes. But the ones I really wanted were not my girlfriends but either someone I barely knew or didn't know at all. For example, once I was simultaneously interested both in a classmate of mine and in someone who sang for the theater where my mother worked. These were women of my age and older.

We were silent. A drunk soldier passed us on his way to the toilet. He leaned too much against us. Asya did not bat an eye. Personal space in Russia is almost nonexistent. I was getting ready to give him a shove, but he just walked on. A soft spot in the corridor floor made him stumble, but he made it to the toilet. The stench descended on us almost immediately as he opened the door.

After a pause she went on.

But did I want a woman physically from the age of eighteen? A woman, exactly? Clearly? A woman and not a man? I still didn't have any experience with girlfriends, beyond a little hug. We may have slept in the same bed, but I had no other experience with them. There was nothing romantic, just friendship. I just never acted on my feelings when I had them. I never permitted that. I don't know why, why I limited myself. . . . My first real experience was with a person who really understood me—that was Lena. For her too I was her first experience. So Lena has been my first and only experience.

I nudged her shoulder and asked, "Tell me what you felt with Lena."

Oyy . . . Sonja, the feelings were so amazing. I tried to write them down. I feel there is the beginning of something, maybe a book, something is there inside me. I am not writing now. I left all that home. My feelings were so great that it seemed like wings grew out of my shoulders. That was my first real love, it was the most wonderful thing that ever happened to me. That's why I don't want to lose Lena.

I didn't feel any kind of confusion or agitation. Maybe a little, the first few hours we all got together— Benjamin, Alexey, Olga, Lena, there was another girl too. When I saw how Benjamin and Alexey were hugging and kissing each other, I felt fogged up or something— I had to get used to it. But I liked it. I really did. Because it was very dear and they were sweet guys, kind. So when I got used to the idea that I was among my own people, that I could speak freely, completely openly, whatever I wanted, I did what I wanted to do—I took Lena's leg and stroked it.

We both laughed. My laugh was unusually loud for Russia. I noticed people tended to be quiet in public so as not to be noticed. An older woman in a kerchief came out of a compartment down the corridor and stared at us. She was the only other woman in our car. Men and women share the same compartments in Russia. At first the idea really repelled me, but toward the end of my stay, I was taking the train and sharing compartments with all kinds of men and women I didn't know. People were polite and considerate for the most part, and very curious.

Asya looked at me excitedly, wanting to go on.

Yes, she wore a short skirt and black boots. At first we didn't even pay attention to each other. I thought she didn't care for me, and she thought I didn't care for her. At first we were a little nervous, then I sat next to her. I couldn't eat or drink or anything. I just wanted Lena, I wanted to be with her, talk with her. I was smoking, smoking, smoking the whole time. Then I jumped up and sat next to her. I put my hand under the table so no one would see. Our hands met for a moment, then I touched her leg and then I understood everything—I didn't have to be afraid, with Lena. I could say anything, do anything.

The compartment door suddenly clicked and slid open. Lena looked at us sleepily, moaning she was hungry. "I'll get the tea ready right away, *kotyonok* [kitten]." Asya brushed Lena's hair away from her face, then kissed her on the lips. The woman with the kerchief eyed us again, then looked out the window.

I loved that we ate whenever we felt like it. And Asya liked fussing over Lena and me. It was quite a switch from my independent single life in the States. Russians take care of each other's needs much more—even to the point of telling each other what they should wear, which reminded me of my mother!

It was late afternoon. At night the train became quite active —the soldiers and sailors drank a lot and joked and argued loudly. The men were generally OK toward women except when they were really rowdy. We'd lock our *kupe* so as not to be bothered. Once we had to call the *provodnitsa* when an uninvited drunk Russian came into our compartment and wouldn't leave. She appeared at the door and very sternly took the guy's arm and yanked him out. He didn't struggle.

I studied the red-haired attendant and thought about an incident a San Francisco friend of mine once told me about. She had taken the Trans-Siberian Railroad across Russia two years earlier and had had an affair with the *provodnitsa*. I was shocked then, but now I could imagine just about anything happening on the train.

The Central Asian soldiers, the Azerbaijanis, and other brown-skinned military men seemed polite. But "the girls" made all kinds of prejudiced remarks about them: "The Azerbaijanis are very crafty. Russians are so innocent and passive, they get hoodwinked by them," said Asya. It was not only that the Azerbaijanis were a darker race but that they were merchants—Russians resented this. "And the Tatars, they can wrap Russians around their little fingers. Don't I have you wrapped around my finger, zayets?" Lena leaned close to Asya. "You're not a Tatar, you're a Russian," said Asya, pushing her away. It was difficult to find any "pure" Russians, especially in Siberia.

Our Lena was a Tatar. Asya was just projecting her own mother's prejudices. We had talked earlier about a boyfriend she had before meeting Lena. Asya said he was from Central Asia,

> from Tashkent. After I met him, my mother and I started having major arguments. She is . . . you already know some about my mother. She doesn't like Jews, Georgians, Armenians, Uzbeks. She only likes Russians. She hates lesbians, homosexuals, drug addicts, prostitutes. She only likes Russians and only the good ones.

I asked what her mom thought of Lena.

> She was purposely insulting her by calling her a nurse. And she always makes remarks about her nationality. She called her "Your Tatar." Of course she's mine. My mother has some psychological problem with this—she

only wants me to be with people who have achieved
some sort of intellectual level.

The woman in the kerchief inched closer to our compartment, curious. I'm sure she could tell I was a foreigner. Sometimes in my travels I would try to pass for an Estonian or someone else who spoke with an accent in Russian—to avoid the trail
of questions and instant friends if I said I was American.

The woman was standing right at our window as we approached the immense Lake Baikal, still frozen in places. It was
the most spectacular sight of the train trip. Huge chunks of ice
were breaking up along its shores; people stood at its edges with
fishing poles. We chugged alongside it for two hours, at times as
close as several yards from the water. Lake Baikal is the world's
deepest (1.6 kilometers) and oldest lake (twenty-five million
years or more). Over 365 rivers fill it, and only one river, the
Angara, flows out of it. People in our car lined the windows rev-
erently.

The woman asked Asya and Lena if they were sisters. "We're
all sisters," Asya laughed, embracing both Lena and me. Small
eyes stared expressionless from the woman's pale wrinkled face.
I told her later that I was American but "please keep it to yourself. I don't want the whole train to find out." She asked me
about what food we ate, about prices, employment, and many
other things. She and her husband, who sat in the corridor seat
and stared zombielike out of the window never uttering a word,
had gone to visit their son and his family in Khabarovsk. She occasionally said things about the man as if he couldn't hear, but
he never reacted. As he shuffled from the seat into their compartment, I noticed his teeth were a shiny, silvery metal.

The woman told me she was a Russian-born German. "I was
taken away from my family to work in factories during the war.
The Germans were treated like slaves, moved from place to

place—Kazakhstan, the Urals, Siberia. I worked on the railroad, in a *kolkhoz*. We were not permitted to speak German. We were only given our freedom in 1956." I hadn't known about the oppression of Germans in Russia.

In Irkutsk we had another adventure—our train was stopped for nine hours. Police were everywhere. Rumor had it that someone was killed on the train. Some of the sailors had been drinking and smoking between cars, and one was either pushed off or fell and died. The police finally picked out four military men and took them away for questioning. I asked Asya if there was a death penalty for murder in Russia. She said only in very rare cases. Most murderers spend about five years in prison if they get convicted.

We went to sleep as the train sped and rocked furiously, making up for lost time. I felt cold; the *provodnitsa* must have decided not to turn on the heat. The next time I woke up, Lena was climbing down from the upper berth to get into her own bed across from me. She noticed me open my eyes, and we both smiled. She bent over and kissed me on the forehead. I felt comforted and happy; they had taken such good care of me and of each other. I didn't know than that this was the start of a long relationship I would have with Siberia—or that Asya and Lena would break up in less than a year.

Evelyn C. White

Egypt: Body and Soul

Sisters (and brothers) of all races who want to experience the full impact of the achievements of people of color should make a visit to Egypt a top priority. It's impossible to believe the negative stereotypes American society perpetuates about the aspirations and abilities of blacks after seeing the great civilization the Egyptians developed centuries ago. People of color have a grand and glorious heritage that has been systematically kept from us for far too long. In Egypt, architecture, books, art, song, science, and agriculture reflect black accomplishments; at every turn, there is something to remind us that African-Americans are descendants of some of the most brilliant and sophisticated people who ever walked the earth. As the late black gay writer James Baldwin said, "Our crown has already been bought and paid for. All we have to do is wear it." I'm here to tell you that they're wearing it big time on the shores of the Nile.

My two-week visit to Egypt was the fulfillment of a lifelong dream. As a child growing up in Gary, Indiana, I was always fascinated by storybook images of the Pyramids. Stylized drawings of Egyptians with their hands pointed in opposite directions never failed to catch my eye. A word and phonics addict, I was enchanted by the secret language waiting to be decoded in hieroglyphics. While living in Seattle during the late 1970s, I got up one morning before dawn to stand in line with thousands of people hoping to gain entry to the local museum's exhibition of treasures from the tomb of King Tutankhamen. "This little brother was *bad*," I thought to myself as I slowly walked past one dazzling gold display after another. "He was something else."

My decision to visit Egypt was sealed by a former lover who has lived in Spain for nearly two decades and traveled widely. When I asked Candace to name the most memorable country of all she has visited, she said "Egypt" without hesitation. I was on my way.

Even for seasoned travelers, Egypt can be difficult to manage because of its unfamiliar customs, perennial delays with transportation, and the heat and language (Arabic) barriers. I took an organized tour, as I felt it best to leave the details to travel industry experts who understood the Egyptian culture better than I. My tour, like most, ensured that I would cruise the Nile and visit the Pyramids, the Sphinx, the Cairo Museum, the Valley of the Kings (where King Tut's treasures were found), and several other magnificent temples. An added bonus was that I was traveling with an all-gay group, led by an outrageous couple of guys from San Francisco. While there were more gay men on the trip than lesbians, the leaders made everyone feel welcome.

The first thing I noticed on arriving in Cairo was the thick smog that envelopes the city. Stringent environmental regulations and pollution controls are simply not a priority in a country whose economy is still primarily based on agriculture. Apparently, the air quality in Cairo, unlike that in Mexico City, has not yet been deemed a health hazard. It is cleansed somewhat by the majestic Nile River, which dissects the city as it does all of Egypt. Bringing forth fertile land, food, and power, the Nile is considered the Mother of Egypt. To see the river firsthand and bear witness to its nurturance of such a mighty civilization is to understand why Egyptians epitomize Rev. Jesse Jackson's rhythmic "I am somebody" affirmation.

Seven and a half miles outside of Cairo, in the suburb of

Giza, are the towering Pyramids. I first saw them out of the corner of my eye as the tour bus rumbled down the road. They span the horizon, appearing larger and more impressive than any photo could ever depict. As we approached, I realized that I was actually *in* the storybook picture that had enthralled me as a child—the image that had maintained its black allure and power even when it was juxtaposed with more horrific images from my youth, like those of German shepherds snarling at black children or of the mule-drawn cart bearing the body of Martin Luther King Jr.

When I stepped out of the bus in front of a caravan of camels sprawled lazily on the desert sand, my jaw dropped and tears sprang to my eyes. All of a sudden I could hear Aretha Franklin wailing, as she does on her album *Amazing Grace:* "My road has been a little rocky on my way home."

The Pyramids (the tombs of the pharaohs Cheops, Chephren, and Mycerinus) were erected as royal burial grounds and are the star attractions of Egyptian tourism. Nearby sits the enigmatic Sphinx, sculpted in the shape of a lion with a human head wearing a headdress, but unlike the massive structures it guards, the Sphinx is actually much smaller than its picture-postcard image. Despite the throngs of camera-clicking tourists who flock to the site, the Pyramids and the Sphinx retain a regal dignity that has left people breathless for centuries. For me, seeing and touching these structures reinforced my belief that any obstacle can be overcome, no matter how formidable. If people of color can accomplish such feats as the building of the Pyramids and the Sphinx, then surely we can conquer drug addiction, teen pregnancy, unemployment, AIDS, spiritual despair, ruthless politicians, and the other contemporary ills we face.

After several days in Cairo, my group flew to Luxor to board a ship that cruised the Nile. In the heart of Upper Egypt, Luxor is the site of Thebes, the "hundred-gated city" immortalized by Homer. Among its many treasures is the divine city of Karnak, a temple of stones, statues, and obelisks that covers more than forty acres. Down the road a bit is the temple of Luxor, which, experts say, the Egyptians used only for their raucous New Year's celebration. Soprano Leontyne Price once performed her signature opera *Aida* in the midst of these sensuous ruins on the bank of the Nile.

Luxor is also the starting point for visits to the nearly one hundred tombs in the Valley of the Kings and the Valley of the Queens. Dug into hillsides, the cavernous tombs once held the mummies of pharaohs and the temples in which they stored the treasures they would need to survive in the afterlife. From floor to ceiling, the tombs are graced with shimmering blue and emerald green hieroglyphics that tell the story of each pharaoh's victories and defeats. The tombs helped me, a product of America's death-fearing and -denying culture, gain a new perspective of on life. The ancient Egyptians believed that life never ended but continued into eternity. They greeted death not with sorrow but with joyous acceptance and the anticipation of an even better afterlife. In fact, the legendary Queen-Pharaoh Hatshepsut was so exhilarated by the prospect of death that she ordered a mortuary temple to be built especially for her embalmment. Carved into the side of a mountaintop in the Valley of the Queens, the huge split-level necropolis is heralded as one of the most spectacular architectural achievements in the world.

From Luxor, the deluxe cruise ship would sail to temple sites at Esna, Edfu, and Kom Ombo before arriving in Aswan. After visiting the Valley of the Queens, our group was dropped off along the commercial waterfront of Luxor, not far from where the ship was docked. We were directed to make our way back to the boat for lunch, after which we were scheduled to depart for Esna.

Until one's body clock adjusts, the combination of early morning outings and the mystical impact of Egypt can leave a first-time visitor disoriented and dazed. Perhaps African-Americans are especially susceptible to this phenomenon because of the ways in which the splendor of Egypt contradicts the denigrating messages we've internalized about our roots. That's exactly what happened to me in Luxor.

Overwhelmed by my experiences at the tombs, I spaced out. I meandered along the waterfront, walking in and out of shops for who knows how long before coming out of my stupor and heading back to the boat. As I approached the dock, I could see a huge cruise ship moving down the Nile. My stomach sank. I knew instinctively that it was the *Ramses*—the boat I was supposed to be on.

There were several men on the dock, coiling ropes, oiling winches, and tending to the other nautical chores. I ran toward them, hoping they'd tell me it was the *Prince Ra-hetep* or the *Khufu* sailing away, not the *Ramses*. No such luck.

Stunned, I stood on the dock, gazing out at the water as the ship moved steadily toward the horizon. "I can't believe it," I said to myself. "I've really and truly missed the boat."

Luckily, I'd made a point of memorizing the ship's itinerary and knew for sure that the next stop was Esna. Lesson learned: when traveling with an organized tour, be sure to know your group's daily destinations. Don't count on the guides to fill you in on all the details. Travelers can get separated from guides. Don't I know it.

I had my passport, driver's license, and plenty of cash in my backpack. I had noticed, during the trip, that folks in the group often divvied up their personal belongings with partners or friends. One person would place, say, both travelers' water bottles, wallets, and cabin room keys in one pack. Then the two would trade off carrying the bag, leaving each person periodically unencumbered during these often strenuous days. Although I was traveling with my then lover Catherine, we'd decided that each of us would keep track of our own money and personal documents. Lesson learned: never leave money, passport, plane tickets, or other valuables in the care of a traveling companion. Graciously decline to be responsible for another traveler's belongings.

Also to my advantage was the decade I'd spent working at a major metropolitan newspaper. As a reporter, I'd covered riots, explosions, murders, earthquakes, and conventions in cities both large and small. I was accustomed to finding myself in unfamiliar situations that demanded my full concentration. Thus, when it sank in that the *Ramses* was not going to make a U-turn and retrieve me, I shifted immediately into reporter mode. My assignment was to meet the ship in Esna without getting raped, robbed, or killed.

My concern about safety was not particular to being black or to traveling in Egypt. Common sense dictates that women should pay special attention to safety anywhere, anytime. In this case, I knew that I'd thrown myself into a crisis situation and was therefore more vulnerable to making hasty decisions. So as I turned from the dock and walked toward a row of about a dozen waiting taxis, I offered a silent prayer to the gods, asking them to help me choose a driver who'd deliver me to Esna in one piece. They brought me to Aesop.

What I remember most about Aesop is that he was wearing a tan, crisply ironed, full-length djellaba, or shirtdress, that contrasted beautifully with his cocoa-brown skin. Indeed, I'm sure I was drawn to Aesop because he exuded a cool serenity in what was by then brain-broiling midday heat. There was not a bead of sweat on his body. Discreetly flashing a twenty-dollar bill, I asked Aesop if he'd take me to Esna. He looked around nervously, as if to fend off other taxi drivers who might have swooped down on me for the fare. Having vibed away the competition, he gently hustled me into the cab. Lesson learned: when in a tight spot abroad, let your greenbacks do the talking.

Off we went. If you're thinking speedy, sprawling interstate highways, think again. We're talking back roads, dusty roads, gutted roads, twisted roads, and to who knew where? Surely not I, for whom Esna could have just as well been Edinburgh for all I knew of its whereabouts. For two hours, Aesop and I rambled through rustic villages and lush Egyptian farmland that I would never have seen had I not missed the boat. Along the way, he explained many of his country's customs to me with the whimsical pride that I came to recognize as characteristic of Egyptian people. Delivering me to the dock where the *Ramses* would arrive in several hours (land travel is much faster than water), Aesop suggested that I visit a nearby temple and purchased an entry ticket for me. As he drove away, I thought about the often fractious relationship between black men and black women in America and how we've become so far removed from our best selves. My time with Aesop gave a meaning to the word *brother* that I'll carry with me for the rest of my life.

After visiting the temple, I found myself strolling through Esna's open-air market. I was soon greeted by Nubie, a barefoot Egyptian boy of about ten who ran to my side and asked, in halting English, if I knew Mike Tyson, Bill Cosby, or Michael Jackson. Quick to shrug off his disappointment when I answered no, Nubie lit a cigarette (quite common among Egyptian boys) and offered to take me on a carriage ride through town. With the grace and charm of a refined gentleman, he took my arm and led me around the corner to where a speckled gray horse, hitched to a black carriage, stood in the sun swatting flies with its tail. Just as we were about to start clip-clopping down the street, a thin boy with a thatch of dark curls, wearing a soiled and tattered djellaba, came running toward us, shouting excitedly. The boy, apparently a friend of Nubie's, was begging to join us on the ride. With an officious nod, Nubie granted permission, and the boy, all arms and knees, scampered into the carriage.

The horse's hooves tapped out a steady, syncopated beat on the pavement as we rode along Esna's waterfront. After a while, Nubie pulled the reins and we turned left into a dusty, mazelike neighborhood of whitewashed houses with tightly shuttered windows. Stopping at an intersection, Nubie leaned back and asked if he could take me home to meet his mother. I said sure, and his face lit up like Times Square.

Nubie's house was a plain, primitive structure crafted out of baked earth. The peeling paint, rickety door, and other signs of poverty were offset by its coziness and the fact that the temperature inside was a full twenty to thirty degrees cooler than outside. Nubie's mother, a short, dark-skinned widow dressed in black, responded to Nubie's Arabic commands by extending her weathered hand to me and then scurrying to the kitchen to make tea. His sister, a girl of about twelve, grabbed a broom made of palm fronds and began sweeping a patch of dirt in front of a battered gold couch on which she motioned me to sit. When the sweet, fragrant cinnamon tea was ready, Nubie's mother poured three glasses—for me, Nubie, and his friend. I waved my hand toward Nubie's mother and sister, encouraging them to join us; they both giggled nervously, shaking their heads from side to side. In a flash, I understood what was happening. Though only about four feet tall, Nubie was the man of the house. And I, the smiling, polite, then thirty-four-year-old black woman from America, was being showcased to Nubie's mother as a "love interest." It was so poignant I nearly started to cry.

Word must have gotten out about Nubie's "girlfriend," because the next thing I knew a stream of neighbors was outside the house. Smoking a cigarette and speaking proudly in Arabic,

Nubie opened the shuttered windows and allowed the people to peep in. Soon a huge crowd was gazing lovingly at me, including several women in brightly colored wraps who were holding babies. These women were especially animated and seemed quite eager to enter the house. After a rapid-fire exchange in front of the window, Nubie went to the door and ushered the women with babies into the living room. One after the other, they came forward with their kicking, cooing infants and held them out for me to touch. For this, I needed no translation. The Egyptian mothers clearly considered me a sign of good luck.

I snuggled, nuzzled, bounced, cradled, and rocked a good two dozen babies before realizing that if we didn't leave soon, I might again miss the boat. I gestured to Nubie (who was now standing about six feet tall) that it was time to go, and after making my farewell to the glowing crowd, we climbed into the carriage and left. As the horse made its way back to the waterfront, with both Nubie and his friend beaming, I reflected on my amazing afternoon. Missed boat, fantastic taxi ride, adorable babies, and ten-year-old Egyptian "boyfriend"—what a life!

About fifteen minutes after we arrived at the dock, the *Ramses* pulled in. I waved—as cavalierly as I'd walked through the shops in Luxor—to my lover and other friends on the ship who had come out on the deck and were leaning over the railing, looking for me. I wondered how I could possibly thank the gods for such a memorable day. While I knew it was meaningless in terms of the cosmos and my profound sense of gratitude, I handed Nubie a wad of bills before I walked down the gangplank to the *Ramses*. He took them, kissed me on the cheek, and lit up with a smile that is forever etched in my heart. A blazing, magnificent smile that captured the body and soul of Egypt.

Rebecca Shine

What I Will Never Be

When Alexandra and I embraced outside my apartment building in Portland, I smelled her hair, like warm bread and lavender, and knew this visit wasn't going to go as I had expected. That smell collapsed her three months' absence into no more than a moment. In her arms, I could imagine that she had never left. In fact, this was her first visit back to Oregon since she'd returned to her home in Greece equipped with a Ph.D. in psychology from America.

Standing in the cool January air, our arms remained firmly around each other, holding on to that sense of contiguous time. Though we could hear people passing across the street, we paid them no attention. Seldom had we ever—not when we had walked in the neighborhood holding hands nor when, finding we couldn't resist a kiss until we were inside, we had disclosed our passion on the doorstep.

I felt safer about being out in Portland than anywhere else I had been, even after living through seven years of Oregon's antigay initiatives. Rather than keeping gays and lesbians in the closets, those political struggles had propelled large numbers of us out of them. The bitter attacks gave rise to equal and opposite forces of solidarity on our part and to increased sensitivity from the wider community.

Walking up the stairs to my apartment, we ran into my next-door neighbor coming down. Linda had known Alexandra casually when she was my lover and had treated her hospitably from the start. That night on the stairs, my neighbor smiled at both of us and asked Alexandra how Greece was.

"Good," she said, though I could tell by the way she kept moving, that there was a much longer answer she was not inclined to give just then.

Once inside, we sat face to face on my living room carpet, surrounded by bookshelves, a desk, and a small couch. Plants stood atop most surfaces. On the walls hung a Georgia O'Keeffe painting, a family portrait from the late 1800s, and a collection of fifteen black-and-white postcards of people I admired, from Amelia Earhart to Toni Morrison.

At first, all I could do was cry. Alexandra grasped one of my hands, put the palm of her other hand on my thigh. She reached over and nuzzled my neck with her nose, kissing my skin. I leaned back to keep myself from leaning forward.

She said, "It's like yesterday I was here."

"Except," I said, "we're over."

"Doesn't feel like we're over."

"But we are," I said.

To keep from kissing her, I suggested we move to the kitchen. Pictures and postcards I had accumulated over my seven years in Portland covered the refrigerator door. My favorites included a photo of me in Yosemite; a "Safe Sex Is Hot Sex" postcard with two naked women sitting face to face, the legs of one wrapped around the hips of the other; and a photo of Alexandra and me, the only one I still kept up—the two of us sitting in front of a museum in eastern Oregon, me leaning back into her, her arms around me, both of us smiling.

In the kitchen, I sat on the counter, Alexandra on a chair at the table. We drank white wine and smoked her Camel cigarettes, telling stories: what we'd thought this reunion would be like; how it wasn't what we'd imagined; how she had still not come out to her father, though this was one of her goals in returning to Athens; how her friends had taken care of her during successive illnesses in recent months.

I told her about having left my job as a political organizer for a gay and lesbian organization and about what my life was like now that many good friends had moved away. I spoke of how I'd begun to feel I was letting go of her—but the next moment I was sitting in a chair face to face with her and we were kissing familiarly, passionately. She told me, as we took one another in—eyes, voices, smiles, each other's body so near—that she wanted to make love with me. I cried again, telling her how mad I was that she'd left and now had come back for a visit, only to say that and then leave again.

"I don't know whether to hit you or make love with you," I said.

"How about both?" Then she added, "But if you hit me, be careful."

We couldn't help but laugh.

That's when she offered me the invitation: "Come to Greece. I wasn't ready to offer that before. Now I am." She tried to persuade me. She said, "Let's not think about the future. Let's just think about now."

"Why do I love you so much?" I said, running my fingers along her cheeks.

I told her all the reasons why I couldn't live in Greece, how I couldn't be happy there, all the things she had told me about Athens, the noise, the pollution, the traffic, the sexism, the homophobia, the anti-Semitism, the anti-Americanism, how a relationship was not enough to sustain me, how I was just beginning to establish a life without her. The more she persisted, the more we disagreed, the more I wanted to kiss her.

"Let's not talk about this anymore," I said.

We sat quietly for a time, something we had learned to do together, something that made me feel I had known her much longer than a year and a half. I looked at her black curly hair resting on her shoulders, her dark eyes against pale skin. I looked at the way her nose arched and her chin jutted out slightly, characteristics I imagined were very Greek. My own Semitic darkness reflected her Mediterranean looks. She was wearing my favorite dark blue lamb's wool sweater with her usual black jeans. I remembered the feel of her skin, her large, luxurious breasts, the wide expanse of her belly. I remembered grabbing her hips and pulling her to me.

"What you do to me," I said.

"Tell me."

"OK," I said, standing up, taking her hand, and bringing her to my bed, "I'll tell you."

After we had exhausted our bodies, Alexandra fell asleep, drained from her flights from Athens to Copenhagen to Seattle to Portland. For a time, I watched her sleep, sitting between her legs, my feet warm along the sides of her breasts. I realized that in our time as lovers, I had never watched her sleep, as she often went to sleep after me and always woke before me. I watched her eyelids and mouth twitch from time to time, her hands clasping my calves, her legs pressing against my hips, a murmur, a moan, a hand tightening its hold on me.

Later, I sat alone at my kitchen table, smoking a cigarette and drinking a glass of wine by candlelight, studying her black watch and silver rings perched on top of a Kristin McCloy novel I had recently begun reading. "Where would I ever get lesbian novels anyway," I wondered, "if I lived in Greece?"

Throughout the following week, I found myself considering a visit to Greece. I had not yet found a new job, I had money in my savings account, I wanted to be with this woman, even if temporarily, and most of all perhaps, I didn't want to wonder, two or five or ten years later, why I didn't go, what would have happened if I had, how it would have changed my life.

"I want you to come if you'll check it out to stay," Alexandra said when I brought up the idea of visiting. "If it's just a trip and you know already that you won't stay beyond that, I'd rather you didn't come at all. I'd rather we make the break now. Save some pain." As if pain could be meted out by will.

My first few days in Athens, I am repeatedly taken for Greek, a misconception I welcome. I don't want to be a tourist, simply traveling the surface of this country. During these first few weeks, I imagine I am going to stay. I will believe this until it becomes true or until the situation proves otherwise.

I study modern Greek with a tutor, progressing steadily, so that I can converse, albeit slowly and simply, with anyone from the bus driver to one of my new friends. In Alexandra's apartment, I put my books on the shelves and rearrange the kitchen cabinets. In the neighborhood, I learn how to shop at the *laiki*, the weekly fruit and vegetable market where you buy by the kilo, never simply picking two oranges here or three bananas there as I would have in America.

As I explore the neighborhood, I find my favorite spots within walking distance: a British World War II cemetery and a sea wall at the end of a nearby marina. As I walk through the cemetery, looking at the multicolored flowers along each of the white headstones, I can still hear the nearby traffic. But I can almost imagine its constant roar to be the sound of waves.

To get to the sea itself, I must navigate the highway that runs between Alexandra's apartment and the marina—four lanes of fast-paced cars in a city where pedestrians never have the right of way. But sitting on the sea wall, watching the boats, away from the cars and the buildings and the noise, is worth the trip. I find that I make such deals often: bearing the sound of traffic in the cemetery for a chance to walk among the flowers, crossing the highway for the sea. It is a matter of bartering daily for beauty in a city no one but Alexandra has recommended to me. When her friends ask me how long I am staying, I tell them I do not know, that I will have to see.

After my first month in Athens, Easter arrives, by far the biggest holiday in Greek Orthodoxy. Godmothers and godfathers throughout the country buy their godchildren new Easter outfits and *lambáthes,* candles to carry on Easter night that are decorated with everything from a simple ribbon to a stuffed bunny to a full-size Barbie doll. All week long before the actual events and for weeks afterward, people greet and leave one another with "Kaló Pásxa," Good Easter.

Alexandra has a break from the psychology classes she is teaching and wants to take me to the island of Lésvos. Though Alexandra grew up in Athens, she spent summers on the island where her father was raised and considers it her home village. Her father now owns the house where he grew up, and Alexandra is comforted by the thought that she will always have this place. She has never taken a lover there, and she says she wants me to see it.

I know this is a chance to learn more about Alexandra. I also look forward to quiet time on the island to read Cavafy's poetry, write letters to friends in America, work on the sweater I am knitting for a friend, and rest. But when we arrive, I find that friends walk through the back door all day, multiple neighbors extend invitations for the same meals and never fail to ask where I am when I don't accompany Alexandra to the *cafeneío,* to their house for a meal, or on a walk in the hills. In this village where neighbors' doors open a mere five paces away in every direction, my hopes for solitude vanish.

The closest I get is a walk with Alexandra among the olive groves. I follow her quietly along the grassy path. At one point ahead of us, a man herds his sheep from the seat of his motorcycle. Watching this modern shepherd at work, our laughter entwines in a way our bodies do not when we walk through this village where no one knows that Alexandra is a lesbian and that I am her lover. I want to return to the house, to be within the privacy of our own walls, to have permission to touch her.

But even in the house our affection is restrained, as neighbors arrive steadily, bringing us food: fried fish, cheese pies, or Easter *tzouréki* bread, which looks a lot like a challah but tastes much sweeter and has a red hard-boiled egg set in it. Discussions ensue about whose house Alexandra and I will eat at each day; she knows how to navigate these conflicts. "I've told Eléni and Yiórgos that we'll have Easter at their house," she tells me, "so we'll just send anyone else who asks us to see Eléni and she can have it out with them." This turns out to be the best method, to let the villagers negotiate with other villagers about where we will end up, instead of us, the visitors, negotiating with them.

Following Christ's casket around the village one night and listening to fireworks and prayers the next, I am acutely aware of being a Jew, albeit a closeted one. It is not a fact I am eager to disclose in a village of Christians who are marking the death of their savior, a savior I imagine most of them have been taught was killed by Jews. When everyone carries a lighted candle around the church on the night of the Resurrection, I carry one too, though I wonder if my conformity is a kind of betrayal. Still, I am relieved to get through the activities unscathed and, for the most part, undetected. I do ask myself if my choice is any different from Alexandra's concealment of her lesbianism and her lover, but I don't come up with an answer.

On Easter Sunday, we have lunch at Eléni and Yiórgos's. Their kitchen could just as well be my own grandmother's in Rhode Island. An off-white tablecloth covers a plastic flowered one, and the chairs don't match. Some of us sit on the couch, which has been pushed up to the round table; the others are in chairs. A television, an old fridge, and an oven crowd the room. The sink sits in another small room, which is good as space is already tight here. Ceramic, porcelain, and glass vases and dishes, probably given to them by daughters and friends, sit on a shelf near the ceiling and clearly haven't been moved in years, except to be pushed closer together when new ones have been added.

I think about the last holiday I celebrated, Tu B'shevat, the Jewish festival of trees. Three lesbian friends and I sat on their living room floor and read stories that made metaphors of all the different kinds of fruits that grow on trees, those with pits, those with skins, those you eat whole. We followed each reading by admiring and then savoring the fruits, from avocados to bananas to strawberries. I can see by the preparations that food is going to be just as central to this Easter celebration.

While Eléni finishes cooking, turning occasionally to smile at her husband, her round face reddened by the oven, Yiórgos tells us how sweet the lamb, one of his own, will be as it has eaten only grass its entire life.

Soon their daughters arrive, Chrisoúla and María, in their early twenties, both in from school in Athens. I wonder if they will understand that Alexandra and I are lovers, catch a glance or a comment that alerts them. Since this secrecy makes me feel awkward, I want the daughters to discover us. But I also hope, for Alexandra's sake, that they don't.

The girls have long brown hair and olive skin and wear sweatshirts and blue jeans. Their parents appear more like grandparents in their seventies than a mother and father of fifty-six and sixty-one, respectively. Especially Yiórgos, a farmer, with his tough and darkly tanned skin. Charging in between them, tangled among their arms, is Dushko, a nine-year-old Serbian boy Eléni and Yiórgos have taken in for six months. I find myself excited to be in the company of another foreigner. With a smile on his smooth, young face, Dushko leans into

Chrisoúla as she sits down, so she will keep her arm around him.

Dushko, we have learned from everyone we have spoken with, has been a blessing for the couple, and this proves true. "There hasn't been so much laughter here in ages," Yiórgos tells us. But when he begins to tell us about Dushko's having been in hiding with his family for four years with the bombs exploding overhead, Dushko runs to Yiórgos's side of the table and cups his hands over the man's mouth so tightly I can see that Yiórgos cannot unclench them.

But nothing in the room stops: María is helping Eléni serve, Alexandra and Chrisoúla are talking, and I am watching the boy, who wordlessly covers the older man's mouth. The scene stays like this for a long time, longer than is comfortable, until finally, without warning, Dushko drops his hands and returns to Chrisoúla's side, tugging her for a kiss before she goes on with the conversation. I can understand his insistence. I have the impulse to command the same from Alexandra.

The boy seems to have accomplished his goal of preventing Yiórgos from speaking, as the man stops talking when the meal begins. Fried potatoes, wild boiled greens, lamb chops, feta salad—we are in fresh-food heaven. During the meal Yiórgos turns to Alexandra and explains that the boy doesn't like to hear about the war. He speaks too quickly, so Alexandra translates for me. I wish they would speak slower so I could understand more.

I imagine Dushko and his mother and brother concealed in their house for so many years. I have been in a sort of hiding with Alexandra for only four days, a confinement without any physical walls, and yet already I am despondent. Unlike the boy, I am aching to hear Alexandra tell our story.

Meanwhile, Dushko is circling the table, getting hugs and kisses from the girls and their parents. There is just enough room for him to squeeze around all of us sitting at the table.

When Yiórgos tells Dushko that I am a visitor from America, the boy slumps sideways in his chair and stays like that. Then he pops up again. The older man translates: when the boy hears America, he thinks of the planes. They dropped bombs on his neighborhood. He's playing dead.

"Good American," Yiórgos tells Dushko in simple Greek, since like me, the boy is just learning the new language. "She's a good American, not a bad one," but already I feel I've lost Dushko as an ally.

For dessert, Eléni serves us fresh *mizíthra,* a cheese still warm from the making, which we cover with honey and cinnamon. Chrisoúla hands Dushko a large chocolate egg. He turns it in his hands, smells it, and then, suddenly, smashes it on top of the table. Pieces of chocolate fly all around the table and onto the floor. For a moment everyone is frozen; then Yiórgos, Eléni, the girls, Dushko, and finally Alexandra and I break out in laughter. After he picks up the pieces, he begins to hand them around to everyone. When Dushko gets to me, he extends his hand with a piece of chocolate. "Thank you," I say, wishing I had the nerve of a nine-year-old boy to smash this invisible egg I hold, send it flying in front of everyone.

As we leave the house, Yiórgos says I am welcome any time and tells Alexandra she must bring her friend back in the summer. As we return to the house, I see that though we came to Lésvos as lovers, we will leave as "friends." Somehow, without our realizing it, this place has changed us—the distance we have had to keep from one another publicly, the number of times neighbors have called me her friend. Not that anything in our private life appears particularly different, but I am learning how the lack of a clear reflection of the truth can blur it. All of this has altered our relationship, perhaps forever and, it seems, without our consent. Maybe we allowed it, maybe not. I cannot tell.

On the journey back to Athens, Alexandra and I sit on the deck of the ship, talking. I am eager to have her all to myself again and so lean forward, without thought, to kiss her. She leans back to avoid it.

"There may be people I know on the ship," she says. Though her words could be taken to imply shyness, her tone belies anger with me—for not respecting her choice, for pushing her.

After a silence, she continues, "You have to understand what I've done here, Becky. You wouldn't have believed how my friends in Athens acted five or six years ago. They were disgusted by the simple fact of me and a woman lover touching in front of them. And now, with us, we can be ourselves around them. That is my doing, my work." Tears gather in her eyes and then in mine.

"I know," I say. "I want to appreciate what you've done, what you do. It's a lot. But it's so different from the way I've lived, the way I think I need to live."

"Do you think it's easy for me?" she asks, her voice rising, the tears advancing.

Alexandra may not like being closeted, but unlike me, she is accustomed to it. Having had a secret woman lover from ages nineteen to twenty-one, she didn't have another woman lover until she was twenty-six when, traveling, she met an American who brought her to Portland to live. Since then, her lovers have been American, Swiss, biracial, Jewish, and just once, Greek.

Soon after my arrival in Athens, Alexandra removed most of the obvious signs of this last lover from her apartment. But even though she has taken down the photo of Sophía on the bulletin board next to the computer and the poster inside her closet of two mouths kissing with a personal inscription at the bottom, even though she has replaced the photo with one of herself and two friends on motorcycles in Australia's gay and lesbian Mardi Gras and the closet door remains bare, I still keep finding things. Well, to be honest, I am looking for them.

I look at the names on the pad next to the telephone to see if Sophía's name is there. When I don't find it, I feel relieved that they haven't talked recently. When I do find it, I am relieved to know that I wasn't crazy to wonder. I get nervous every time Alexandra plays with the silver circular charm around her neck, a gift from Sophía. Every time I glance at the message board and see the Mykonos Island poster, I think of their trip there together. And every time I choose a tape to play, I look at the homemade mixes Sophía once made for Alexandra, open up the tape boxes, and read the titles and inscriptions. Sometimes I understand them immediately: "You left too soon." Others I need to look up in my Greek-English dictionary: "We are both islanders." I am never quite sure if I'm translating that one correctly.

I select a tape with the red construction-paper cover and a title I don't understand to listen to on the way to see my friend Ándriana one Wednesday morning. While on the train I think about how I'd never be able to understand these songs if they were in Greek. I am aware more and more these days of how much I lose in translation, wondering if I have missed anything essential so far. I would not say I am particularly prone to paranoia, but I am a talker, a listener, a reader, a writer, and residing in a foreign language sometimes leaves me feeling not just disoriented but helpless. I know what I want to say but can't form the words, can hear people around me talking but can't make out their meaning. By the English song titles, I know this is a tape full of love songs, but I continue to listen. By the time I walk through Ándriana's gate, I feel sick, as if I've stuffed myself with food far past being full.

I ask myself over and over why Alexandra's relationship with this ex-lover pains me more than any of her others. I have met Sophía, seen her long, wavy auburn hair, her handsome freckled face, the silver bangles on her arms, the fashionable clothes that suit her work as a graphic artist, the black cowboy boots she wears out to the bars each night. Do I think she is more beautiful than I am, or smarter, or more intriguing? But this is not it, at least not all of it. While much of what I feel is jealousy of the way Alexandra seems to keep Sophía on a pedestal in her heart, the tension springs from something deeper still.

What I finally come to see is the place where Sophía and I differ inalterably. I come to see that what Sophía is and I am not, what I will never be, is Greek. And while this has its benefits— for I do not feel I must live in this country or in the closet, as Alexandra does—it also means I will have to give up my lover in exchange for my own home, a place where I feel I belong, a place where I can be wholly myself.

After all, it doesn't really matter if Alexandra and I make each other laugh, if we cry at each other's stories, if we find the simplest satisfaction in a meal together, a walk, a talk, a bed. In the end, none of it really makes a difference if she is a Greek who wants to live and work in Greece and I am an American who wants to live and work in America. No matter how many times I whisper endearments to her in her native tongue—*omorfiá mou, máttia mou, agápi mou*—it will never be my first language.

The day before I leave for home, we are reading newspapers in an empty *tavérna* by the sea, not knowing if this parting is for good or not. We've had all the conversations about when and what if and how would it be possible and so on. Now we sit, two women, both dark, both Greek looking, though one belongs and one doesn't (our respective Greek and English newspapers give us away), swapping news clips—"Study of Soccer Hoodlums at the University of Liverpool," "Dole Leaves Senate to Pursue

Presidency"—as I try not to think anymore about the longing that will set in a few days, a few weeks, a few months from now.

The waiter covers the green-and-white-striped tablecloth with a paper one to keep the cloth one clean and holds the paper down with clips on all four sides of the table so the breeze doesn't take it away. The *tavérna* is empty because it is a Wednesday and only one o'clock, too early for Greek lunch.

"The European Community OK'd construction of a new airport outside Athens," I read aloud to her.

"That," she says. "They've been talking about that for decades. Who knows if we'll ever see it." That's the difference, I realize, between reading about a place and being from there: you know what's propaganda and what's the truth.

We look up when the waiter comes over, and I order in Greek. As he walks away, she smiles at how I have used the slang instead of the tourist's Greek. We are laughing again and reminiscing about the first time we came to this *tavérna*, a forty-five-minute motorcycle ride south of Athens.

It was on the first of May, a union holiday in much of Europe, when many people strike from work and, in Athens, set off for the sea. We head for Ayía Marína, navigating through the stagnant traffic, weaving between cars, sometimes heading up the opposite side of the street. The cars hardly move, but we keep going, passing churches and marinas until we turn right into a seaside *tavérna*. The sea is *yalázia,* a word used to describe the blue of the Aegean—a word we do not have in English, I think, because we do not have such a sea. The taverna is full, inside and out, so we must wait for a seat. But we don't mind, because it's beautiful out, warm enough finally to sit outside, because the anticipation of the *calamarákia,* fried zucchini, and *tzatzíki* is part of the pleasure, because it is a holiday, and because there is no end for us in sight.

Linda Smukler

Looking at a Map of the United States

1. LOOKING AT THE MAP OF THE UNITED STATES

Looking at the map of the United States I close my eyes and try
to place myself   a big land reduced to pale yellows and greens
and pinks   of state and forest and desert and plain   I write
plain on my paper and think that's what I'd like to see   a stretch
of grass and field   a place without danger or disease   a long
round of earth I could touch and hold under my palm like a
pitcher's mound   I open my eyes and suddenly I'm in the Blue
Ridge   a green diagonal near the coast and the sky a dark dense
gray because there are storms all throughout the region   so the
radio says and my hand pulls me to the right and up to the
farthest tip of Maine an island and mud sucks at my feet as I
bend down to gather mussels for dinner   marinara and corn at
our home which hangs off the cliff into the east-facing sky   the
storms will make it here by tomorrow morning and we will simply sit and listen   our house securely bolted to the rock   but
nothing is secure enough over the years from some freak storm
or a hurricane and one year we did almost lose it all   that is
Maine and life suddenly feels very short to know all the places I
see when I look down at the map of the United States   to say
nothing of Baffin Island and the Faroes and icebergs off the coast
of Patagonia   but not today on this map this hand this palm
singing in Memphis or lying down somewhere in the Texas dirt
never mind that I've never really laid down in the Texas dirt   in
a week I will do so and that takes my breath away for the chance
and the curl of my toes against paper then of actual experience

and grit   That is a gift she said   to make a map a dream then a path and tires on the road   in a week I will know that Texas smells a little like old cat food and dog beds and a lot like Texas   an air I've never smelled before   somewhere to the west   the first breath of a new home

2.   6 A.M. TOMORROW MORNING

6 A.M. tomorrow morning and today is July 20   the day we were supposed to leave but we are leaving tomorrow so it's here roundabout not quite precise but precise enough   6 A.M. to-morrow morning we will pull out of the driveway driving away from the sound of the stream and we will cross a line   a mark   a true before and after   a monthlong note of endings and revelations   of tying up bags and packing boxes   of deci-sions and rearrangements   of coasts and other coasts   of past lovers and trails   of what can be thrown away and what has to be kept   what is kept is you   our kisses going west   our god-pushed travel   our fuzz-filled truck and the fuzz-covered ani-mals that inhabit it   at 6 A.M. tomorrow morning we will drive away to red mountains   to cactus and hidden waters   at 6 A.M. we will be on the road and each breath will count as the next until we land ourselves and all we have   really just our-selves and the things we protect inside the cab of a little green truck   at 6 A.M. the wood thrush will call to us good-bye and half a life will wave and half a life will beckon   at 6 A.M. at dawn the sun to our backs over the eastern hills

3.   THE BUDGET POST

At the front desk a kind woman with one of those signs *if your dog can vouch for you . . .*   and the swimming pool is a welcome sight and all bodes well for our first motel of the trip   not as far as we thought   a mere 400 miles away from home   you can get to Woodstock VA from Woodstock NY in seven hours so

why hadn't we ever gone before?   such an easy romp and you
joke about teaching positions in Tennessee and Roanoke and I
think silently No I will never leave where we are going after we
work so hard to make a home there   but then that is two years
away and here we have passed the Mason-Dixon line into a foreign country   overwhelmingly white on the highways and in
the brochures and we cannot get off the road because it's summer and we have two cats in the truck who will not survive the
heat   so we drive on and even the Blue Ridge and the Appala-
chians are too shrouded to see from I-81   we're taking the route
designated by AAA because the long roads through Indiana and
Ohio seemed too familiar and known   we have yet to see one
other New York license plate but there is Comfort Inn and Super
8 Days Inn Wal-Mart Citgo and Cracker Barrel   McDonald's
and Quality Inn   a billboard that asks WHO'S THE FATHER?
CALL 1-800-DNATYPE

4.   THE RAMADA INN

The Ramada Inn in Morristown but we are not there now
we're on our way to Knoxville at 7 A.M.   you in the driver's seat
two cats by our side and a dog in the back   a Bimbo's billboard
advertising for fireworks   75 mph going south to Chattanooga
and I-40 and NPR a familiar and comforting voice as long as we
can get it   long roads with a short sight line because of the heat
and the mist and the large yellow truck just ahead   the day
much more hopeful than it was at 4 A.M. or even 9 P.M. last night
much more than exit signs and campers   surrounded by unseen mountains and camouflaged men who scared us at first but
were really quite harmless   quiet in their rooms   the Tennessee governor's task force to find and destroy fields of marijuana
in the midst of corn and tobacco and orange earth   last night I
saw Hardees and Phillips 66 signs floating in the thunderclouds
and Babka chased sticks on an abandoned road   Tyne Daly was

on TV and I watched her strong and tragic face and wanted to
cry in her ample breast with her justifiable anger and I thought
of the mail we've been sending out and wondered if our friends
noticed the boredom and fear I went to sleep with and woke up
with too   finally I woke you with the loudness of my sighs and
I talked to you for a while about people who paid attention and
seemed to care and people who did not   about public performance and private acts   and just your touch brought my anxiety and homelessness to a pause

5.   THE SATELLITE INN

The Satellite Inn   Jetsons' lettering and a solar system   the
center of our world for another night in Alamogordo   military
and Harleys   Trinity to our west   the father the son and the
holy death   closed except the first Saturdays in October and
April and if we go the guidebook warns us to *leave our testicles
and ovaries at the gate*   Tularosa   Trinity of the roses   signs
for *Small* and *Large* Missile Range   we walk barefoot to touch
the spirit of the sands hard-packed by storms and we wonder
what poisons come up through our feet   dirt roads climb the
ancient volcanic cones to gunneries and observatories   the
woman at the desk tells us about her tabby who looks like our
Smudge   how when you first see them they look like *nothing*
then when you really look they are *just beautiful*   you lie on the
bed ready to sleep exhausted from cramps and driving   I
spread your legs and feel bits of sand   I brush you clean to
enter you   the lights are on and maybe someone can see so I
say Wait and get up to turn them off   Smudge and Max lie content with us on the bed and Babka groans in her sleep   the dark
becomes our world   contained at first and not so large as the
sands and Trinity   but then a rapid light and then vast again

Sarah Grossman

Adios Paraguay

"*Adios,*" they greeted me as I walked toward them. They were the Paraguayan children in the barrio I was now calling home. Their greetings were long and drawn out on the first syllable, "Ahhhh-Di-Ohhs," so it almost sounded as if they were saying "to God" instead of "good-bye." In the beginning of my two years as a Peace Corps volunteer (PCV), I wasn't quite sure what to make of this greeting that I would hear ahead of me in the distance before I could recognize the person talking to me. Good-bye before hello. Was it prescient of what was to unfold? Or were they really saying "to God" as a warm South American "hello"?

The children became bolder and tried out their rudimentary English. Now I was greeted, "Good-bye, how are you?" amid giggles at their own mispronunciations. The English erased the doubt of the translation but not the confusion. Was this some Zen koan about impermanence and a practice of nonattachment? And how did this fit in with "si Dios quiere"—"if God wants it"—which followed nearly every statement and was really a question, "No?"

Doubt and confusion would be my constant companions throughout my Peace Corps service. In 1983, just shy of twenty-four, I had left my on-again, off-again lover of nearly a year and joined the Peace Corps. I had been ready to make a difference in people's lives. I would help handicapped children truly in need of my physical therapy skills. This work would overshadow any need for a lover.

My earnestness had fed my expectation that I would be the only lesbian in the Reagan-era Peace Corps. And as a PCV in a country run by a Nazi-harboring dictator, who had renewed a state of siege every six months for nearly three decades, I hadn't anticipated any Latina lovers. I had thought this path of service and celibacy would enhance my inner growth. I had banished from my consciousness the fact that after six months without the attention of a lover, my loneliness would start to itch like dead skin insisting to be scratched off and that I had always found someone to soothe the itch. In my pursuit of enlightenment, I had ignored the differences between celibacy by choice and celibacy by circumstance.

During the first three months of training, the Peace Corps boards you with a host-country family while you go to classes every day for language, cultural, and technical training. It was during this time that I found out that I was not the only gay person in the Peace Corps. In my group of fifty *aspirantes* (aspiring to be PCVs) I found a gay man and a lesbian and suspected a few others. We were relieved to discover that we weren't alone, as we had all anticipated being, especially after learning the Paraguayan slang for gay in one of our early cross-cultural training classes.

Our trainer filled us in on gringo innuendoes, gestures, and language that could be misconstrued sexually by Paraguayans. But the discussion was heterosexual, and since I was still aspiring and not yet a full-fledged PCV, I didn't ask any questions about lesbianism. For some reason, though, our trainer offered the slang for "gay" as another important piece of information for surviving in Paraguayan culture—like boiling the water or checking your feet for the pica parasite that burrowed into the skin and lay eggs.

Ciento ocho—"one hundred and eight"—for the list of one hundred and eight prominent businessmen suspected of homosexuality that had been published on the front page of the newspaper some years back. The trainer laughed telling us the story, and said there was still some confusion about whether the original list was actually one hundred and nine, followed immediately by a suicide that dropped the number to one hundred and eight, or whether the original number was one hundred and eight followed by a suicide. Regardless, *ciento ocho* was the slang. After hearing this story and its accompanying laughter, I became more cautious in revealing my sexual orientation to people. *Ciento ocho* was much more ominous than the *maricón* I had heard in high school from my Puerto Rican friends. As derogatory as *maricón* was meant to be, still the image of a butterfly was much less weighty than that of a man killing himself.

I made it through training and, now a PCV, moved to Pilar, a small town six and a half hours south of Asunción, the capital. I overlapped with a volunteer in special education who would be leaving soon, and she helped me settle in, assisting me with finding a place to rent and a bike to buy and introducing me to the teachers and special education students and their families. I tried to explain what I could do for them as a physical therapist, but my rudimentary Spanish and only basic greetings in Guarani limited our initial meetings. We all smiled and nodded "*Sí*" to one another and waited for *mañana, si Dios quiere.*

Tranquilo (peaceful), *paciencia* (patience), and *así es la vida* (such is life) quickly became a part of my vocabulary, if not my sense of being. I was intent on offering my help and had little *paciencia* when I knew there was so much work to do. But the Paraguayans seemed more interested in my translating Michael Jackson songs, leading a Jane Fonda workout, and just settling down with a nice Paraguayan man. I blushed, smiled, shrugged my shoulders, and feigned more ignorance of the language when it came to introductions to single men. In my worries about being able to survive as a lesbian and most likely a celibate one at that, I had overlooked the most obvious of relationships that would undoubtedly arise in my two years, being with a man. After all, I was getting old by Paraguayan standards, and I had the allure of being *Norteamericana*.

Having slowly built my acceptance in the community, I wondered how long it would last if I repeatedly denied my Paraguayan suitors' advances. Hector, the son of a wealthy rancher, a strapping European-looking young man who had all his teeth and owned a motorcycle and jeep, was one of the first to come calling. I was inside writing in my journal, yet again recounting my frustrations with the lack of progress toward any real work and my increasing size, when I heard clapping outside the gate, the Paraguayan announcement of a visitor. I opened the shutter, looked out, and saw Hector. I couldn't recall from my training which days were the ones that were reserved for dating and which ones were just social calls, but I did remember that there was a distinction.

I walked out to greet him, and we chatted briefly at the gate. The conversation consisted of basic greetings and repeated questions on his part, as I was still caught up in figuring out what the significance of visiting on Thursday was. I smelled his cologne, which clued me in that this was a formal calling night, and not knowing what to do next I agreed to go for a walk with him, which seemed safer than inviting him in. We walked to the center of town, he bought us ice cream cones, and then we sat in the plaza and talked about life. My language skills at that time limited me to the present and simple past tense, and since my past was not so simple to discuss in Paraguay, we spoke mainly of the present.

The next day my landlady asked me about my date with Hector. I tried to explain that it wasn't really a date, but I could see in her smiling eyes that she didn't believe me. She congratulated me on my good fortune and asked when he was coming again. I said I didn't know, which was the truth, but she said he'd probably be by again on Sunday and that if I wanted she would make up some of her special rice pudding for us. I thanked her and said she didn't have to do that, then returned to my room and my journal writing as there was no one to talk to about my dilemma. The special ed volunteer with whom I had overlapped briefly was now back in the States, and the friends from my training group were days away by bus.

Hector persisted in his courting of me, and I went along with it while our dates didn't proceed past hand-holding and a kiss good night. But I knew this time was limited and that he would soon begin to insist on something more. People in town were already discussing wedding plans for us when, one evening, the good-night kiss beckoned for more. After many months of no sex I wavered briefly, but knew that I couldn't continue this with Hector. I pulled back and answered his pained face with "I already have a *novio* (boyfriend)."

He looked even more stunned, and I apologized, stumbling my way through a lie about dating a volunteer in another town. I told him that I was sorry I hadn't told him sooner, that I really enjoyed his company, that I hoped we could be friends, and that in North America men and women can be friends without there being a sexual aspect to it. At least I tried to convey all that, but I don't really know what he understood of these ramblings in my limited Spanish. Always the gentleman, he was respectful. But as time passed with no sign of my *novio*, he began to question my fidelity and suggested I have two *novios*, one in Pilar and my PCV *novio* whom I had met, supposedly, in Asunción.

Initially my PCV *novio* had been a total fabrication, but as the story grew, I replaced this fiction with my gay friend Don. I figured that basing the lies on something true to life would help keep me from getting more entangled than need be. Now my *novio* had a name, a face, and even a job in another town. I explained to Hector that I was faithful to *mi novio*, wondering how long I could pull this off. Even my landlady was beginning to question my story, especially with such an eligible bachelor courting me. Luck was on my side: I soon discovered that Don would actually be moving to Pilar, as he was not happy in his site and there was an opening for another volunteer in my town. With this good fortune, I began to feel that I could deal with translating Michael Jackson songs while I waited for my job to evolve.

Don and I quickly became the talk of the town, and I enjoyed our masquerade, walking arm in arm with *mi rey* (my king). I was his *reina* (queen), and because our personalities were different, we played up the fact that opposites attract. He is tall, handsome, and refined, more cultured and more of an introvert than I, preferring time by himself to read, write weekly letters home, and listen to opera. I am tall, nearly as tall as most of the Paraguayan men but still seven inches shorter than Don. Siesta filled my needs for solitary moments; the rest of the time I was out visiting families, playing soccer with the men and basketball with the women.

Luckily for me, Pilar, being so close to Argentina, was more progressive than most towns in Paraguay. Most parts of the country had no organized sports for women, but Pilar had an entire basketball league with various teams. The exercise helped me retain some sense of self, even if playing soccer with the men rendered me *un poquito más hombre que mujer* (a little more man than woman), as some elderly women said when they passed by the field where we played.

Meanwhile, rumors also started circulating that perhaps Don was a spy for the CIA, since he spent so much time reading and writing. Friends started approaching me with questions about his "real work" and cautioned me to be careful. I assured them that Don was not a spy, and although I don't know whether they believed me about that, they did seem to believe in our relationship.

Now that I had a *novio* living in my town, I didn't have to deal with the Paraguayans courting me and I had the freedom to look for a *novia*, although I didn't dare look beyond the circle of volunteers. I knew there was at least one assured lesbian, but she and I remained "just friends." *Así es la vida.* On the other hand, the distance from family and friends and perhaps the heat and humidity and abundance of passion fruit and papaya seemed to encourage many doubting women to explore their desires to be with another woman. Their curiosity would turn to a newly discovered truth while embracing a woman for the first time under the mesh tent of the mosquito net.

I had a few *novias* over the course of the two years, most of them adding our tryst to their list of new things experienced in a foreign country. It was difficult sustaining a relationship in Paraguay with volunteers coming and going every six months. We were scattered throughout the country with no sure means of communicating or even seeing each other. Some towns didn't have phone service, and even if there was a phone office, one had to rely on the office in the other town sending out a messenger on foot or bike or horse to find the volunteer and hurry her back to the office for the call. Telegraphs were a little more reliable but had to be sent in Spanish. And since you were giving the message to an operator, who would later tell all her friends, the message had to be cryptic. Creating yet another language in this country that already had two was a challenge. Mail was slow and hardly reliable, but at least one could write in English and hope that your outpourings found your lover before the relationship ended. Visits were thus hard to arrange and often happenstance. A scheduled meeting in the capital might be rained out, as the dirt roads leading to the three paved highways would turn to impassable mud, leaving you stranded at home or on the road.

But on the rare occasions a lover made it to Pilar for a visit,

I had advantages over my heterosexual PCV friends. Since I was perceived as being heterosexual and living alone, which was unheard of for single Paraguayan women, the townspeople, who worried about my living arrangements, looked out for me. Having a girlfriend spend the night brought me blessings and a sense of relief from my neighbors. My reputation as being a chaste and faithful *novia* to *mi rey* was intact, so everyone could sleep better when I had someone with me to protect me from the evils of the night. My other PCV friends who had visits from friends of the opposite sex—regardless of the nature of the visit—were assumed to be wanton and immoral. But here in Paraguay it was almost as if I were sanctioned for having a lover stay with me as long as we were quiet about it. Besides, we were women and what could two women do together anyway?

By the end of my service, the only lasting love relationship was my fictional one with Don. He and I remained *novios* and had the blessings of the community. Or so I thought. In my last few weeks in Pilar, I was given two farewell parties. The first was from the women's basketball team I had played on. The team was a mix of high school–aged girls and a few women my age or a little younger.

Two of the women my age were single, shorthaired, and also *un poquito más hombre que mujer*. The three of us would often linger on the court after the others left practice. They both knew Don and asked many questions about us, waiting for me to tell them something other than my standard retort that our relationship was solid despite our differences. Many times I wanted to tell them that, yes, I was *ciento ocho*, but every time I came close to disclosing the secret that wasn't so secret, I thought about my reputation in town. I had spent many months working toward projects that were just beginning to materialize, and I had new ones I still wanted to start, so I kept on lying. Slowly our talk would turn from the personal to the game, as we dribbled, spun, and shot our way through the hot afternoons.

The farewell party was hosted by our captain, Ludy. Her husband helped with the grill, and the rest of the team brought salads, cakes, and beer. The food, beer, and music kept the spirit of the party upbeat, and I was able to focus more on the good friends I had made rather than the good friends I was soon to be leaving. Don and I sat side by side in the patio sharing stories and laughter about our basketball season. As the party progressed, I became more aware of the impending good-byes, so I started to help clean up and divert some of the attention away from me.

I carried a stack of dirty dishes to the kitchen where Ludy was washing things. Marta, one of the suspected lesbians on the team, followed me in. The three of us cleaned and dried dishes, making small talk, when a drunk Marta threw her dish towel down and hugged me from behind, saying how much she was going to miss me. She rocked me side to side, pressing her belly and breasts into my back. She kept talking, slurring her speech, although I was able to understand that she had a going-away present for me. I told her she didn't have to give me a present, that our friendship was enough.

"No," she said, "I want to give you something special," and then she slid her hand down inside the waistband of my pants. I immediately grabbed her hand and pulled it back up before it went inside my underwear. I hugged both her arms around me so she wouldn't persist in her gift giving, and tried to think of a graceful way to get out of her grasp and this situation. Ludy watched us, waiting to see my response. I smiled as I felt Marta's hot beer breath on my neck and told her again I didn't need any presents. I struggled and turned us around. I looked out on the patio. Surely *mi novio* would rescue me. No one on the patio noticed anything going on in the kitchen. I could see Don talking with some of the others, but he couldn't see me. Yet he could still be my out. I told Marta that Don was the jealous type, and I'd better go see him. She laughed, rocking us both off balance. She leaned against a wall, still holding me tight, and said, "Jealous, ha! Your *novio* is *ciento ocho*."

At that revelation and with no interjection from the curious Ludy, I realized there was no graceful exit from this scene. I broke out of her grip and walked out to the patio, speaking loudly in English, "We're getting out of here. Now!"

My remark, understood only by Don and the few volunteers who happened to be in town, was followed by a chorus of "*¿Que? ¿Que dice?*" I answered their inquiries in Spanish with "I'm sorry, but I feel sick and have to go. Thanks for everything. I'm really sorry."

After a year and a half with Don, this was the first time I discovered that my *novio* cover was not as foolproof as I had thought.

A week later, at my next going-away party, I learned the slang for lesbian. Never before had I heard anything other than *ciento ocho* to refer to someone who was gay. I hadn't noticed that it was always men that people were talking about.

The Paredes family invited Don and me to dinner at their home. They had become good friends through my rehab work with the community. Augusto was a physician, and his wife was born and college educated in Uruguay. Her lilting Spanish, effusive energy, and broader worldview than that of most Paraguayans had been quite a welcome relief in this slow little town. Don and I had shared many meals and discussions with the Paredes during our time in Pilar; now this was to be our last meal together.

We were to bring the makings for burritos, with recipes, and they would provide the traditional Paraguayan food—*asado* (grilled beef), *chipa guazu* (a heavy, rich corn bread), and plenty of *cerveza* and *vino*. Prior to our visits they had never tasted Mexican food and had become quite fond of the spicy beans wrapped in flour tortillas. Don was in charge of the beans, while I made the tortillas and salsa.

Before I went to Paraguay, I had never made tortillas, as there had never been a need. I experimented with flour and water despite lacking the necessary utensils, but being a good PCV, I used appropriate technology. After patting the balls of dough in my hands into a rough approximation of a tortilla, I laid them on my floured table and rolled them out with my water bottle. Then I cooked them in a skillet on my miniature tabletop stove. The little two-burner propane stove always reminded me of playing house with my sister's Suzie Bake Oven. My chipped enamel plates, jam jars for glasses, small tins of tomato paste, and film canisters filled with spices added to the feeling. This was the last time I'd be making tortillas in Pilar, but the enormity of the situation was diminished by the size of my kitchen and utensils.

After making enough tortillas and salsa to last us the night, I headed over to Don's house. My *novio* was ready with the pot of beans, and we walked the half mile to the Paredeses', each carrying a handle of the basket that held the food. I tried not to think about this being the last dinner with the Paredeses, the last week with my *novio,* the last week with all my friends in Pilar. Tried not to dwell on how kind the Pilarenses had been in opening their hearts and homes to this *gringa* and of how accepting they had been of my relationship with Don. So many times I had felt overwhelmed by the deceit of my relationship but had felt I couldn't come out in a country where the slang for gay was *ciento ocho.*

Don and I arrived at the Paredeses with smiles and only a little dust clinging to our sweaty limbs. My fingers were stiff from the plastic-coated wire handle of the basket. Patricia greeted us at the gate with her two young children running up behind. We exchanged kisses and greetings as Augusto walked up, his round belly covered by an apron smeared with grease and blood.

We milled around the kitchen and patio until Augusto shooed us away from the barbecue. Patricia, Don, and I then sat at the table while the children played outside. We mostly listened, as Patricia, always longing for company, talked about the sadness of tonight's dinner and shared the town gossip. I loved listening to Patricia talk even though I didn't always understand what she was saying. Her Spanish was singsongy, rising and dipping on syllables I hadn't expected. Her *ll* sounds were soft and chewy compared to the Paraguayan *y* sound, and she spoke at a speed that defied the workings of my tongue. Don and I sat back, nodding, interjecting short phrases here and there, while Augusto sang off-key in the background.

Then Patricia, apparently tiring of gossip, asked about our food, what would she ever do after we left, how would she prepare such *comida?* We laughed politely at her melodrama; then Don reviewed the bean recipe with her. Sitting across from him, I watched as he smoothed the wrinkles out of the paper he had folded and placed in his breast pocket. He slid the paper toward Patricia and told her which *mercados* were the best for beans. Beans were hard to come by in Paraguay. They were what the poor ate, but even the poor, not wanting to be considered poor, stayed away from them. A doctor's wife buying beans would probably be suspected of being on a mission for the *clinica*, providing food for the needy. After Don's precise instructions about the preparation of the beans, she looked up at him and asked, "¿Y Las tortillas?" And the tortillas?

He answered, "You'll have to ask Sarah, she's the *tortillera.*"

Patricia looked at me, looked at Don, and then laughed. A big laugh, open mouth, exposing her gold- and silver-filled cavities. She wiped her eyes and took a sip of water. Don and I gazed blankly at each other, clearly missing the joke. Patricia stifled a giggle, inhaled, and looked at both of us again, asking in her lilting Spanish, "You don't know what *tortillera* means?"

We both shrugged our shoulders, answering, "No."

"Ay, *una tortillera* is a woman who loves other women, you know?"

I nearly choked on my water and kicked Don under the table, feeling my face flush. He kicked back, looking at me with incredulous eyes. We both laughed, now getting the joke and so much more. I couldn't believe that I had been here this long, had even made some Paraguayan friends I suspected might be lesbians, and still never knew about *tortillera*.

After wiping the tears from our eyes and catching our breath, I shared the tortilla recipe. Augusto joined us shortly, and we stuffed ourselves with food, wine, and stories the rest of the evening. We laughed at ourselves much of the evening, reminiscing over the past two years and how our cultures and languages had sometimes collided and twisted, resulting in tragicomic events that now were truly humorous. When the wine had been drained from the bottles, Don and I stood up to go. We all hugged, cried a bit, and laughed a little more at the *tortillera* incident. Another story that would be retold with much laughter in the months and years to come.

Don and I walked home arm in arm. The night air was cool, a clear winter night like the ones I'd first experienced two years earlier, arriving in this semitropical winter from an East Coast summer. I leaned against Don's tall frame, needing the warmth and extra support after all the *vino* and the discovery that I was *una tortillera*, not *un ciento ocho*, like my boyfriend. We laughed again at the revelation and mimicked Patricia's singsongy Spanish on the empty streets, "You don't know what *tortillera* means? It's a woman who loves a woman!" More than a decade later, I can still recall perfectly her burst of laughter and the pitch and intonation of her question and answer.

In the last two weeks of my two years as a Peace Corps volunteer, I had discovered that not everyone believed my relationship with Don and that if anyone were to talk about my true loving, I would be referred to as *la tortillera*. In a country where no food even vaguely resembled a tortilla, I found this an odd term for lesbian. And even if there had been tortillas, it would have seemed strange. Apparently it came from Mexico, as someone told me later, slapping her hands together like a woman making tortillas. "See, it's like women pressing their bodies together." I nodded, but didn't really see myself as a flip-flopping, slapping kind of lover. I was disappointed that the slang had made it down from Mexico while the food hadn't.

Don walked me to my door, forever the gentleman. He kissed me good night but instead of wishing his *reina* a pleasant sleep, he wished his *tortillera* sweet dreams. I don't remember what I dreamed that night, but I do remember waking and wondering what else I thought I knew and really didn't.

Carole Maso

The American Woman in the Chinese Hat

Everyone here is kissing everyone on the cheeks—once, twice, three times—this summer, one of the hottest in years, I'm told, on La Côte d'Azur, where I have come to write. But I'm not kissing anyone; I'm waiting for her.

She has written to me: "How much I miss you! Beneath all I do is an undercurrent of sadness at your absence. I think of you without knowing I am thinking of you, until I spring into consciousness and you are before me as clearly as the road I am driving or the fork I raise to my mouth—that close, that immediate, I love you so."

And I have written to her: "Come here and I will make you lamb with anchovy butter. Courgettes and tomates provençale. Soupe de poissons. I will wrap you in French cottons. I will bathe you in perfumes made from flowers not far from here."

I have come to Vence, a small resort town, ten kilometers from the sea, between Nice and Antibes, and I am sitting at the bar called La Régence.

La Régence. Everyone here is sitting under white umbrellas, drinking their drinks, tossing their heads, talking about le cinéma or la poésie, or the great thinkers of France, in this beautiful place ten kilometers from the sea.

It had been a moody June, a month of cold and rain and wind, but now the luck has changed and everyone is out in full force to celebrate, to talk, talk, talk, to flirt, to languish in heat and light and I am caught in it all, in a whirl of polka dots and lace, in high heels and perfectly shaped legs, of light and stripes and sunglasses. Ooh là là! At every table, salut! Ça va!

Waiters and waitresses glide by with trays of many-colored drinks. The drink that is grenadine and beer, an intense rouge, the bright green drinks of menthe and the yellow citron pressé. The cloudy drink that is pastis. And vin rosé. Les glaces fly by. Marvelous ice cream concoctions arrive at the marbled tables, topped with fan-shaped cookies like wings.

Vacationers pose for photos, the small adored dogs on every arm. "Tootsie, viens!"

Children run around a circular stone fountain. Old men race by on mobilettes. People pass carrying gâteaux and extravagant bunches of flowers. And on the street the large, expensive cars of summer drive by slowly for all to admire.

The young are engaged at every table in animated intellectual conversation. "Mais oui! Mais non! Mais bien sûr! Voilà!" They fling around cigarettes and run their hands through their tinted hair. During a lull they look around. They are not afraid to stare. I feel their eyes on my exposed back, on my shoulder, my leg. My foreign face.

"Ça va?" they say. "Ça va bien," and "à demain." I love the way their voices rise at the end of their sentences, the way they sing their language.

She has written to me: "I was so sad there was no letter from you today. I wait every day for the letters to unfold, the French stamps, the pink paper. If only I could open one of your letters, put my lips against it and taste you. I must tell you, my dove, that I feel somewhat lost without you."

Pink drinks, sea-green drinks float by. Children in designer French clothes dart in and out of the palms. "François, viens!" A gloriously sculpted head goes by. All kinds of hats. It's the kind of light that makes you feel like you're seeing things for the first time. And on the radio Sade sings about Paradise.

"One feels safe from grief here," I write in my notebook.

The albino midget passes and waves.

I am known as the American woman in the Chinese hat who writes.

A girl passes who reminds me of her ten years ago. She must have Basque blood, I think.

I close my eyes and picture her here, sitting under a white umbrella at La Régence.

In three months she will leave her job in finance and come here to live. We will stay in a stone house with a red tile roof. We will live on olive oil and tomatoes, bread and figs, a few small fish. We will drink rosé from Bandol, white wine from Cassis, Côtes du Rhône. I will work on my stories. Find the arrangement of words for all this. She will learn French. Learn to love this place as I have come to love it.

And I have written to her: "The dollar today is worth six francs and suddenly, mysteriously, magically, I am richer. I'm sure you could explain all this to me—but here alone, going to the bank, it feels like another small miracle in a place of miracles."

We will live safely together in a house of stone. Surrounded by a grove of orange and lemon trees. Surrounded by roses. I will live in a house in France with her. It is finally what I have come to want. After all this time.

La Régence. The plane trees cast an incredible shade. The young move in and out of light, singing American songs— Michael Jackson, Taylor Dane—this glorious day. I order another drink.

And I write to her, "I wish I could send you a hazelnut torte or a tarte au citron. I wish I could send you the way the sunlight falls on the baskets of women in town, or make a gift of the sound of bells on dimanche."

I tremble when I hear a bit of Spanish, the language she still speaks in her sleep. Or when I see a cat that reminds me of our cat. To touch a cat. She will bring the cat, of course. And the absentee ballots.

And she writes: "Today Dave caught a sixteen-inch trout, that's almost twice the length of this paper, twice my poor trout that we ate on the porch dreaming of Nice. Dreaming of Antibes."

I miss her. I am acutely lonely here without her. I am the American woman, toute seule, in the Chinese hat. But it will not be long now. It's our last separation. It seems inconceivable to be apart anymore. I see it with the clarity only this kind of light makes possible. The two of us together, forever. I have given up too much, I think, to write the handful of stories I have written. I have given up too much to be the person capable of writing them. I have almost lost her as a result.

I write to her: "You are my dove. My colombe d'or."

And she writes to me: "I am going to plant the small plants we bought." She is going to make an herb garden. She is going to grow her hair.

I am trying to improve my French before she comes. Venir is to come. Choisir is to choose. Attendre is to wait.

They call the cats mignon here—little and sweet and dear, all in one word.

"Tiens!"

And she writes to me: "Be careful when the mistral comes. You know how distracted you can get. You know how sometimes you slam into every tree. Be careful. Remember how easily you bruise."

They call the children les petits. Everywhere there are French babies. Little François has wandered away from his family again, this time to pet a white bird. "François, viens!"

I order another drink. I stare back at the young French man

when he stares at me, and I hold my notebook for courage because so much courage is required. How the day dissolves in
salut and ça va. How the day dissolves in pastis. My eyes rest on
a girl who has seated herself next to the young man who stares.
She laughs with the carefree joie de vivre of a pretty young girl
in early summer. She calls out to a friend passing through the
square, "Pascal, attends!"

Attendre is to wait.

Another man comes up to me. I steer clear of desire. It's a
choice I'm learning can be made. His eyes graze my leg. I want
only her now. Still I write in my notebook, "One does whatever
one must. One walks through fire if necessary, through light.
Attracted to it like moths. One swims in treacherous waters like
poor trout, brouchet. Attracted to it like salmon to their deaths."

What is this love of the illicit, the forbidden? This love of
oblivion?

I'm drifting off. These strange hours of writing in the cafés
and bars of Vence.

"Tu es toute seule?" he asks.

"Oui."

I feel my ankle and then slowly the rest of my body begin to
go. I look back. I guess I'm curious just how persuasive this
blond offering Gauloise might be.

There is so much longing in me.

"Non. Merci." I am waiting for her.

A fish, a woman, a vulture appears before my eyes. I can't
stop from seeing this. A spear. Goats gambol around a dancing
nymph. Fishermen devour their catch of sea urchins in darkness. I think of the great Picasso, who has given me this, painting in Antibes. It is 1946 and he has just met the beautiful Marie-
Thérèse in the Galeries Lafayette and they are lying on the beach
at Juan-les-Pins and they are about to go for a swim.

Something here is slightly dangerous. These strange hours of writing. Sometimes there's vertigo. Sometimes I lose the way home.

You bruise too easily. You go under.

Home. Everything had left its mark: the paper tearing, the cry of concrete, the red sign that said PSYCHIC lighting the dark city. I was too afraid there. My older brother in a white bed.

What is it that is so dangerous under this bright surface of saluts and kisses and ice cream and many-colored drinks in the dazzling afternoon?

I look up. Love should be like this: a blond boy in a striped shirt tipped back in his chair on the dazzling surface of the afternoon. A boy framed by bamboos and palms and large cars, eating a sandwich jambon. Only his eyes on my leg. Love should be like this. But it is not. Love is too imperfect, too hard. I think of our ten years together. I'm losing my concentration. I close my notebook. On the cover of a magazine at the next table it says, "SIDA: les chats aussi." One must take care in a foreign country. Without language there is no preparation, without familiarity things pop into your vision seemingly out of nowhere. Without warning, magazines like this one. "AIDS," it says, "cats too." One must take great care.

I was too afraid there. My older brother and me in a white room erasing our names page after page.

I am the American woman in the Chinese hat who writes.

Everyone here is talking. Everyone here is flirting. From this perch I can watch all the Vence regulars come and go. Names I would hope to someday know.

Vouloir is to want.

Attendre is to wait.

Manquer is to miss.

How beautiful she would look in white under a white umbrella at La Régence.

I might make her a hat from a paper napkin.

We might order an ice cream with wings.

We might practice our French.

We might tear off the ends of a baguette.

We might drink Veuve Cliquot in our black dresses and try to guess the nationalities of all the people around us.

We might even allow the mistral to make us crazy, safe with each other.

Everyone here is kissing everyone else. My waitress is at the next table taking an order. She is wearing her Day-Glo clothes, her butterfly belt, her necklace of plastic leaves and fish and spears. The bus pulls up from Nice. A man steps off, comes up from behind, and caresses her. She turns. She is wearing her favorite striped midriff top and she is in love.

Two women just off the bus from Nice sit at the table next to me. One is dark, one quite blond. They laugh, twirl lavender between their fingers. They order two sparkling drinks and toss their heads back in the sun. They are American. It is easy to see. Here on vacation—like everyone.

They talk excitedly. I strain to hear: a concert at the cathedral, the Musée Picasso, the marché in Antibes, soaps from Marseille. They practice their French. They talk with their waitress. One feels safe from grief.

A cat, one of the hundred cats of Vence, comes up to me and rubs against my leg. It is soft, the softest thing perhaps I have ever touched. I tremble.

When I look up I see that one of the women has begun to cry. She is frightened suddenly. It's a vague feeling. Impossible to pinpoint. Her friend tries to comfort her. "Don't cry," she says. "There is no reason to be afraid. Look, we have made it!"

Everyone here is talking and flirting, kissing each other. Everyone here is laughing.

"Auto-école," the dark woman says, as the driving-school car passes. "We will send you there." She reassures her as she has so many times before. She directs her gaze to a beautiful bouquet of flowers. "There is no reason to be afraid."

"Yes, of course, how silly of me," she says and smiles.

Every rose trembles.

Whatever it is has passed. I am glad.

"François, viens!" Maybe they will have a subsidized French baby. Here you are given money to make French children. They laugh.

They are not here on vacation after all. They have come to stay.

The one who was afraid tells a story. She says: "In June I went to a village a little ways up from here called Saint-Jeannet. It was raining. I stepped into the church and said a prayer. When I came out the whole town was washed in light. I watched a golden dog in the square. I heard bells as the afternoon slowly turned to evening. From a window I watched three children put on a magic show. They pulled flowers from their sleeves. Eggs. 'Voilà,' they kept saying, 'et voilà! Magique!'"

"I was still crossing out the days until you then."

The dark woman smiles. "Maybe we will live there. I think I would like to stay in France forever."

I close my notebook. I count the days like magic. This is the place we think we could love. It wouldn't take much.

I watch a flower being pulled apart. She loves me; she loves me not. In bright light I watch a woman being sawed in two. Because I do not know how to look away . . .

She loves me; she loves me not.

Dimanche and the bells arrange themselves around the pure desire to believe. Each village rings out. Vence, Saint-Jeannet,

Saint-Paul, Tourrettes. I look into the faces of the faithful as we enter the ancient cathedral.

Inside in candlelight, I look for Mary, her blue robe, her open arms. Elle est vierge toute pure. I memorize her flaring back, her steady gaze. Mary, our Lady of Sorrows. I ask her for peace here. I ask her for patience and courage. I allow the mass to wash over me in French. Ciel is the word for both heaven and sky, I think. I pick words out: Toujours. Sans doute. Sans exception. L'éternité. Such beautiful words.

Last night the bicyclettes racing around and around the square in the heat. Colors. Names: Chambord, Bilot et Fils. Flags. The bicyclettes whirling. A microphone, trophies. Who can make sense of any of it? I miss her.

If I turn my head I can see the great vaulted entrance. Bright light pours in. Luminous vegetables and fruit. Let it be enough for now, I ask the Virgin.

Two children hold a white linen at the feet of the priest to catch fallen hosts.

"Le corps du Christ."

"Amen."

"Le corps du Christ."

"Amen."

Dimanche and the bells. I pass a striped cat pressed against a window screen. A red rose pulsing. In the market framboises Vence, anchois, artichauts violets. I hold the large, globed artichoke, the glowing tomatoes. I go into the pâtisserie for brioche. People buy gâteaux. They'll walk down the peaceful streets this afternoon. Bonne après-midi, bonne promenade, bon appétit, they're all saying. Then suddenly all is quiet.

Déjeuner behind closed shutters. All the streets of France empty. The sound of silverware, low voices. The civility of midday. I'll never know what they say.

I pass two goats. A rabbit in a cage. A man blowing through a reed flute on this odd, beautiful part of the planet called France.

I wish I had someone to bring gâteaux to—or a tarte au citron.

Dimanche—our day to talk on the phone. You are my dove, I will tell her. My colombe d'or. You are my framboise Vence. How the day revolves around the hour of the call. How the day dissolves in white wine and cassis.

Three o'clock. It is three in the afternoon here, but it is only nine in the morning there and she's probably just waking up. She's probably just stepped from her bath. She's wearing my white bathrobe. She's opening the Sunday paper. She's petting our cat. She's drinking too much coffee.

I love her.

When I dial the number I am already drunk. A thousand centimes, those little beautiful coins I still haven't learned to spend, fall from my pockets. They shine like gold.

The miracle of her voice inside this glass booth. It's a shock every time. The miracle of her voice as I look out at the olive trees, the fig trees. The figs just beginning. I tell her all about my week. I can't stop talking. English! I tell her about the Arab music that sometimes snakes around the corner of the old town. I tell her about French pizza, soap from Marseille, about the bicyclettes. She is silent. Talk to me, I say. "Qu'est-ce que c'est?" I ask. "What is it? Last night the bicyclettes—"

"I'm seeing someone else," she whispers.

"No, I don't believe you."

"It's true."

And then she begins. She says she can't stand the separations anymore. She says she can't believe she's put up with so much. She says something about all my affairs. She can't go on. She says she loves me but she is worn out. She can no longer be a slave to my genius.

"My *genius?* What genius?"

"I need a break for a while, that's all. I thought you'd understand. After all we've been through."

"I don't understand."

She says something about my usual anger and arrogance "on display."

I can't match this voice with anyone. I can't reconcile the things she is saying with the brilliant day. Through the glass I watch women with flowers. Gloves. All I can say is I don't believe it. "I don't believe you."

She says I never loved her enough. She says I've been very cruel. She begins to list my crimes. But I scarcely remember being that woman.

I hear the limits of love in her voice. A pact being broken.

And then she is gone. Somewhere far off there are more bells. Centimes fly around my head like some incomprehensible future. I close my eyes and see colors. Last night the bicyclettes—

Donna Allegra

Dancing Home a Stranger

Winter solstice 1993, and sweat inches down my leg like a caterpillar. Hoping for a scent of wind to cool my sopping leotard, I stretch toward the horizon and view an endless expanse of juicy green leaves. Above the treetops, an impenetrable gray-blue sky. Fifty feet away, a coconut palm droops an umbrella of fronds. Down the road mango, papaya, manioc trees shade the grass. I yearn for even a tickling breeze to sniff at me.

I am in the République de Guinée—called Guinea in English —a West African country on the coast of the Atlantic Ocean.

I'd sneaked to the upstairs porch to steal some time alone. The voices carried on the frail wind aren't English or even French. The Guinea boys speak Sousou, and New York City is two days and a universe away. The velvet tones of the balaphone—the forerunner of the xylophone—are more comprehensible than any human language. Its music poses a set of surreal questions and answers. Earlier, djimbe drum calls and replies inhabited my head as I took morning dance class.

I hear feet clambering up the wooden stairs and Itiya's face appears. She carries a plastic bottle full of the oil that I've seen her knead into dreadlocks that reach below her waist. Frustration raises my temperature several degrees higher than the heat.

"The group of us is planning to go into town for a decent meal. You want to come? I'm tired of Mama Epizo's one-trick-pony cooking."

"Nope." Hastily I relent, "Thanks for asking."

Itiya is my least favorite countrywoman, but she's making an effort toward me. How did I get to this touchy place with her and the others?

I'd boarded the flight to Guinea alone, but en route I recognized the five women from Detroit who would be with me during my stay in Africa. Later I'd learn their names—Itiya, Nubia, Sabira, Kahende, and Lacina, who is twelve—and that they are all heterosexual.

"I should kiss the motherland, but it's so dirty," Itiya had said after we'd disembarked from the plane. I stood with the five other African-Americans in the arrival area of Conakry International Airport. We'd all come to study dance on a trip organized by Epizo Bangoura, the man with whom I study West African dance in New York City.

As we waited to go through the customs line, the African checking our passports was high-handed with us, African-American women in our thirties without male companions. The attitude of his attendant guard also walked the border between duty and disrespect. The Guinean woman who inspected our vaccination cards cast her eyes across us with a look of dismissal that made it clear that she was not at all impressed with us American Blacks. While we waited on yet another line, I watched white Americans and Europeans, whom the African-American dancers had faintly disdained, accorded a respect that we Blacks did not receive.

At the baggage-claim area several men rushed over, saying, "*Ça va?*" to start a conversation. They hovered, hoping to establish their claim to help with our luggage and be tipped.

I say dryly to the group from Detroit, "Looks like African brothers see us Black Americans as tourists to hustle for fun and profit." No one replies, but I feel the emotional temperature of the muggy airport descend several chilly degrees.

Oh. I guess that no criticism of Africa is allowed with these women.

Inwardly, I'd raised an eyebrow at Itiya's overblown ideas about returning to the motherland, but I too had had notions that I'd be treated differently than this. The male energy feels lustful and opportunistic; the Guinean women either won't acknowledge me or they frown and stare. Welcome home to Africa.

Outside the terminal, numerous Guinean women rove the area with platters balanced on their heads. These platters hold dozens of white balls just right for playing tennis, and I wonder what manner of egg or dough confection they carry as easily as I tote the knapsack on my shoulders.

Epizo has finally rounded up cabs to take us to the villa where we will stay. I look out the windows seeking stars and they appear as white petals reaching from a black sky. The road is lit with candles from wooden stands where people sell liters of gasoline, loaves of bread, paper funnels of peanuts late into the night.

I awaken my first morning in Guinea to a baby's endless wail. Outside my window, the baobab looks like a person with an old soul. Beyond the tree, goats roam the yard, leaving trails of black turds. A single neighing kid makes the sound like a baby's cry.

The cock crows every fifteen minutes and does so throughout the day. At 8 A.M., my room fan shuts off of its own accord. I later learn that electricity won't return until 6 P.M.

Already the heat is everywhere. I'd tossed all night trying to catch some cool licks from the fan, which churned more noise than ventilation. When I step outside the house, the heat shackles me like a meddlesome parent who won't give a child room to stretch out and grow.

"Those mosquitoes was having breakfast, lunch, and dinner off of me," I hear Nubia say as I enter the porch. As she pores over the table set up with breakfast fixings—white-flour rolls with packets of butter and jelly—I admire her dreads styled into a French braid. I munch an apple, glad for the stock of food I've brought with me.

This morning, our group is to drive back to Conakry to check in at the American embassy. I hope to find fruits and vegetables to supplement my food supplies. The car ride affords me the luxury of marveling at the people of Guinea. The ethnic groups are Sousou, Peulh, Malinke, Baja Kounkouma, Catagui, Toma, K'pele, Konianke, and Coniagui. I wonder how these distinctions are made. Peulhs are the largest population, and everyone in Conakry, the capital, speaks Sousou.

Houses along the road, many like simple shacks, have their doors and windows open wide. A kaleidoscope of African fabrics hangs on clotheslines or dries on the ground. I watch people of all ages engaged in acts of daily life—a woman combs a child's hair, an adolescent carries a bucket of water, a woman in her twenties plays with a toddler who tries eagerly to walk and then stumbles into her waiting arms.

No doubt, with my gazing, I look like a smiling idiot. When I traveled in Europe, I sought art, culture, and beauty in the museums. In Guinea, I find all these in the faces of the people and the clothing they wear.

I say to Kahende, who has brought her twelve-year-old daughter to Africa, "These faces are just like the people I grew up with."

Kahende's smile reveals a gap between her teeth, a trait African people the world over find attractive. "I was thinking the same thing!"

Women wear traditional clothes in fabrics of African design while many men sport contemporary American styles. I haven't seen any women in pants or even a Western dress. To my dismay most of the African women have straightened their hair. The men smoke—Harley-Davidson cigarettes are as advertised as Marlboro.

Like a kid in the backseat, I hope this ride lasts forever, even though I begin to feel nauseous. The road smells of engine exhaust worse than any U.S. city I've experienced. The makes of the cars—Toyota, Nissan, Suzuki—look like models from the 1960s. These automobiles have no emission control standards, and gasoline fumes sicken me away from my desire to shop for food.

"The drivers race like they're out of their minds," Kahende says. "Lacina, don't lean so hard against the door."

"I'm not, Mommy."

"That car was going so fast it'll take a week to stop," Nubia says.

We observe carcasses of streetlights along the highway. Sabira remarks, "Those lights don't work because when the French pulled out of Guinea, they took the technical know-how with them."

"It figures," I snort.

Our villa has electricity, but most people in the area don't have any such supply. Guinea is a much poorer country than neighboring Senegal. Having been in Senegal on a similar dance and drum study tour, I can see that facilities for tourism in Guinea are minimal. And I'm glad no McDonald's or Sheraton Hotel franchises are making this country a theme park. Still, I regret that I can't even find postcards to mail to friends back home.

After we check in at the U.S. embassy, we head for the market in Madina. Our cars stop at a roadside checkpoint for some kind of military inspection. Guinea soldiers look into the car and ask for identification. As one soldier looks over our passports, three others stare, more with arrogance than curiosity.

Itiya speaks irritably, sure the men don't understand English, "If you're gonna look at me like that, y'all should at least say something or pay admission."

Looking past the soldiers, I contemplate a teenage girl wearing a *lapa*—a length of fabric wrapped around the waist to make a temporary skirt. The fabric fairly sings of birds in flight across a rainbow-striped sky. Her head is also tied with fabric in one of the many possible head-wrap styles called a *geelee*.

She doesn't wear a shirt. Many women on Guinea roads do not. Or else they wear tops where their breasts are visible through the sides, and this causes no lustful reactions from males, no insinuations questioning her virtue.

This girl's chest remains bare, emerging innocent as she sits by a bucket of greenish oranges. With a knife she peels off slivers of orange skin until its white underwear is exposed. She places each orange on a platter piled with other shaven heads. I realize that what had looked like platters of eggs in the airport were oranges such as these.

A soldier shifts the rifle at his shoulder and saunters toward her. Men with guns are a common sight, but they don't behave like bullies. To this musing, Nubia remarks, "That's because they're people's brothers, fathers, and cousins."

Our car is parked close enough that I can see the man with a gun hand the girl two hundred Guinea francs for five oranges—that's twenty cents American. He sucks out the juice and discards the pulpy inner flesh, which he tosses to the ground. This is how Guineans eat oranges.

Up the street, a woman carries a plate on her head and calls, "Bien glacé" to those who want to buy her wares—plastic bags plump with cold water about the size of a container of orange juice.

Sabira, whose skin glows in the heat of this tropical country, has bought oranges. She sections one, swallowing the pieces and leaving no remains. A woman passing by sees this and turns around to point at Sabira eating an entire orange. Sabira frowns in discomfort as the woman laughs behind her hand. It touches me that her feelings are hurt.

As we explore the Madina market, people stare at the six dread-locked Black Americans. Curious Guinea men approach us, trying first French, then English words. I note how these Africans, like other people who speak more than one language, are more patient than an American would be at piecing together language and facial expression for fragments of communication.

The women of Conakry seem to glower—if they let on that we evoke any interest at all. It pains me to see the women turn away, then scrutinize us out of the corners of their eyes. In their behavior, I see the way African-American women have scowled over white women who enter a black people's enclave and are welcomed with a sexually appraising friendliness by the men. I don't feel comfortable saying this to my compatriots. These sisters want to hear no evil about brothers. They are independent women who won't put up with jive turkeys but who still coddle men when they'd hold women to account. Instead, I point to the many Chicago Bulls T-shirts and billboards.

Nubia says, "They got a lot of Chicago Bulls fans here. The first thing folks here ask is, 'Do you know Michael Jordan?' And I'm like, 'Do you mean personally?' Oh, yeah, me and Mike are good buddies."

The hubbub of humanity and heat stirs the market scents—urine and fish smells rise from the wooden slats that make up the stalls. The only vegetables I've seen are puny carrots and undernourished kirby cucumbers. I have brought food into Guinea but need vegetables to supplement this country's abundance in peanuts and oranges. Dismayed, I wander to where Kahende is poring over something next to pink Brillo soap pads.

If Conakry is representative of Guinea, then the country

seems to do commerce with merchandise the United States and Europe have discarded. I recognize many products that are long past any fashion, with labels far from contemporary. Market stalls are stacked with Ovaltine, Gloria concentrated milk, Scott tissues.

Seeing me, Kahende grabs my arm, "Look! These birth control pills are expired."

"Oh, Lord. Yankee ingenuity at its best." I mourn with her for the women who'll believe these pills offer them safety.

In the fabric area, market women wearing an extravaganza of African prints descend on us like a flock of birds. Their faces are smooth as buffed leather and they want to sell us fabric, which African-Americans prize. These women know we are not Africans because while the Detroit women wear fairly convincing lapas, each woman's hair is in some manner of dreadlocks.

As I observe my compatriots drawn into the market frenzy hoping for a bargain, I see that American social conventions don't have their intended effect. One cannot smile and convince an African, "No, I don't want to buy this particular piece."

The market people—mainly women—and street sellers seem pushy. Later on I consider how in the United States, the buy-and-sell culture is so pervasive as to seem invisible. People hawking their wares in Guinea seem rude, but back home, I don't give a second's thought to radio and TV programs being interrupted every two and a half minutes for a commercial message. And I simply accept that newspapers are 80 percent advertising that aims to appeal to cultural insecurities.

In Conakry, where you can buy expired birth control pills and other products outlawed in the United States, there are fewer disguises for the fact that commerce is rife with life's underside—hunger, desire, greed, intimidation, fear. Shopping here feels like hand-to-hand combat, and I plan to take home the lesson that the frown is a potent bargaining tool, especially in an America where women are taught to smile forever and be nice.

En route back to the villa, we stop where a group of men are selling mangoes beside the road. Twenty to thirty Guineans press on our two cars urging, "Mille francs, mille francs." The price for four mangoes is one thousand Guinea francs—less than a dollar.

I indicate that I want some, and as the mango sellers push each other out of the way, two men start fighting over who will get to sell me his mangoes.

When our cars pull away, Nubia says, "It's like a war zone and they don't take 'no' for an answer." In the side mirror, I can see the mango sellers still fighting over who should have gotten to sell us four mangoes for a thousand Guinea francs.

"This is their hustle. They're desperate, and as rich Americans, we're cash flow to them," I say.

Indignant, Itiya snaps, "I'm not hardly rich. You say, 'enough' and twenty guys still insist on selling you their mangoes," she complains to her friends.

I feel put-upon by my countrywomen who don't want their vision of the motherland tarnished. Grieved for Guinea's poverty, I wonder how people manage to earn a living from selling plastic bags of water, sweet green bananas, long loaves of bread for two hundred Guinea francs. Along the roads, they hawk gasoline in one-liter bottles, three-ounce funnels of peanuts, and bundles of firewood for less than a quarter. How can women wearing such beautiful fabrics to peddle peeled oranges that earn pennies still have the heart to love their children in a land where an American can buy four monstrous mangoes for a dollar?

To do anything in Guinea takes a little less time than forever. There are always people with whom Epizo must stop and talk.

We visit his mother's house, and our group is quickly surrounded by the neighboring children. The youngsters are so beautiful I can't get enough of their faces, eager with shy curiosity. I wish for a camera and invisibility to capture those lovely stares.

At home I seldom see children in all phases of life. These remind me of people in the Brooklyn neighborhood where I grew up. There, Blacks were the only people; my eyes never went hungry for dark skin. Along with the faces on the Guineans come body types, physical attitudes, and stances that I want my eyes to cram into memory and claim as evidence of my ancestry with these people.

In that moment, I am glad that we six Americans offer a cultural experience for some of Guinea's youth. But I want to hide our gadgets and props. Did our sneakers and cigarette lighters and jeans and knapsacks and fanny pouches and Walkmans spark visions of a richer American life? Was what we had something to strive for, and indeed, was it worth the price?

On our third day in Guinea, Epizo conducts morning dance class. When lunch is set out, the rickety wooden table holds a large bowl containing rice cooked with uncertain vegetables and fish.

"Aren't you eating?" Kahende asks.

I scowl at the meal, which will reappear at dinner and on all the days to come. "I got my own stuff. I carried a good twenty pounds of raw food in my luggage. I'm a vegan who knows better than to trust Epizo's notions of vegetarianism. Fried chicken and small vegetable portions drowned in cream sauce don't cut it for me."

Kahende's twelve-year-old, Lacina, questions, "But we're vegetarian and we eat chicken and fish."

Oops.

Once again I feel the group consensus chill in my direction and don't entirely understand the disapproval. Is it because I'm a lesbian and they need ammunition to bolster a bias against me? Or do I arouse questions they don't yet want to consider with each other?

Later in the afternoon, Sekouba Camara, our master teacher, arrives. Sekouba is the artistic director of Ballet Djoliba and a minister of culture. Today he wears a red beret, though sometimes he sports a baseball cap turned backward.

Each day, he works us long and hard, teaching us folkloric dances. In morning classes, he shows us the steps from kookoo, sosolay, yankadee, macoo, dundunbah, and mandgiani. Though he builds an increasing opera of folklore, we still haven't scratched the surface of Guinea's dances for such occasions as the harvest or for life passages like initiation and marriage.

Two African women, Beau Sara and Aminata, are generally on hand to assist Sekouba; their every move fascinates me. My body thrives on the dances that I've been doing for years in New York studios; now it has the stamina to push my physical intelligence to learn the new steps. Still, after several days, my body-mind can't take in any more information and won't execute the steps. I crave time alone and wish the young men drummers would go home.

On a break from dance class, Kahende says she "needs" an apple from me for her daughter. I don't like her demanding tone of "asking," but give her two from my dwindling supply of food.

The drummers who provide the music for our workshop relax in their circle. I guess these young men to be between thirteen and nineteen years old. Foeday, Malay, Abdolaye, Nabi, Pico, and Mohammed are flirty in a way that feels harmless and sweet. They are young and lovely; initially my ego is flattered.

The men in Guinea, like the men in Senegal and those I met

when I traveled in western Europe, aren't so aggressive with their sexual interest. Nor are they so hard core in their ways of being men. I even perceive that Africans feel a love for the very nature of women that doesn't match my experiences with American men.

Frequently on the streets of Conakry I see two men who walk holding hands or with arms linked in affection, kissing each other on the cheek. Such freedom of affection stirs a longing in me for companionship.

Every time the toddler in the villa cries, one of the boys goes to pick her up and comfort her as a mother would do.

"These men don't disdain having to care for children. You can trust a teenager with a small girl—a situation I'd feel mighty anxious about in the U.S.," I say to the dancers at rest.

"What's that supposed to mean?" Nubia asks, a suspicious look creasing her face. "Men never bother me."

Inwardly I roll my eyes. Like the others from Detroit, the context for Nubia's political coming of age was a Black nationalism where women step to the rear. The way I see it, Nubia was well trained to keep to a cheerleader's role.

I speak cautiously and level my tone, "I see these boys give maternal energy to babies, and they don't act like doing so is an offense to their manhood." I hope this sounds reasonable. I don't say how I prefer the company of African men to American—that the Africans have more humanity in their freedom from macho poses.

The Guineans on the porch are discussing something in Sousou. There's some French mixed in that makes me think I can understand. In Guinea, just as in Senegal, Africans have no social prohibitions against showing anger, expressing impatience, arguing. I see them bicker and settle with each other, then continue the established relationship.

"And another thing," I go on. "The times I've seen someone getting mad here haven't felt dangerous. Children receive adult displeasure and aren't wounded by it. This seems highly civilized."

Nubia frowns again, but I don't care. "What a revolutionary concept where a father's anger is not a serious threat to life and limb, where a mother's annoyance doesn't signal emotional devastation to come." Lacina shows some interest, and I plow on. "Such a people are incredibly evolved."

Kahende smoothes her daughter's hair. "Well, the children here get to grow up and feel welcome in the world."

The Guinea folks call the drum *tam tam*. Even though I first came into African folklore as a drummer, playing is hard labor on my hands. Still, I like being in this energy field. As I play in the afternoon drum session, watching the dancers, I want to join them on the floor. I've always felt dancers were holy—these were the women I worshiped, the men to whom I gave the benefit of the doubt. But there's a joy conjured by the drums that calls me to play here. I also bask in the veiled admiration I get from the women of Detroit and Guinea when I drum. Pocketing this attention gives me pause in my impulse to reject them.

After one particularly long afternoon dance and drum session, I head for a place to be alone. So many people are at the villa all the time that I'm hard-pressed to find privacy. Beau Sara, for instance, frequently enters my room without knocking.

I make my way to the roof, even though the sun has the presence of a petulant boss. The sky is neither clear nor fogged. It remains a filmy gray that has yet to show a full face of clear blue.

The young drummer Nabi has followed me to my sanctuary. Speaking French, he asks if I am married. I say "Yes," thinking of my girlfriend. It takes a suspicious few seconds to come up with an occupation for her, who is assumed to be a him.

Shortly after Nabi leaves, Nubia and Sabira arrive. "I need some rest and to get me some sun. I want people back home to ask where I've been to be so sunstroked," Nubia says.

They talk and I'm glad to hear I'm not the only one who feels tuckered out only a week into our stay. Nubia says to Sabira, "I don't like these little boys acting like they're our peers."

This surprises me coming from Nubia whose attitude seems to deny that there is any wounded space between Black men and women. She rises a notch in my estimation, and I try to make a little more room in my heart.

I'm shocked that the boys whom I thought were thirteen to fifteen years old are actually closer to eighteen to twenty-one.

"I tell 'em I'm married. It works like insect repellent to keep the buggers off." Sabira slaps her forearm.

"I am truly sick of being a sacrificial lamb to these mosquitoes. And these flies are about to drive me crazy," Nubia says.

"That's their job," says Itiya, who has also made her way to the upstairs porch.

"To drive me crazy?" Nubia demands.

"That's their job," Itiya playfully refuses her buddy sympathy.

At times like this I enjoy eavesdropping on the Detroit women. But it takes only a moment before I again hate their concerns and am glad to be on the outs with them.

Itiya starts her ritual of one-hundred sit-ups, the old-fashioned kind with legs straight, which I know to be ineffective. "You gotta look good to keep a man trained," she says.

"Well, them days are over," Nubia says.

In the yard below, I watch a Mandike woman washing clothes and laying them on the high grasses to dry. I admire her hair—thin braids gathered from two-inch-square sections of scalp. Each braid extends three to four inches from her head, like a tree with its own characteristic twist.

Fifty to a hundred yards away, three women cook over a fire pit surrounded by rocks. An iron caldron, one yard wide, bubbles with a mustard-colored, soupy mass.

One of the Guinean women pounds a pestle as tall as herself in a mortar the size of a washbasin. Her effort reminds me of a jackhammer breaking up the pavement. I think back to African-American folklore—John Henry with his hammer—as I watch this African woman prepare food. But in this precinct of Guinea, no paved road is within easy reach—only the orange-brown earth around the compound where our villa is situated.

"It seems like women here have to marry if they want to survive," I say.

"So, what's wrong with getting married?" Itiya says, but she's not interested in any answer from me. I shut up, embarrassed at my need to talk when I'm not listened to.

"What I don't understand is how they control the fire like that. It's not like turning the knobs on a stove. All they have is rocks and that wood. That looks dangerous," Itiya says.

"They grew up with this. They know how to work it like we read the dial on the oven," Sabira tells her.

"It's not healthy breathing in that smoke. That little woman looks like she's about to faint." Itiya sounds aggrieved, as if she were the one inhaling smoke and ash.

Farther afield, some people are burning a plot of grass with their garbage, and I focus on the sounds that pop like grease frying. You don't see garbage pails for refuse in Guinea—people regularly sweep up and then burn litter—plastic bottles, paper wares. I've even gotten comfortable with the local custom of throwing my fruit skins and pits to the ground where one of the young men who works around the house will sweep it up.

The Guineans burn grass to clear land little by little; it's too expensive to bulldoze when they want a clearing. One of the boys has told me that burning also kills off a poisonous herb. I think how the smoke we don't inhale rises like heat and colors the sky forever gray.

"Whatever it is they're cooking smells good, but I haven't had an appetite since I got here. It's too hot to be hungry," Itiya says. "I wanted to experience Africa on a different level, not just this underdeveloped shit."

All three Detroit women actually agree when I say, "African nations remain underdeveloped because of a thousand varieties of European and American imperialism." It feels nice to be part of the gang for a minute.

"Colonialism keeps the whole continent in poverty and extended slavery." Sabira shakes her head like a neighbor over a fire-gutted house.

"I still say that we're 'rich' Americans, privileged even in our second-classness back home." Itiya is frowning at me again, but Nubia and Sabira listen. "It kills me how so many folks here want to be like Americans and take on our bad habits—smoking, polluting the environment with leaded gas. Then there's the gigolo syndrome when these boys jockey for a rich woman to take him to America." Let them dislike me again, I think.

Some time later, as they make to leave the roof, Nubia turns to me and says, "'Guinea' means 'land of women.'"

After aeons of waiting for Epizo to get organized, our group heads out for a *dundunba* party in a Kissoso neighborhood. Dundunba, the name of particular drum rhythms, means "dance of the strong men." When we arrive around 9 P.M., it seems the entire village awaits us, as if for a huge block party. My irritation over the three-hour delay is humbled by the realization that we are guests of honor.

The children start up to dance when the drum orchestra assembles. In the center of the circle, sixty or so adolescents dance joyously to the sabar rhythm, doing sabar steps and moves from other dances I recognize—mandgiani, a dance of young girls; kakilambe, a harvest dance; kookoo, a social dance.

A little later, the drummers gear up for the adults to take over the dancing ground. The community forms a circle and not everyone dances, but those who do return again and again to the center to leap jubilantly before the drummers. I feel awed and shy on the sidelines. I am chagrined, then grateful when Beau Sara pulls me into the circle to dance.

I'm not ready for this and fall back on steps I know my body can do. Dancing before all these people leaves me exhilarated. It's a rare gift to be drawn into such ecstasy and emerge feeling entitled to a place in community. I feel powerful in my body—a power that isn't personal, like property. Rather, this is something communal that everyone has a share in.

When I leave the dancing ground to stand with the Detroit women, their cheers claim me as one of their own. Smiles invite me to share the circle of good feeling.

I've been granted a victory for answering life's call with appreciation, and in that moment, I feel poignantly how I will miss life in Guinea. I haven't come looking for a long-lost home, nor would I consider remaining in Africa, still . . .

While I had a hard time with this taste of communal living, I garnered some valuable lessons. I will take back to the United States many Guinea ways—the frown, an even greater love for the dance and music, more acceptance of my African face and physique.

Already I grieve the loss of the sight of so much clear brown skin. I'll even miss the uneasy connection with the Detroit women, our common ground in American blackness. As determinedly heterosexual as these women are, we all come from that cultural enclave of middle-aged Black women who continue to wear their hair dreadlocked despite the new age of hair relaxers for African-Americans.

My time in Guinea had me living as part of an extended family with twenty younger boy cousins and five sisters my own age. Travel always bestows pieces of myself I can't find in mirrors at home. I hold up for scrutiny my fears, strengths, accomplishments, judgments, and values.

My last night, I turn off the fan to enjoy the night sounds—crickets, the cock crowing, a lone bird's call, a dog barking. Outside my window, the Guinea moon is a gleaming coin that in a little while, will buy dreams from the store at the edge of the sky.

We are leaving Guinea. As we ride into the evening toward Conakry Airport on a road fetid with car exhaust, I look forward to a fresh smell—New York City air. Hot water with the turn of a knob will be a luxury. I think about the tension between the individual and the community, private and public life, as I puzzle over the billboards along the roads, reflecting Guinean culture: "Prudence—notre préservatif contre le SIDA" (our protection against AIDS), "Budweiser—la vrai Americaine."

Toward dusk, the sun becomes a fluorescent ball gleaming in the fevered indigo sky. For a short time, the moon hangs in that sky as well, its appearance like a peeled orange sharing the horizon with the sun. As dusk fades, I watch a pink halo dim the orange sun, and heaven turns gray to cover the ends of the Guinea earth.

Susan Fox Rogers

Traveling with Desire and Father

The night before I left for Alaska, I called five different women to say good-bye: the butch softball player from Idaho, the butch softball player who lived down the road, the counselor at a small college, the editor at a magazine who spoke French to me, the triathlete who wrote poems. I loved them all, each a slice of who I was, but none of them was *right,* this we all knew. (And what was this thing I had for butch softball players?) For the first time in my life as a lesbian I was single, and I had been behaving like a teenager, dancing every weekend until four in the morning, smoking cigarettes just to stay awake, and drinking more beer than I wanted to. Alaska was far enough away from my home in New York to offer the distance I needed to sort out how I felt about desire and sex. The only problem was that my father was traveling with me. Desire is not a family member.

When I called my parents to tell them I was going to Alaska, my father said, "Maybe I'll go too."

Every time I spoke with my mother after that she would say, "Your father really is thinking of going with you, encourage him a little." My mother has always orchestrated our lives.

His inviting himself was not out of line, given our family. When I was a child, we often traveled as a family. There was the wonderful trip to France in 1964 with grandparents, parents, and me and my sister, ages three and five, proof that we could travel three generations together. Photos of carside picnics next to twelfth-century churches showed wide smiles, a group happiness. I wanted to believe that was still possible. But part of me knew it was ridiculous to hope for what was clearly gone—the past.

We hadn't traveled together in years—probably not since I had come out in 1983. Since then, family time had been remarkably brief, whether planned by me or my mother. And certainly my father and I had never traveled alone. In fact, I had spent years avoiding being alone with him; earlier I hadn't wanted to get into a conversation where intimacy was possible, a conversation where he might learn I was a lesbian. And then after I came out (and he asked, Why didn't you tell me before?) I was still programmed to run, to avoid conversation at all cost.

Going to Alaska was to be a sort of personal pilgrimage, a journey into land and self that I had always envisioned as a solo venture. So I didn't encourage my father.

He decided to come.

My father and I met in Vancouver, planning to take the ferry north through Canada along the Inside Passage. It was late when I arrived at our downtown hotel. I unlocked the door to our room and smelled right away the rich mixture of sweat and garlic that laced our home in Pennsylvania. That familiar smell was startling in this white clean room in this far northwestern city.

I closed the door, cutting off the thin ray of light that shot in from the hallway, and stood for a moment listening to my father's heavy breathing, which was almost a snore. I thought of the time now over ten years past when the sound of his breathing irritated me. My father had taken the brunt of my late-adolescent rebellion: everything about him irked me. And now for the next two weeks I was going to sleep next to those same breaths, magnified in the night air. I shook my head and switched on the bathroom light, stepped into the clean white space already littered with my father's toothbrush, a white undershirt, a wet towel looped over the shower rod. I looked at myself in the large mirror: short brown hair cut neatly over my ears, gray-green eyes sunk into my head, asking for sleep. But it was a Saturday night and for the last nine months that had meant dancing. I snapped off the light, slid out the door.

Down on the street, I circled the block hoping that by some wild luck the gay bars I knew existed in Vancouver were right here, just around the corner from our hotel. But after passing several bars where men and women clung to each other and kissed openly, I turned around, let exhaustion walk me back. As I rode the elevator up, I worried that it was my father's sleeping form that was drawing me back to safety. I certainly felt like a good child as I crawled between the thin starched sheets.

"Is that you, Susie?" my father asked.

"Yes," I said.

He got up, leaned over my bed, and kissed me on the top of my head. "Hello," he said.

I smiled. "Hello."

We had been on the ferry for over ten hours and there were eight more to go. I had imagined these ferry rides as great youthful migrations north, had figured I would feel old amid twenty-something adventurers camped out on the deck. Instead, I was surrounded by couples all over sixty discussing how they had gotten senior-citizen discounts for the trip. My fellow travelers had installed themselves behind the glass windows at the front of the ferry and were watching the remarkably monotonous landscape go by—beautiful, but green, green, green. Whenever we passed something that interrupted this rolling empty sameness, everyone stood up and took a picture.

I took my father by the arm. "You can't ride inside here," I said firmly. "You may be retired, but you're with me."

So we stood on the deck, the sharp, clear sun beating down, the hoods on our parkas flapping in the wind. Near us stood a large woman dressed in baggy flowered pants who was traveling with her mother. The mother sat cocooned in eight layers of sweaters on a deck chair while her daughter stood at the railing videotaping the whole voyage, every green hill, all that blue cold water. "Isn't this incredible?" she sighed. I looked toward shore while my father laughed, intrigued by her enthusiasm. He learned she was from California, worked in health care, and that the next day she would take the same boat back south because she only had a short vacation. She was looking forward to it. "There's so much to see," she exclaimed.

"She reminds me of my cousin Ann," my father told me. "She can get excited about anything." He told me how he and Ann had dug tunnels together in the Indiana Dunes as children, and how every summer she had a different diet. The most memorable was one where she would bang her hips against the walls at dawn. I watched our deck companion now like she was family.

She went home with a videotape of eighteen hours—maybe thirty-six—of green, and a few smiles from her mother and from us.

At the twelve-hour point I decided that it was worth splurging on a small cabin, a place to rest, to get away from the wind and sun. The cramped room was located in the bowels of the boat and smelled of engine fumes. My father went down and had a nap, emerging with his green-blue eyes clear. Later, I went down and lay on the bunk, knowing I wasn't going to sleep. I put my hands between my legs and within minutes came, quick and hard. It wasn't about desire or sensuousness, but about being a bad girl with several hundred grandparents so close by.

We got off the boat at Prince Rupert and spent the night there. After the first of many salmon dinners accompanied by wine we walked through the empty town, absorbing the night air that felt clean because it was cooler. I looped my arm through my father's. I was surprised at how natural this felt, the comfort of his narrow soft frame. A short dark-haired man in a rumpled suit weaved toward us. From a distance I could smell the whiskey. As we passed, he lurched toward me, grabbing at my free arm.

"Hey," my father said, swatting at him, brushing him away easily.

I tugged at my father's arm as he spun to be sure the man was moving along. I thought for a moment that he might go after him. "It's nothing," I said as I moved us along quickly. I realized my father did not know the me who was an adult, the woman who traveled the world by herself, who knew how to avoid drunken men on empty streets in foreign cities. He was still protecting his little girl.

We spent the next day hiking to the reversing falls. The trail there was mossy, cloaked in tall trees, wild oversized vegetation springing up along the spongy path. This was a new landscape, foreign to us, and we finally had the sense that Alaska was near.

My father in his khaki pants and checked shirt strolled along, his arms clasped behind his back as he bent to examine a leaf, smell a flower. I loved how he was appreciating everything—a lovely stroll through the woods. But I could feel the tightness in my legs, ready to go, to stretch and really move through these trees.

We had been together every minute for three days, so to separate seemed natural but felt more complicated than it was. As I shot off through the woods and looped down to the water, I felt free, no longer a child or daughter. We met at the beach and picnicked, marveling at the falls—how they really did reverse—and he told me names of plants that he had seen. I tried to picture these plants, but all I could remember was the freedom of movement, the return to myself, no names.

We separated again on our return, and I got back to the parking lot ahead of him. Two women I had seen on the ferry were loading into their camper; one was tall and thin, long wavy hair, the other with short hair, broad shoulders, and strong arms. I watched how they rearranged their things, touched each other on the arms. I walked over and started a conversation, found out they were driving back to Vancouver, camping along the way.

I did not want to say good-bye to them. As we pulled out of the parking lot, I stopped the car, jumped out, and ran back to give them my card. It was as if they were the last lesbians I might see for the month, and I had to know more about them, let them know about me.

As I climbed back into the car my father looked at me. "Do you think they were a couple?" he asked.

"Of course," I said, and smiled. I was pleased he had noticed, more pleased he had asked.

My father is a writer and notices the smallest details about people: a tic around an eye, how they hold their hands. He sees flowers and trees. But for years he didn't see me, and he claimed, when I finally came out, that he'd had no idea. My being gay didn't seem to make him sad or angry. In fact, I realized, I had no idea how he felt. Except that he loved me.

That evening, we continued our journey north on a ferry headed toward Haines. I had reserved a cabin for the two nights we would be traveling—a light-filled room not much bigger than its two bunk beds, where I slept up, he slept down. But there was a bathroom and a square wooden table where we could sit and look out, write postcards to friends, play solitaire. Later when I told a friend about sharing a bunk bed with my father, she opened her eyes wide, raised her eyebrows, and asked, "You did what?" But at the time it seemed natural, a part of the adventure we were on together.

In Wrangell the boat docked for half an hour and we were allowed to get off. We walked out the long wooden planks of the dock, single file, my father in front. I noticed his weight landing heavily on his left foot with each step, how his arms spread out to give him balance as he tried to ease the pain in his right knee. I looked at the back of his head, gray hairs mixed with brown blown in the wind, making him look like a mad professor. His beige parka covered his long torso, the waist that was no longer thin. I had that same long torso. Brown work pants covered his still-thin legs. Things I had always taken for granted I was now seeing anew. I slowed my pace, walked with my hand clutching the railing. Tears formed in the corners of my eyes.

In Haines we grew dizzy from looking up, spotting eagles and then insisting that the other look. "Over there, do you see it?" "Magnificent. Ohh, look there."

My father wanted to have a martini, to sit and watch the eagles flying by, but I wanted to go for a kayak paddle. So he installed himself before a large picture window (off to the side was a TV airing a baseball game he didn't want to miss) while I paddled through the icy waters with a local guide. Seals popped their heads out of the water, dolphins arced in front of me. Thousands of scoters bobbed in the water, and always there were eagles gliding in the air above me or perched in the towering pine trees.

Dinner in a waterside restaurant was salmon so fresh it didn't taste like the sea, and for dessert we shared the best rhubarb pie we'd ever had. We drank a bottle of wine, and I began to ask questions about cousins, uncles, grandparents, what happened in 1968. Asking didn't feel hard or awkward, though these were the same questions I had carted around with me for what seemed like forever. They had haunted me, taken up a lot of time during therapy sessions. What made it easy now for me to ask and him to answer? The salmon? The wine? The big sky and fresh air? The shared bunk bed? The eagles? Maybe all of it. But I felt so relieved that the silence I had been knocking around in for years was shattered.

We flew to Anchorage via Juneau in a small four-seater plane. There, we spent one night before heading out onto the Kenai Peninsula. That one night in town I thought I needed a fix: desire had become a drug and I needed some. So I headed to a gay bar I had heard of, the Blue Moon. When I entered the bar at eleven that night, the sun was still hovering in the sky. There was no chance of slipping in and out of bars in the darkness, unnoticed.

Two women were shooting pool. The one with short hair leaned over the table, stuck one leg behind her in the air, looked up, and winked at me. I smiled, and she bought me a beer. I took that beer and walked around the bar, noticing the men in their leather pants leaning into each other, the bartender talking too loudly, pouring gin into small glasses. I sauntered back to the pool table, my tour of the room completed in less than five minutes.

"Do you know where you are?" the pool player asked, leaning on her cue. I looked at her blankly, amused by her question but wondering if I did know where I was.

"Are you in the right bar?" she clarified. I smiled and nodded. But I wasn't in the right place. I didn't want to be in a gay bar in Alaska. I had come to get away from bars, because I knew I was not going to find what I wanted here, in this music-filled room. What I wanted was more complicated than a beer and a kiss. What I wanted was still about as clear as the smoke in that room, but I knew I wasn't going to find it by leaving my father—my family—sleeping in a hotel room. He had to be a part of my desire, as did the eagles, the questions I had asked about family, our salmon dinners and walks in the woods. I no longer wanted to compartmentalize myself, my lesbian self not communing with family, my love of the outdoors not mixing with the rest. Alaska was giving me not just distance and perspective but dimension.

Still . . . I had to stay to watch the weekly drag show. The half dozen six-foot-tall Alaskan men in high heels parading across the dance floor were like drag queens anywhere, only maybe taller, bigger, and when they left this bar their dresses would shimmer in the northern light for all to see on the main street in Anchorage. When I left at two in the morning, it felt odd to have the light expose me, wake me up. But I was exhausted when I reached the hotel room; I slid quietly into bed, yet it still roused my father, who asked without sitting up, "Where were you?"

"At a gay bar," I said, and went to sleep amazed that I didn't feel I needed to explain myself.

We drove down to Homer the next day, checked into a B & B right on the bay, the white walls of our spacious room reflecting the cold-green water. As we unloaded our suitcases, we marveled at our luck, at the bite in the summer air. We walked out onto the long wooden dock where fishermen were bringing in their catch and commercial stores tried to sell us T-shirts and hats announcing "Homer."

As a birthday present for my father, soon to turn sixty-seven, I bought tickets for a boat ride that would take us out to see the puffins. We were both giddy, pointing at the comic seriousness of puffins. My father's curiosity and delight was kidlike, his enthusiasm contagious. I thought, *I could not imagine sharing this with anyone else.*

That was the night we decided to try and reign in our eating and spending. Yet we ended up ordering a shrimp appetizer, the halibut dinner—Homer is famous for its halibut—dessert, and a bottle of wine. We couldn't help it: every meal seemed not just a celebration of Alaska and its wonderful food but also of something much more.

At one point I said, "Mama will never accept me as a lesbian, will she?" That I could ask told me something: *he* had accepted me.

"If you find a partner she likes, she will. Then it will make sense to her, your happiness will seem more real," he said.

My father had always made a huge effort to like—or at least understand—all the lovers I had insisted on bringing home for Thanksgiving, Christmas, or long weekends. I saw now this was a part of my never-ending effort to combine who I was as a Rogers with who I was as a lesbian.

I nodded. *If I find a partner I like*, I thought, *I will probably accept myself too.*

On the way out of Homer, my father said, "Tell me more about the bar you went to in Anchorage."

I began to tell him about gay bars: Prime Time, the local club where I spent my weekends, and then the Clit Club in New York, about girls in leather with soft exposed bellies, pierced or tattooed.

"Oh, so there's the same sickness as there is with gay men," he said.

I wasn't sure I understood or had heard correctly. "Sickness?" I asked.

And then my father and I had our first ever conversation about sex.

Sex was about beauty and tenderness, he said.

I said it was also about power, and that pain had a place there, sometimes a healing place. We talked some more, our words at first hesitant then more sure. After a while we were quiet, my father at the steering wheel, his head nearly brushing the roof of the small rental car. I looked over at him, at his high forehead and large nose, which were clearly my own. Then I turned back, looked out the mosquito-dotted windshield at the huge mountains around us, the endless sky. *Alaska is big,* I thought. *This is why we came to Alaska.*

We never came to an agreement. But that didn't matter. I felt a loosening in my jaw, and then my heart, that felt like freedom.

Three days later I drove my father to the airport. I was staying on and suddenly I was deeply unhappy to be alone. I had come to treasure the pace of our lives together, the comfort of his presence and the surprise of our conversations. But I knew that I needed to keep moving, into the interior of Alaska, where I would begin the journey I had originally set out to take. Now there was a difference: this journey was no longer a running away, a rejection of where I came from. It was more a running to (or running into). And somewhere around Denali I shed my old skin and emerged: lesbian, Rogers; desire and family.

Gerry Gomez Pearlberg

Driving for the Fast and Faithful:
First Five Days in Kathmandu

DAY 1   Missed the dog blessings but did find a few mutts with yesterday's *tika* powder, pink and red, rubbed on their heads. Today Lakshmi, Hindu goddess of wealth and prosperity, is honored, and everywhere red and ocher mud paths are smeared from the unpaved streets into household doorways to help her locate and confer good fortune on the faithful. Offerings abound: coins on a tiny copper platter loaded with cooked rice, anthill piles of *tika* powders in every sunset hue, plus raw lentils, apple slices, bright orange marigolds.

This evening we paid a visit to M.'s colleagues at Save the Children. Fittingly, the accounting department is hosting this gathering in Lakshmi's honor, doing what they can to ensure a fiscally sound future for the agency's Kathmandu field office. Scores of red, yellow, and white candles burn along either side of every step of the cold stone staircase leading up to the office, like oversized birthday candles on an enormous rock-solid cake. They also adorn the terrace wall and the outdoor walkway to the office. In fact, the entire city is entwined with lights; strings of what in another context would be Christmas-tree lights dangle from shop signboards and the second-story windows of homes, and candles flicker in every niche and crevice, this being the third day of Tihar, Festival of Lights.

DAY 2   Cows and dogs and goats everywhere; they seem especially fond of dozing on or inside shrines, but the middle of busy streets, traffic circles, and intersections run a close second as favored napping locations. Cars and bicycles and rickshaws just veer around them. The absolute integration of animals and worship in the lives of the people here is a joyful shock, given my culture's thorough alienation from both.

L. has observed that one is forced to think of the color orange very differently (and with increased respect) in this part of the world: marigolds are ubiquitous, and here they actually mean something, carrying a sacred weight when wound into a necklace to confer good fortune upon the wearer or lovingly arranged on a shrine. Girls wander down the street with bowls of them mixed with the same purple globe-shaped flowers I like to buy at the Brooklyn farmers' market. Everything here is re-contextualized: the color orange, the dozing dogs, those purple flowers, the handsome young men walking arm in arm.

In Kathmandu's Durbar Square, a throng has gathered to make purchases for the last days of Tihar. Piled on the ground or hanging from strings are apples, bananas, cauliflower, and many things I don't recognize. Burlap sacks bulge with red and orange spices—curries, saffron, cumin. Brilliant Chinese-red confections shaped like bridges and dragons shimmer like glazed ceramic. Raw greens are piled next to neat boxes of incense and sparklers, tinsel wreaths, and tiny children's masks shaped like frogs, elephants, dogs. Toy guns made of hammered metal glisten alongside dozens of T-shirts reading "I Survived the Plague, India '94." A radar dish rises like a black moon behind an edgy pagoda rooftop. Kids toss blue marbles into the complex of smooth mazes they've spooned out of the dirt.

An exhilarating ride in an auto-rickshaw brings me "home." One asks to be taken to a neighborhood here, rather than a particular street, since the streets are for all practical purposes nameless—that is, if they have names, no one knows them. Darting through traffic so recklessly forces me past anxiety into a puddle of pure thrill. The driving here would be terrifying except that all the mayhem occurs in slow motion: it's a laneless, lawless, multidirectional tangle of cars, tractors, bicycles, motorbikes, pedestrians, rickshaws (man-powered and motorized), trucks, cows, dogs, children, buses, wagons, ducks, and more dogs—each moving on its own timetable with an amalgam of heightened awareness, single-mindedness, obliviousness, and what M. describes as "blind faith." And it works! Which leads me to think that it's here, on the dirt roads of Kathmandu, that the deities really get to show their stuff. It'd make a great virtual reality game: "Gunning the Engine in Kathmandu" or, taking the name of a local driving school here, "Driving for the Fast and Faithful."

DAY 3 Nightfall at Boudhanath Stupa, one of the world's largest Buddhist stupas, a "tangible symbol" of the enlightened mind of the Buddha. Here monks gather at low tables to buy Western-style underwear from street vendors, and boys cluster around candlelit game boards painted on sheets of cloth, tossing coins into mazes of icons and color. Circumambulating the stupa in a clockwise direction are hundreds of monks and nuns, some chanting, some chatting, some carrying bright red boxes filled with—incense? prayer scrolls? Calvin Klein boxer shorts? I've happened on a major Buddhist festival. One shopkeeper explains, "That's why it's so dusty here today—all those walking monks."

Above me, dark sky, new moon, and a barn owl passing, also clockwise, over the stupa, disappearing over the rooftops of the "Buddha Arcade."

DAY 4 Daylight at the stupa: a boy runs by rolling a bicycle tire with a metal stick, wheels it up a ramp, and disappears into an open doorway. A motorcycle guns by—clockwise. Two teenage girls, arms entwined, giggling and eating sweets. Under one monk's robes, a business suit. Two men push a cart piled impossibly high with fresh greens. A tiny kid in a mustard-colored shirt stands smoking a cigarette. Another, dressed in burlap, clearly destitute, wanders by. An ancient man with a long gray beard limps along, chatting with a teenager wearing a bright yellow baseball cap. A couple of women pass, then stop to stare at me. When I smile, I am greeted with two tremendous, divinely cheerful, toothless grins. A monk on a bike with a hot pink backpack. Long shadows of walkers on the stupa, cast by early sun. Shadows like syrup. A smirking monk chewing bubble gum (my kind of monk). Dogs pee on the base of the shrine, then curl up to sleep in the path of the faithful. A baby monk, running and kicking his sandals ahead of him. Blaring Hindu pop music infuses the air.

DAY 5—MORNING   An hourlong ride to see the botanical gardens leaves me in Godavari, a village that completely alters one's urban and Western conception of time. There's not a telephone pole or radar dish in sight: this could be any time. Voices of women and children echo across the valley; roosters crow; hand-operated farm implements strike the earth again and again in a drumlike rhythm; crickets sing. Women in sky-blue sarongs pass by carrying enormous loads of hay and vegetables. A man shuffles through the inch of grain spread over his rooftop to dry in the sun.

The gardens are just the kind I go for—in full-bodied decline, with cracked stone pools, tiny crumbling bridges, and enormous, ancient-seeming moths clinging to lichen-gray tree trunks. An almost prehistoric quality—sheer ruin in all its gorgeous glory. The greenhouse windows are more spiderweb than glass, and what glass remains is mottled with desiccated spiders and beetle wings, the ghost furniture of a thousand insect lives. Makes me think of Coney Island, old mirrors, and men's shaving kits—those barriers between shimmering loops of time and obsolescence, that tinkling chandelier. Decline makes you see a place or thing more deeply, attaches it to you like moss or a microbe, forms a mystical link between what's happening "outside" (decay) and the open secret of what's happening to us.

DAY 5—AFTERNOON   Built along the banks of the sacred Bagmati River, Pashupatinath, Nepal's most sacred Hindu shrine (to Shiva, in his Pashupati—or Lord of the Animals—form) is actually more like a little city of temples, ashrams, statues, and ruins—a treasure trove of art and architecture. And of spirit—the sight of people ritually bathing in the river to ensure release from the cycle of rebirth and the smell of smoke from cremations taking place on bamboo pyres along the riverbanks give death (and its aftermath) as powerful a presence here as the goings-on of the living: worship, prayer, laundry, tourism.

I've come to pay homage at the Guhyeshwari temple, dedicated to Shiva's "girlfriend" Durga (or Sati), who is said to have immolated herself over a family feud. Heartbroken Shiva hauled her corpse across the skies, and as pieces of her body decomposed and fell to earth, they created sacred sites. Her vagina fell near Pashupati; Guhyeshwari means "secret" or "hidden" goddess. Non-Hindus are not allowed past the temple gate, but what a gate! Frenetic with cartoony images: elephantine Ganesh, golden dragons, a monkey with an erection, green serpents, a dancing skeleton, and three munchkin-like characters merrily riding in a tiny yellow boat—or is it a candy dish, the sticky-sweet center of a red-hot goddess?

Which brings me to a useful quotation from *Insight Guides: Nepal:* "Opposed to contemplative meditation, Tantrism substituted concrete action and direct experience. But it soon degenerated [*sic*] into esoteric practices, often of a sexual nature, purportedly to go beyond one's own limitation to reach perfect divine bliss. Shaktism is such a cult, praising the Shakti, the female counterpart of a god. Some ritual Tantric texts proclaim: *Wine, flesh, fish, women, and sexual congress: these are the five-fold boons that remove all sin.*" I couldn't agree more, and were a sixth boon to be added to this Tantric list, I suspect traveling would be a strong contender.

Terri de la Peña

Beyond El Camino Real

Almost a decade ago, I sifted through haphazard piles of size 6 jeans and tiny muscle T-shirts, remnants of another time—my life with Jozie. I worked quickly, emptying the stuffed dresser, packing possessions into cardboard boxes, deciding what to keep, what to toss. New bedroom furniture would be delivered the next morning. As usual, I had waited until the last minute.

I sat on the edge of the queen-sized bed and pulled out the creaky bottom drawer. Inside I found a neat stack of journals and several packets of photographs. Sighing, I reached for the journals and placed them on my lap. I stared at their dog-eared covers for several moments. When I flipped open the top one, my hands shook.

> 7/4/84   I'm on the plane winging home. Jozie got paranoid over what I'd scribbled so far about our trip. She said I've been too specific about our relationship. I told her she had no business reading my journal in the first place, and I really hate being censored. Why doesn't she understand I'm recording my thoughts and reactions? This is *my* journal!

I slammed the journal shut. Why was I wasting time reading that? Four years had passed since our cross-country trip. Jozie had left for good almost ten months ago. What was the point of dredging up memories?

I set the journals and photos aside and turned my attention to the next drawer. I had so much junk—what a convenience it would be to have additional drawers and a platform bed with more storage beneath. But I still needed to throw some things away. I dumped a colorful collection of camisoles and panties on the quilted bedspread and immediately tossed several pairs into the wastebasket. I needed to get on with my life; buying new underwear seemed a perfect way to start.

Jozie had selected those lacy camisoles and bikini panties. Her smoky blue eyes had promised unspoken pleasures, and she had not disappointed me. Lolling against her, I had felt sexy in those scanty things. There had been such passion between us. . . .

"Stop remembering." I scowled at myself in the dresser mirror. But since when had I ever taken my own advice?

Beyond El Camino Real, I had found the land vast, often threatening. I had not expected that. A fifth-generation Californian, I had been eager to plunge across America, to explore its diverse communities and to visit Jozie's native New England.

During our first weeks together, we had meandered up the California coastline. Jozie had dubbed those early days "M & Ms" because we had stopped primarily for meals, museums, or missions—and motels. In that carefree time, we had learned each other's habits and preferences, and I had begun to fall in love.

In California, I had not felt like an outsider. Nearly every town had a sizable Chicano population. Traveling from Los Angeles to Santa Barbara, from San Jose to San Francisco with my Anglo lover, I had anticipated some curious stares, some homophobic and racist comments. But we had rarely encountered any—or maybe we had been too distracted by each other to notice. Yet I had noticed the difference once we traveled beyond El Camino Real.

Past the continental divide, where America's geography changed from majestic Rockies to flat Midwestern plains, where towns with Spanish names diminished, I had experienced the

first stirrings of alienation from my homeland. Away from the
ethnic mix of California, far from the brown people of the
Southwest, I had faced the daily reality of being a woman of
color in a white-dominated land. And I had not liked that sudden confrontation.

"She thought I was Native American." I glanced at Jozie across
the Mazda's cab.

"Who?"

"That waitress back there in Julesburg. That's why she was
rude."

Jozie did not take her eyes off the highway. "I thought it was
because we're—together."

"Probably that, too, but she was ruder to me—slamming
down dishes, talking only to you. She wanted to pretend I wasn't
there, Jozie. She saw my straight black hair and brown skin and
pegged me for what I am—or for an American Indian. Neither
is welcome around here."

Jozie's soft hand pressed mine. "Don't think about it, honey.
It's over."

"No. It's just starting."

In an Omaha restaurant, we stopped for dinner. In the rest
room I met hostile stares from the white women waiting to use
the facilities. A little girl was particularly curious, peeking from
behind her mother's dress to gawk. Uncomfortable with the attention, I passed the time combing my hair and tucking my
Napa Valley T-shirt into my jeans. The tension in the small
room made my head ache. Finally, I turned and smiled at the
blond child.

"I don't bite."

The mother whisked the little girl into the next empty stall,
leaving me half amused, half resentful.

6/20/84   We argued last night. I wanted to sleep in a bed instead of camping again, but guess I didn't make that clear. Jozie aimed to drive straight through to the campground in Anita, Iowa. I was tired and cranky when we crossed the Nebraska-Iowa border. By that time, I had slithered my skinny frame through the cab window into the camper shell and curled alone in the sleeping bag.

Jozie was surprised by my annoyance and got miffed herself. Matters grew worse because the campground wasn't easy to find. Hours later, we lay together in the camper and didn't say much at first. Then she kissed me, and I started to soften up. Whenever she touches me, I can't stay angry. We talked about our feelings after we made love, but I don't think she really understands how alienated I feel in the Midwest. I don't fit in. I don't like being stared at, even by kids. I'm so aware of being different from everyone else, and this becomes even more obvious because I'm traveling with her, my white dyke lover.

Jozie tries to understand, but she doesn't help by saying, "I don't think of you as being Chicana—I just think of you as being my lover." Hearing this, I wonder if she can ever really know me. *I am Chicana!* My identity evolves from being Chicana *and* lesbian. I don't even know which comes first. I'm not like her and never will be. Jozie seems to close her ears to my bitter words; she seems hurt by my anger. I didn't mean to hurt her—I love her. I just wish she would understand. Maybe things will get better when we get to the big cities on the East Coast. . . .

I pushed my shaggy bangs aside, and let my fingers drift down to the edges of my eyes; they were wet. Just thinking about the identity crisis I had experienced during that trip depressed me. But this did not stop me from picking up the packet of photographs and spreading them over the bedspread.

In the Grand Canyon shots, Jozie with her Slavic cheek-bones and curly hair looked the transplanted Easterner. I appeared native to the canyon's north rim, although I really was an urban dweller. My brown skin and black hair complemented Arizona's ruddy earth tones.

In the later Chicago photos, I seemed out of place, awkwardly seated by Lake Michigan, the blustery winds disheveling my hair. My smile was unnatural, the tension evident in my face. I rubbed my thumb against the photo, as if trying to soothe my former self, and the memories overcame me again.

6/27/84   We left Boston today and headed for New Hampshire. In Massachusetts, I began to feel more anxious, knowing I would soon meet Jozie's family and Nell, her college friend. I was overwhlemed by a deep sense of inferiority, for lack of a better term—something I have not felt for a long time. I wonder if I'm having some sort of breakdown—I feel out of control, crying constantly, for seemingly no reason. Jozie's finding out how neurotic I am.

. . .

"Maybe I should take the first plane home. I'm spoiling your fun." I buried my face against Jozie's warm breasts and sobbed again.

"Honey, I've never seen you like this. Can't you talk about what's troubling you? You clam up, and the next thing I know, you're crying as if your heart is breaking." Jozie cradled me and gently kissed my damp face. "Tell me, please. I'm worried about you."

I sniffled and tried to stop my tears. "I just don't belong here—can't you see that? You love this part of the country. It's where you grew up, but it's completely foreign to me. I look around and there's no one else like me."

Leaning on my elbow, I made myself meet Jozie's concerned

gaze. My voice was shaky and thick with tears. "I've felt alienated before—being the only Chicana in my office, for instance. That's different—I can walk around the medical center and see Chicano patients. If I walk outside, I see Chicano gardeners and Chicana employees on their lunch breaks. I even have a Chicana bus driver on my way home. But here, I'm the only one of my kind."

Jozie frowned at my words but did not interrupt. I took a deep breath and continued. "Remember how nervous you were that time we got lost in San Jose and wound up in the barrio? All of a sudden, you realized you were the only white person in sight, and it scared you, didn't it? Well, that's how I feel—off center, out of whack—and it really scares me.

"Jozie, when you talk about living here someday, I get even more scared. I don't want to lose you—but I don't want to lose myself either. That's what would happen if I ever moved East."

Her frown had not vanished. "You're just nervous about meeting my parents."

Sighing, I sat up and pulled the motel blanket to my breasts. "I can't deny that, but don't belittle the rest."

"For God's sake, sometimes you're too damn sensitive." Jozie rose in one abrupt motion and went into the bathroom. I leaned against the headboard and rested my chin on my upraised knees. I felt miserable.

6/27/84   Nell's farm is in Plainfield, out in the middle of nowhere. Kurt, another of Jozie's former classmates, was house-sitting until we arrived to take over. I had to go into my "friend" routine because Jozie isn't out to Kurt. I despise pretending—it's so hypocritical. My spirits fell even lower when Kurt explained about maintenance of the hot-water tank and the details about feeding the sheep and chickens. I should've flown home from Boston.

6/28/84   Jozie's parents came to the farm for lunch. They are pleasant, unsophisticated folks, a bit wary of strangers—especially people of color like me. They scrutinized me closely, and I didn't have much of an appetite as a result. The ice was broken when Jozie's mother miscalculated the edge of the picnic bench and landed on the ground instead. We all enjoyed a laugh over this—it certainly relieved the tension! Jozie left us outside while she prepared lunch. How could she expect me to entertain them? I was so nervous, especially because her mother asked several times how we'd met. I think she was trying to catch me in a lie. Wonder if I passed inspection . . .

To clear a space on the bed, I moved the journals and photos aside. I lay back and closed my eyes, remembering those summer days in New Hampshire. After Jozie's parents had left, we had wandered inside and spent the rest of the afternoon making love. I recalled our precious intimacy, her soft breasts against my face, her pink nipples budding at the touch of my lips. We had connected at once as women, but why had our cultural conflicts been insurmountable? I still did not know. I only knew I missed her.

6/29/84   Jozie's grandmother suffered a massive heart attack early this morning. Jozie cried in my arms after her mother's phone call. Then she resolutely got up and went to the hospital. She would not let me go with her. This makes me sad. I'm too emotionally drained to be angry.

I'm alone at the farm, miles from any town. Jozie took the Mazda, so I'm stuck. Maybe this is good. I'll have time to reflect on our situation. This trip has been traumatic—nothing like seeing the U.S.A. while on the verge of a nervous breakdown.

None of this is Jozie's fault. She wanted to show me New England—how were we to know this would happen? I love her so much and feel helpless over her grief. Her grandmother is the family matriarch—Jozie had really been looking forward to visiting her. . . .

After washing the dishes, I walked the dogs, one a keeshond, the other a collie-shepherd mix. The air was so clean and fresh, but the sky had begun to darken. I did not want to stay out long. I couldn't get used to the silence of the country; I'm more familiar with city noise. And I kept thinking, what if one of Nell's friends or neighbors drives by and sees this brown stranger with the dogs. How can I explain who I am? There are no people of color in this area—I haven't even seen any black people, much less Latinos. I not only feel culturally isolated but also, while I'm here, I can't even call myself Jozie's lover—only her friend. Women here look like dykes, but Jozie says they aren't; they just have that unadorned, outdoorsy look— which is what I find so attractive about her.

In this land of the Yankees, I have no identity. And I'm so homesick for Los Angeles—especially for *comida mexicana.* I'd give anything for a warm *tortilla de maíz con mantequilla.*

In the afternoon, I wandered into Nell's study. She has an impressive library—at last a chance to read Gertrude Stein's *Q.E.D.* and Djuna Barnes's *Nightwood.* The day had turned dismal—a heavy rainstorm complete with thunderclaps. *Nightwood* depressed me, but it filled the lonely hours until Jozie's return.

When I heard the phone ring, I did not budge from the bed. In moments, I heard my friend Elisa's voice on the answering machine.

"I thought you might need some company. *Llámame, por favor,* so I can help you move the old furniture out to the patio. And I'm great with a vacuum cleaner, *amigüita. Hasta luego.*" The machine clicked off.

I lay still. Ever since Jozie had left me, I had withdrawn, kept mostly to myself. I had a hard time trusting in and believing anyone. Some of my friends had given up on me, but not Elisa. Maybe I would phone her back later. Right now, I had to deal with the memories by myself. The best way to do that was to finish the task at hand, but I found I could not put down the journal.

7/1/84   Jozie's grandmother died this morning. Jozie is shaken, but since Friday she has been pretty much resigned to her grandmother's condition. Before getting up for breakfast, we cuddled a lot. I held her for a long time and wished I could ease her grief. She's cried so much. I have to be strong for her. This isn't easy since I'm still full of anxiety about being here. I steeled myself for a long day. . . .

7/2/84   I'm alone again. Jozie is spending today with her family. I stayed in bed most of the morning and read back issues of the *Women's Review of Books.* I'm very concerned because Jozie is adamant about my not attending the funeral; she feels she would fall apart if I'm there. I know there is much more to it than that. How can she explain me to her relatives? Is she ashamed because I'm Chicana? How can I confront her about her racism and internalized homophobia in the depths of her grief? This makes me feel angry and so helpless. . . .

Nell phoned from Frankfurt; her plane has been delayed. I like her voice. She told me she has difficulties dealing with Jozie's closeted life and seems worried about my being at the farm alone. She asked if I'm all right. I appreciated that. Not sure if I am. . . .

With all the commotion about the funeral, I've decided to stay a day longer. Don't like having to leave Jozie at this traumatic time. I want to be here for her as much as possible and now am desolate about going home. I feel very conflicted.

7/3/84   Jozie is at the funeral. I'm so depressed about being away from her today. I hate these feelings of powerlessness. It cuts me to the core that I'm not at my rightful place beside her. She must be feeling alone, too. She's been so quiet lately, mourning, remembering. . . .

Nell arrived while Jozie was gone. An awkward meeting—she's tired and I'm depressed. Somehow we managed to make a tentative attempt at friendliness. I like her—she is a robust-looking dyke with long sandy hair. She's known Jozie for years, quirks and all. We wound up talking for hours.

I sat up and rubbed my eyes. At the bedroom window, I studied the bright summer sky. Such a difference from that other July in New Hampshire. I remembered the long drive to Logan Airport, sheets of rain nearly obscuring the windshield. Jozie and I had been too numb to talk much. I had put my hand on her thigh and kept it there for hours.

When Jozie'd returned from the funeral, she didn't have much time for me. She needed to talk with her longtime friend. I had felt left out, abandoned, and had gone to bed alone.

Sometime during the night, Jozie had awakened me, wanting to make love. I had clung to her then, knowing it would be seven weeks before we would be together again. We had wept, and I recalled thinking that seven weeks is as long as Lent.

In the morning, our time at the airport went too quickly. I was the last to board the plane to Los Angeles. With a shaky voice, Jozie called out, "*Hasta la vista.*" With her New England accent, she tacked an *r* at the ends of the first and last words.

I blew her a kiss before boarding and cried most of the way home.

I carefully packed the journals and photos into a box. Then I dumped the remaining contents of the bottom drawer on the bedspread. A packet of letters fastened with a silver elastic band bounced inches from me. Frowning, I made myself look away from it.

I did not want this task to take all afternoon. Glancing at my watch, I thought about phoning Elisa. We could make quesadillas after moving the furniture to the patio. Over *cervezas,* we could sit and talk. Elisa was such a good listener. She understood about Jozie.

Yet, without even deliberating, I reached for the packet of letters. My fingers peeled off the elastic band, and I chose a letter at random.

7/18/84   Today I write to you on my birthday—lots of thoughts on this, the beginning of my thirty-third year. Our year together has been wonderful for me. You are "the gift that heaven sent." I have often wondered what I would have done without you during these months of continued tragedy. I do know how fortunate I am that your strength has buoyed mine, that you have pulled for me, nurtured me through dark hours, listened to me cry myself to sleep. I also know the happiness of your smile, our laughter together. . . . When I am with you, my dear one, I feel happy inside, content, wanting you, wanting you to share your emotional and physical beauty with me and I with you.

Yes, I miss you. I miss your body next to mine, the smell of you, my arm resting over your shoulder in the night. I had sort of a minifantasy about our first meeting when I return—obviously, I won't tell you 'cause we shall live it—if you don't mind. I'm making the plans for both of us, as usual a bit hoggish on control.

Honey, do take care. I think of you often as these long days pass. Kisses, hugs, and much love—Jozie

I stuffed the letter back into its envelope. I did not want to read anymore. Tears blurred my vision; I blinked them away and put the letters into the same box with the journals and photos. The lid fit snugly as I pressed it down.

Yet how could I forget those days with Jozie on the road— that dark journey that led me to recognize our differences? With Jozie, yes, I had learned to love. With Jozie, yes, I had celebrated my lesbian self. And with Jozie, I had also discovered that my Chicana self had threatened the insular world we had structured around us. When we had been alone, safe within each other's arms, we had been happy, compatible. But when I had felt alienated in the Midwest and in New England, when I had reached beyond Jozie to Elisa and my other Chicana friends, Jozie had balked.

She had been jealous of my need to socialize with and enjoy the company of other Chicanas. Closeted, with most of her friends living on the East Coast, Jozie had resented what she considered to be the Chicanas' intrusion into her life with me. She did not understand their need—my need, too—for bilingual joking, boisterous ranchera music, and our strong family ties. She had moved to California to be far away from her own family. *I* was Jozie's family in California—she had no need for anyone else here. At first, I had been content with that exclusive arrangement—but then I had begun to feel submerged, lost, invisible. Jozie had not understood that either.

I carried the box to the hallway and opened one of the top cabinets. Standing on tiptoe, I pushed the box onto the highest shelf and firmly closed the cabinet door.

"*Hasta la vista,* Jozie," I whispered.

In the years following that tumultuous cross-country trip with Jozie, I have often traveled beyond El Camino Real, either alone or with Gloria, my life partner. Once in a while, I have felt a sense of isolation, of being out of place in a different environment, but never to that same extent. In 1984, newly lesbian, newly in love, I was perhaps more vulnerable than I have since allowed myself to be. With maturity, self-acceptance, and yes, even with a stronger sense of humor coupled with a better understanding of others, I have learned that traveling beyond El Camino Real need not be frightening or traumatic but can actually be informative and exhilarating.

Nowadays rather than being gawked at, I am more likely to be approached in a museum gift shop by a curious Native American asking who "my people" are, or by a friendly Latina with the same surname wondering if we could possibly be related, or by a smiling dyke in a feminist bookstore. Through the years, whether traveling on Amtrak or on a Pacific Northwest ferry, viewing New York City from the Empire State Building's observation deck or browsing among exhibits in the Smithsonian, I have learned that people like me are all over this vast country, further beyond El Camino Real than I would ever have imagined.

Witnesses to a Revolution

Nisa Donnelly

Looking back, it was Nike's fault, or Reebok's—one of the sports-shoe companies, definitely. Or maybe we owe it all to Yuban. Either way, television definitely was the start of it.

Going to the Yucatán was Ellyn's idea. (Going to Chiapas, the poorest and most remote state in the country was, I admit, mine; but that came some weeks later.) We were watching *L.A. Law*, I definitely remember that, when the Nike commercial came on. At least I think it was the Nike commercial, maybe it was Reebok. Anyway, some overly ambitious Americans—not all that different from us, we would rationalize later—were scaling a pyramid in the jungles of Mexico. And then, not thirty seconds later, the Yuban panther growled, his eyes glowing yellow through rain-forest mist—1993 was obviously a big year for jungle settings.

"You want to go to the Yucatán for Christmas?" Ellyn was still in graduate school and I was working for a university that all but shut down over the holidays. We'd been debating the rigors of going "home" to the Midwest, although home for us has been a flat in San Francisco since 1989.

"Sure, why not?" If the options were San Francisco again, family again, or a trip to Mexico, I was choosing Mexico.

"OK." With that, we went back to staring at the television.

Three days later, I came home with two guidebooks and the number for the Mexican Tourist Board. By the end of the week, I'd become accustomed to reading sections aloud from *The Maya Route* while Ellyn cooked dinner.

We'd already decided on Mérida as a base, although we were

having more than a few problems convincing the travel agents that the city had anything resembling an international airport. "It must have an airport," I'd told one that afternoon. "The pope was just there and you can't tell me he got there by donkey cart."

The travel agent had been unmoved by my analysis of the pope's methods of transport. "The pope?" he'd echoed.

"Yes, the pope. He was in Mérida a couple of months ago—it was on the news—when he apologized for the church's role in wiping out the Mayans." I hadn't bothered to mention that there were still considerable numbers of Mayans in the Yucatán, a fact that had apparently escaped the pope's notice, as well.

"Uh-huh," said the travel agent. "Well, I still don't show any flights to . . . where was it you wanted to go in Mexico again?"

Ellyn was chopping cilantro. I remember this clearly, because she stopped midchop, little leaves sticking to the knife, when I announced my new dream destination: "Chiapas." I'd been jumping ahead in the guidebook.

"Which is . . . how far south did you say?"

I held up the map. Suddenly, it looked further than I'd imagined. Flying into Cancún and taking a four-hour ride on an air-conditioned tourist bus to Mérida was one thing. Chiapas was at least another couple hundred of miles further south. It might as well have been in Guatemala. In fact, it had been. It was one of those tracts of land that countries periodically pass back and forth. At the moment, it belonged to Mexico but borrowed much of its politics from Guatemala. We didn't know this yet, however.

Ellyn looked at the map. Just the year before she'd trekked through much of southern Europe and was adept at estimating distance and time. "Too far," she declared, and went back to chopping. I spent the next week recalculating days. We were already stretching beyond two weeks, which was our target. Seeing

Chiapas would add—what? Three days? Four? Still, I was fascinated by the idea of Palenque, rumored to be the most beautiful of the Mayan ruins, and San Cristóbal de las Casas, and the churches with their uniquely Mayan interpretation of Catholicism. Two weeks rapidly grew to three.

"If we can't go to Chiapas, then I'm staying in San Francisco," I announced finally.

Ellyn sighed.

"According to this book, the finest indigenous weavers in the world are there."

Aha! Ellyn was starting to look interested; if there's one thing she loves, it's weaving. We negotiated, then renegotiated, recalculated, and eventually settled on an itinerary that included Chiapas in the middle of the trip. I was elated. As far as I could tell, Chiapas had everything: jungles and ruins and indigenous weavers and the possibility of weird religious sites . . . and a revolution in the making, although we wouldn't find out about that until later, either. And the best part, it was easily accessible by a six-hour or so bus ride from Mérida, at least according to the guidebooks. We'd see Palenque. Be in San Cristóbal for New Year's Eve. Check out the indigenous weavers, drop by Agua Azul for a day's swimming, then back to Mérida and over to Isla Mujeres for snorkeling.

"Very cool," observed one of our friends. The year before, she'd spent her honeymoon in Cancún and she'd loaned us a video of the trip. Endless shots of her girlfriend's backside on the beaches were punctuated by an occasional view of the sea, of marketplaces, of fishermen and swimming pools and mariachi bands. "Those resorts at the beach are absolutely the best. You don't even have to change your money if you don't want to, and everybody speaks English. It's not like being in another country at all."

"We're not going to the resorts, we're just flying into

Cancún; from there we're going south to the jungle to climb pyramids," we told her.

"If I were you, I'd stay in Cancún," our friend said, convinced that we'd gone mad. "They have day trips to the pyramids." She fast-forwarded the film to shots of her girlfriend's backside going up a series of steps that might or might not have been part of a pyramid.

DEAR DIARY: PARIS IS STILL IN FRANCE

We weren't expecting the cold. That was the second shock; the first, of course, came at the sight of San Cristóbal itself. Dirty and gray. The guidebooks had promised us a "colonial jewel" and a city "reminiscent of Paris in an earlier century or Santa Fe, New Mexico." Paris of which century, we wonder. It is too hungry. Too cold. The streets of Paris and Santa Fe are not filled with barefoot Mayan women, young but with eyes looking already older than the oldest woman you've ever seen, dragging children through the streets. Too many children. Too thin. Too dirty. Eyes too desperate. Hands outstretched. "Help me, help my child." But they do not say this, at least in no language the tourists understand. They, like us, speak only enough Spanish to get by, only enough to conduct the simple business transactions of the marketplace. We do not speak Tzotzil.

"Chiapas is not Mexico." Walking these narrow streets, I hear the words of my Spanish teacher. Faced with the formidable task of teaching a half dozen San Franciscans enough of his language in eight weeks for us to survive as tourists, he would entertain us with tales of a wild ride through the mountains of Chiapas and Guatemala, sleeping in hotels with bug-infested beds for a quarter a night, trading his Hard Rock Café T-shirt for tamales. I have no gift for language, but I learned because here even Spanish is the second language. Chiapas is not Mexico. I decide he was right.

Mérida, with its cosmopolitan grace and sophistication, spoiled us. In the Plaza de la Independencia—site of the ancient Mayan city of T'ho until the Spanish came and destroyed the temples and pyramids—are Christmas lights and politics. Talk of secession. Tourism and oil and NAFTA that are sure to bring untold riches to the Yucatán, Campeche, Quintana Roo. "But what about Chiapas?" one of the men in the crowd wanted to know. The speaker's face contorted, he spat, a dull sound like bird droppings on the sidewalk. "Chiapas? They have nothing but poor people. Let Chiapas go back to Guatemala." Laughing, nodding, they ignore the American tourists with their dictionaries, their strange accents, imagine that we do not understand. They are right; we will never understand what we are about to witness.

DEAR DIARY: ON THE ROAD LESS TRAVELED

Leaving Mérida, we press south, tourists and some of the Mexicans wealthy enough to travel by the luxury buses that are a part of this country's class system. We are the only Americans. The rest must be content to stay in the resorts of Cancún, we tell each other, arrogant with our independence. First, to the ruins of Palenque, then on to San Cristóbal de las Casas for New Year's Eve. On the daylong bus trip, we talk of ruins, of jungles, of the people who by night steal into the park, the ancient city of their ancestors. "There are five hundred or so Lacandones people left," I tell Ellyn. "They do not allow themselves to be photographed. Only the men interact with tourists and at that just to sell their arrows." The guidebooks have made us walking encyclopedias of trivia.

We arrive at Palenque a few days past the winter solstice, the time when the sun appears to set into Lord Pacal's tomb, the centerpiece of the site. Not that we would be allowed to stay and witness this miracle of engineering and astrology; tourists are scuttled out long before sunset, when it again becomes the domain of the Lacandones, the white-robed, long-tressed, barefoot, jungle-dwelling people who have kept the sacred site free of overgrowth for generations. They live much as they always have, planting corn by gouging holes with sticks, hauling water from streams, casting darkly mistrusting eyes on the tourists whom they tolerate, but just barely. They are rumored to still use the site as their ancestors did on religious holidays, moonlight washing over their white robes, over the white-rocked tombs and temples. We are the intruders. We know this without any guidebook having to tell us why.

This jungle, which sprouts leaves larger than any person, which guards the secrets of a people as ancient as the land itself, is giving birth to a revolution. We do not know this yet, do not know that the revolutionaries are training here, even as we climb the Temple of the Inscriptions. All we know is that we want to come back, want to feel the peace of this place that is more beautiful than any place imaginable. Yes, we tell each other, we will go on to San Cristobál, then stop here again when we come back. When we come back.

The next morning we are again the only Americans on the bus that leaves Palenque for the more than five-hour trip required to travel fewer than a hundred miles on roads that curl like ribbons through the mountains. Eventually, we will reach seven thousand feet.

Finally grinding to a stop at a dusty crossroad village called Ocosingo, the bus waits to take on a few more passengers. I stand on a dirt street, watching a livestock auction. A few children stop to stare. *Alemana*, they speculate. No, I tell them, *Americana*. They shake their heads in disbelief. They see few American women here, apparently fewer still standing outside a bus smoking cigarettes. In the coming weeks, we will be increasingly mistaken for Germans, and we will stop correcting those who make that mistake.

Back on the bus, Ellyn rouses from a Dramamine-imposed stupor and asks, "Anything here?" No, I tell her, nothing to see, just a marketplace across the road and some men auctioning off a pig. She passes me the Dramamine. The bus lurches on. It is the next to the last day of 1993. The next time we hear of Ocosingo will be when we see newspaper pictures of boys not much older than the ones who mistook me for a German, dead in that marketplace, their blood staining the dirt and concrete.

DEAR DIARY:

WHY THEY DON'T PUT REVOLUTIONS IN GUIDEBOOKS

"When I write of this revolution," I tell Ellyn on New Year's Day, "I will say that it came with hot water." We are on the roof of our hotel, sitting next to the large solar water heaters and reduced to telling bad jokes, any jokes at all to try to break up the boredom, to dispel the fear of not knowing what will come next. She smiles, turns her face toward the sun, listening for helicopters. They have been buzzing over the hills for the last twelve hours, maybe more; we can no longer remember. They remind her of the war, she says, meaning the Vietnam footage on the evening news twenty years ago. Neither of us has ever been to Vietnam. Neither of us has ever been to a war. Before now.

"Do you think the embassy will send helicopters in to get us out? I've seen that on television," she says, "the tourists getting on helicopters." I don't answer. We are Americans, but the American embassy is far away in Mexico City. There is nothing here the Americans would want; our government would not be interested in rescuing tourists like us.

The *zócalo*, a half-block from our hotel, is filled with guerrillas who appear to be nothing more than poorly armed boys. The streets are alternately deserted and filled with terrified men and women. I do not tell her that this morning when I ventured out of the hotel's colonial courtyard, I saw a knot of men carrying a screaming woman through the streets, her leg broken, her face contorted. How had that happened? I don't know anyone to ask. The few questions I manage are met with silence and distrusting stares.

Lining the sidewalks surrounding the *zócalo*, the guerrillas watch the tourists, anxious but not afraid. How could these poor boys from the mountains have anticipated the high level of boredom tourists experience when there is nothing to see? How could they have imagined that with the shops barred, the museums locked, the churches closed that they would become the tourist attraction?

Outside the sacked city hall, where the day before we were reading announcements of plays and poetry readings, a press conference is going on. We will find out later that the main speaker is Subcommandante Marcos, the EZLN's charismatic, ski-masked leader. We come as close as we dare, careful not to disturb the local residents who have gathered to carry away city files. A couple on a nearby park bench puzzle over an upside-down map of the city's sewer system; two boys push each other through the street on a rolling desk chair. The guerrillas watch with unamused eyes. The tourists' cameras click-click and whir against the afternoon.

The women, the ones dressed in the identifying colors of the small mountain towns that gave birth to this revolution, no longer haunt the streets, surrounding tourists with their out-stretched hands, selling folk art, small weavings, dolls, resin fashioned to look like amber. Perhaps they and their children are huddled in their cardboard and stick shanties that dot the hillsides of San Cristóbal, across the highway that is closed by the revolution. The finest indigenous weavers in the world live in Chiapas, selling their art in the shops, in the market by the old convent. But the shops are closed and the market empty, save for the truly desperate.

Following the cobblestone streets, we work our way toward the marketplace. Hansel and Gretel have gone before us, leaving behind their markers of banana peels and orange skins. Mayan women dressed in the sky-blue blouses and rough black woolen skirts that identify their village as San Juan Chamula, sit in front of stalls with warm oranges and thick-skinned melons. They talk only to each other in subdued voices. They have nowhere else to go, except maybe back to their shantytown. Their village has turned them out for following the American missionaries. In their world, there is only one way to dress, one way to pray. Now they survive by selling oranges and melons, embroidered blouses, and small, finely crafted woven scarves. Some let tourists take their photographs—for a price. The world has stolen their dignity; they are desperate enough to sell bits of their souls to the cameras of pale strangers. An aging American couple, the woman in the kind of tailored linen suit that bespeaks position and power, is attempting to buy a few oranges with American cash. Worthless here. The vendor reclaims her oranges, shaking her head no. Who knows when the money changer will be open again? The husband opens his wallet displaying the greenbacks. He offers her a five, then a ten. She shakes her head again, turns away. He looks at her in disbelief. We stumble on, past the mostly closed stalls, the stench of rotting fruit rising up around us, forcing us back to the street, deserted except for tourists like us. There is no way out.

The next morning, the guerrillas are gone as silently as they'd arrived, and in their place is the Mexican army, equipped with modern American-made war toys. The soldiers are less kind, less tolerant. They hold large guns loosely. They smile at tourists. We do not smile back. We are looking for other

Americans, for answers, for a way out of this city. A low-level bureaucrat from the American embassy has finally arrived. We find him in a bookstore. "Are you Americans?" the bookstore owner asks in Spanish. The bureaucrat offers to contact our parents. And tell them what? we wonder. He does not offer us a way out of San Cristobál. There is no safe way out. The guerillas and the army are fighting in the hills—and the hills are everywhere. Some tourists have hired private cars to take them north. The road to Palenque is open, we hear. Some go, driving into the heart of guerrilla strongholds. They are the unlucky ones; they will have to run again. All of Chiapas is in a state of war. Go west to Tuxtla Gutierrez, the men who run our hotel tell us; they do not tell us how. The television cranks out endless reruns of 1960s American movies. The city is emptying of tourists, filling with journalists. We are too ignorant to be afraid.

"NAFTA," we hear whispered as we pass through the streets, "NAFTA is to blame for this." On the wall of the bank opposite the *zócalo* is what remains of the handbill, the Zapatistas' declaration of war, pasted up on New Year's morning. I translate for Ellyn in my faltering Spanish: "After five hundred years of oppression by the North Ameri" is all that is left. The rest has been torn away. "I guess that would be us," I say. We trudge the streets, careful to avoid the guns of the soldiers. In a small *tienda* I have found a saint painted on a board. Which saint, I wonder. I ask the shopkeeper, but my accent is too harsh. She misunderstands, tells me it is from a village in the mountains. I recognize the name of the village, still do not know the name of the saint. We pick through the crafts market outside the convent, but the whir of sound and color of a few days ago is hollow. An old woman approaches with a white-on-white embroidered *huipil.* Delicate, intricate, many hours of work, she tells me. I recognize the pattern on the blouse as one from the temples. The patterns pass down from generation to generation, reaching all the way back to the Mayan ancestors of more than a thousand years ago. I show her the saint, a gift for a dying friend who has found strength in God. She crosses herself and points toward the church.

Dark and rough-hewn, the floors covered with pine needles and the wax from the long white tapers used by the Mayans in prayer, the old church is cold and solemn, thick with smoke from copal and candle wax. Saints with gaunt faces and haggard eyes peer down on us. A Mayan family kneels in front of a trio of saints with bloody faces. The men pray loudly, the women sway. At the far end of one alcove is a figure of Jesus, a rope around his neck, being led by a pair of conquistadors. "Doesn't need a whole lot of translation, does it?" Ellyn asks, motioning me toward the far side of the church where, in shadows, another figure of Jesus is laid out in a glass coffin, paraffin hands crossed over its velvet-covered chest. A woman with angry eyes rolls toward us, cluck-clucking, shooing us toward the door, fanning her skirt behind us the way my grandmother herded chickens.

DEAR DIARY: WHERE DID ALL THE TOURISTS GO?

It is Wednesday, the fourth day of the revolution, the last day San Cristobál will be open. Determined to leave, we have finally found a way out thanks to a taxi driver who has brought journalists into San Cristobál and is looking for a return fare to Tuxtla.

On the highway, hundreds of tanks filled with Mexican *federales* pass us, heading toward the town we are fleeing. We are stuffed into a Volkswagen Beetle that bounces past hillsides dotted with poor villages. Mayan houses of thatch and stick, with dirt floors and no doors but built in the style of the royal cities, cluster at the bottom of steep hills. Barefoot women and children, dressed in the colors of birds and rainbows, walk along the sides of the road oblivious to the passing tanks, gathering sticks that they carry on their back. Sparse stalks of corn struggle for life on craggy hillsides. Men lounge on the steps of a public building, drawing patterns in the dirt, their white trousers and shirts shining like lost moons. There is no work for them, has not been for a long time. The finest indigenous weavers in the world sell work that takes weeks to make for pennies, sixty cents for two days' work. And those are the lucky ones, who are able to sell anything at all. "What will become of them now?" Ellyn asks. "Who will buy their weavings? How will they live?" I watch the landscape. I am trying to see it all, trying to forget nothing, trying to understand. Two women and three children follow the edge of the highway in a raggedy parade. I am a spoiled American; I have more of everything than these people will ever have. Suddenly I feel dirty and very, very cold.

We pass through another security checkpoint, our sixth in two days, but this time instead of ordering all the men off the bus, the soldiers board. Their guns slap against the torn dirty seats. Across the aisle an old woman coughs. Coughs, coughs. Tuberculosis is rampant in Chiapas. We know this, we try not to think about it. Two soldiers shine flashlights into the faces of the Mayan boys sitting in front of us, then turn their attention to the couple behind us. These are the refugees. They speak only to each other and to the soldiers when pressed. The couple behind us has two hundred pesos, they tell the soldier. How will you live? he asks. We do not hear the answer as he pushes them off the bus. We hold up American passports. The soldiers are not interested in us; they smile at our stupidity. We wait. Ten minutes pass. Then fifteen. How long will the bus wait for the couple? We strain to see, but only our own faces are visible in the dark glass. I doze, imagine I see guerrilla encampments in the mountains. Finally, the couple returns. The bus lurches on down the mountain.

The first newspapers we see are terrifying. The boys who had sat on the bus with us huddle close in the station in Villahermosa, carefully dissecting the pages before them. They read slowly, the way the near illiterate do, the way we do, piecing the words together, focusing more easily on the photographs. Color pictures of the dead in the Ocosingo marketplace; of guerrillas or maybe just those believed to be guerrillas being held in makeshift prisons, their faces bruised and bloodied; stories of villages bombed, of house-to-house searches conducted by the *federales* in San Cristóbal the day we left, of guerrillas routed from the jungle and mountains. Already, rumors are beginning to spread of torture: prisoners forced to drink urine, men suffocated when hoods loaded with hot chili powder were put over their heads, their skin burned by cigarettes, cut by knives, lacerated by pins.

They were children, we tell each other, no older than those boys on the bus. We saw the guerrillas; they were just hungry-looking kids armed with sticks and machetes and old hunting rifles held together by rope. We were in San Cristóbal on New Year's morning; we saw Subcommandante Marcos. And if that was the seat of the rebellion, if those were the elite of the guerrilla fighting unit. . . . The thought is difficult to finish. We put the newspapers away. The boys from the bus have disappeared.

DEAR DIARY: IT REALLY DID HAPPEN, DIDN'T IT?

We welcome Mérida like an old and tired friend. The streets are still garishly dressed in colored holiday lights, the beggars still huddle in the shadow of the great cathedral, the horses still clomp-clomp through the street, pulling tourists in white carriages. It is all the same—only we are different. We do not yet understand this, however.

The first hotel we try turns us away. Three days on buses have taken their toll. Seeing our reflection in the lobby mirror, I am not sure I would rent us a room, either. At the second, I try a different approach. "We just got out of San Cristobál . . . please rent us a room." The desk clerk looks skeptical, relents, and sends us to the very back room on the very top floor of his very empty hotel. He is obviously sympathetic or maybe just intrigued, but not enough to give us a front room on a lower floor, just in case. When we emerge an hour later, the dirt of the buses and the revolution spun down the shower drain, our fetid clothes tied in a plastic bag, he looks genuinely relieved. "Ahh, you look so much better," he sighs. We hadn't let him down after all.

The revolution has toughened us, scraped away the wonder. By the time we arrive back in Cancún, we no longer have patience with taxi drivers who want to overcharge us the way they would ordinary tourists, tourists who haven't witnessed a revolution. "Ha!" I tell one. "I got from San Cristobál to Tuxtla for less than you want to charge to take me to the airport." He shakes his head in disbelief. *Alemana,* he says in disgust. "No," I correct him, "*Americana.*" And when I pay him in pesos, he is convinced I have lied. After all, Americans never travel further than the big resorts and pay in greenbacks . . . that's what they love about Cancún, it's not like being in another country at all— why, you don't even have to change your money.

Mariana Romo-Carmona

Between the Andes and the Sea

One day I found myself in a land where I had been for so long the soil had a rightful claim to my bones. Thirty years in the United States, or nearly thirty, yet sometimes I still walked around this new country feeling like the adolescent girl who first arrived here. Most of the time I was a grown woman who counted the disparate parts of herself and gathered them in one integrated fold, living life consciously, purposefully—but not always.

The truth is, I am an odd kind of immigrant, or maybe a very common one. Leaving the land of my birth, I prepared for adventure in a new place, to learn a new language, and encounter a wholly different culture; gaining a new sense of existence in a world in which we have the ability to forge relationships with the land and the people who will meet us in our journey. In the mid-1960s, our family's emigration was completed when my parents, my younger sister, and I arrived in Connecticut. Our brother was born a year later. What I didn't know was that there was little that could prepare me for being an immigrant. Even so, a few years later I could feel roots growing into this new ground, friends, a kind of ease in understanding the coming of new seasons, in knowing their fragrances, their moods, and the nuances in the language of my neighbors. Meanwhile, in Chile in 1973, the hope of the people had been destroyed, the government was replaced by a dictatorship, thousands upon thousands were dying and disappearing, and my beloved land was in the grip of a horrible fate. We were exiles.

In 1996 I contemplated my journey as an immigrant—a journey that was perhaps always slated for me, like the fact that I'd grow up to be a lesbian and a troublemaker, a born outsider. In this adopted land, I became an activist, protesting and organizing against the war and nuclear power and for the rights of lesbians and gay men, of people of color, of Latinos and Latinas. I also became a writer, and perhaps this made me more keenly aware of how much I had lost in the process of just becoming myself. When I came out in 1975, I lost custody of my son. As I gained understanding of a new language and a new culture, I lost much of my hold on that with which I was born, on all that would have defined me once. The truth is that as I breached the dividing line between my forties and the rest of my life, I knew it was time to undertake a journey home.

Home, of course, is a word stuffed full of emotion for the immigrant. I have seldom been comfortable when I hear the word being used in the most ordinary contexts. "Are you going home for Thanksgiving?" I would be asked by other students who planned to travel during the holidays to the opposite coast or at least to the next town over from where we were going to school. Why would I go home? Which one? The one where I lived alone? Or the one where my parents lived, which wasn't my home and certainly wasn't theirs? Our home was six thousand miles away and we didn't celebrate Thanksgiving there.

As I plotted a course for my return, twenty-nine years, three months, and seven days after we had left, I wasn't sure that my old country was still going to be my home. But the *idea* of home still haunted me; I have always felt that if I could return to the place where I was born, something unusual would happen to me. Something astonishing, such as losing the fear of making momentous decisions, of writing with my whole heart, of living.

Maybe just that. To just live. Regain childhood. Become an adult. Just live.

For this trip, I talked to a travel agent months in advance, as I would be going during the height of the travel season and it would be hard to get reasonably priced tickets. The decision to go, finally, was easier than I thought. My lover June and I had talked about this journey ever since the dictatorship had ended and a democratic government had returned to my country. She knew everything that returning there would mean to me, had seen the photos I kept, the small mementos, had heard the stories and heard me sing the hymns of the Nueva Canción, the new song movement; she had even learned the words. And she had been part of the nostalgic talks that I'd had with another Chilean friend who had also been away for twenty-some years.

We determined that we would go on the eleventh of January, June and me, my friend, and her American lover. Somehow this little expedition party of four lesbians would pack their bags and actually make it aboard a flight bound first for Buenos Aires and then for Santiago.

On the plane, the hours began to accrue, bringing us closer to a country that was by this time a dream to me. Or a sheaf of memories, painfully blurry with time. There is a specific one that I have hoarded because it seemed to hold a clue to the recognition of myself as "a person who writes."

In this memory we are in Santiago in 1958, when I am about six years old. My mother has brought me to my future teacher's classroom in the school that she and her two younger sisters attended. Since I already know how to read, the teacher accepts me in second grade, though she looks at me doubtfully. "She's very small," she comments. "I wonder if she will be mature enough."

Life feels slow, predictable, even somewhat safe. Quietly, steadily, school becomes everything to me. It is my entire world, and my teacher is my only love next to my mother. One day, she announces that she wants us to write and gives us a task: to write a poem. A year has passed, but I have never forgotten that she was not sure whether I was mature enough to remain with her class. Now it would be unthinkable to leave, to go to another class without her and my friends. But I have also become confident, and when I hear what the assignment is, I believe that I can do it.

I write in pencil in my notebook. I am now a third grader; we know that only in the fourth grade will we be allowed to write in ink. I long for the smell of ink in the bottles and for the ink stains on my fingers that will identify me as a student who uses a fountain pen. I become distracted, and I begin to look out the window, watching a tiny sparrow flying gray and brown in the thin breeze of autumn in Santiago. I don't know what poem I will write. *Write impressions*, the teacher has said. I disregard her advice and decide to write something fantastic, a magical poem. Something tells me I can embroider with words, that I have the ability to fool with them and get them to do what I want. I don't know why. There are quite a few books in my house, and I have begun to read them all. Cervantes, Neruda, Mistral, and a number of books for children, books of adventure. *Arabian Nights*, and translations of Robert Louis Stevenson and Louisa May Alcott. No one has told me how it is possible to create with words, but I have some thoughts about this. I write some words about a fountain, water, and fairy creatures. I think it's a poem.

My deskmate cannot write her poem. She almost cries with worry and pushes her notebook to me. "Here, you write it," she says. And I do. *When the sparrow's wings close, she seems to wear a little gray overcoat*, I write in Spanish, hearing the lilt of the words in my language, the impulse of the images to take written form in my mind, on the paper, coming surely from the sharp-pointed, fragrant, graphite and pine pencil.

A few days later, another teacher comes to the class. Young and pretty, she is in charge of the school newspaper. She explains that the best poems of every class will appear in print, and my teacher tells us she is pleased that one of her girls has written a poem that has been chosen. She says my deskmate's name.

When we stopped for a layover in Buenos Aires, I had to ask myself what the hell I thought I was doing. Having slept on a plane is not the best way to ponder momentous decisions, but I was more than pondering. I was a wreck, pacing, looking again and again through the airport shops, and talking nervously with the waiter when we finally managed to sit down for some tea. I wanted him to tell me something that would at least give me a sign that I was back, so close, almost there. I asked him about certain kinds of cakes that I know they have in Argentina, little pastries called *masitas*. I had eaten them when my mother took me on a trip to Mendoza, and I never forgot how light and delicious they were. The waiter does his best. He brings us four different kinds of *pastelitos* and some comforting *Nescafé con leche*. My friends realize that from now on they're not going to get New York coffee; we are in tea country.

The sweets almost hit the spot, but not quite. They tasted like airport pastries, of course, and I don't know why I expected anything different. So there we were, sleepy, wired from the sugar, and still on the other side of the Andes. After an interminable wait, we hear our flight being called. The other passengers have dispersed; the only ones boarding now are the ones who are really going to Chile. I try to distinguish the Chileans from the visitors, and I sort of think I can. Especially if I eavesdrop on their conversations and listen for the unmistakable Chilean inflection. June gets antsy and says she can't bear the humidity in Buenos Aires, that it's worse than New York in August, and it really is. Finally, our plane takes off as the sun is setting, and it is our good fortune to be flying west over one of the most impressive mountain ranges in the world. As light sinks down over the Andes, we can see the peaks rising out of the summer snow, bathed golden at first, then deepening into blue and purple. The highest peaks are draped with clouds and it is hard to make out their shapes, but what we see is enough to make me hold my breath. I try to look for the Aconcagua, the tallest peak at over twenty-two thousand feet, but in that ghostly range of giants draped in white it hardly matters whether I've seen it or not. Night falls.

In Santiago, summer is dry. The night feels gentle and I'm no longer anxious, just hungry for day to come so I can see everything. Going through customs has a dampening effect, so that when at last I meet my aunt and my cousin, I am walking with my feet somewhat touching the ground. June and I stay with my family, and our friends depart for a cozy little hotel in downtown, to meet up with us later in our trip. My aunt has brought me a rose, and having visited New York once before, she already knows June without really knowing what she means to me.

But I haven't seen my cousin in all this time, not since she was about six and I was fourteen. We look at each other in amazement. We touch each other's faces and hair, hold each other's hands, and end up laughing at the habit each of us has of placing a right hand on the hip.

On the ride to my cousin's house from the airport, I sniff the night, looking for my life. I touch a tree and smell a leaf. No one seems to think that what I do is strange. I don't find what I am looking for until the morning, when I run outside and find the highest peaks of the Andes silhouetted, blue and lavender as always, in the hazy light. People rising early sprinkle their sidewalk with water and sweep the dust away. I tingle from head to foot, smelling that particular scent of earth in the breeze, while from far away, the aroma of eucalyptus trees stirs and mingles with my memory. A bird flies into the dark leaves of a persimmon tree, singing loudly, and I, who know little about birds, hear my adolescent voice saying, *Zorzal—That is definitely a zorzal.*

In my body that is made out of lines a line was crossed, by me or by the part of me that had been asleep. I began to feel with my whole body the experience I was living, not just experiencing with my mind what I was seeing, tasting, feeling. There was so much that was becoming unveiled for me in those few days that I didn't want to miss anything.

In the days that followed I tried to reacquaint myself with the city of my childhood. Santiago was beautiful in the early summer. Buried just underneath, though, one could sense all the sadness, the anguish, the betrayals, and the deaths brought on by the coup d'état and the dictatorship. It was impossible not to feel these things. But above all what I felt was the love for the land, the spirit of the people I was meeting. I walked with June through Santiago trying both to learn and to recover what I already knew. I had been so young when I left that it seemed the city had been lying dormant within me. As we walked, I was seized by the feeling of ghosts awakening, as if I were recalling a previous lifetime, though I had never felt that before; but I could only imagine that it must be something like what I was experiencing. I was reliving all the dusty dreams I had been having during all this time of nostalgia, when I was trying to hold on to what I knew of this country I loved so much.

I was feeling things I wouldn't have imagined. The names of the streets sometimes brought back entire conversations I must have had with my mother when I was young, or words that I must have heard or read. Bandera, Huérfanos, Catedral, la Alameda, the streets of downtown. I began to recognize buildings, *el congreso, la iglesia de San Francisco, la Universidad de*

Chile. We sat down in the Plaza de Armas and I looked around to find the bandstand. It was smaller. I didn't remember what buildings were around the plaza, but I remembered playing there on a Sunday outing when I would have gotten peanuts as a treat, or even cotton candy. After the band left, the small round enclosure became the province of children who met there for a day, an afternoon, and became lifelong friends in a still, sunny hour while the parents sat talking on a bench. I showed June where I jumped from, the edge of the stand down to the sandy path by a palm tree. Not a high drop, maybe three or four feet, but I was daring and the other children had been duly impressed. I had kept the tingling in my legs to myself, and the dull headache that came later.

We walked through some side streets; I found a church that looked so familiar I felt dizzy, and outside, I saw the vendor who had candles, silver medallions, and stamps of the Virgen del Carmen for sale. I bought a little medallion, tied with a red ribbon and held with a small safety pin, ready to attach to a baby's clothes to prevent the evil eye from affecting the child. La Virgen del Carmen is the patron saint of Chile, I explained, but the little red ribbon I suspect derives its powers from Chile's indigenous culture, always a feature of popular lore, powerful but conveniently hidden, obeying the laws of an unspoken racism.

And then we stood on a street called Moneda. From there we glimpsed *el palacio de La Moneda,* the presidential palace, with its mended wounds still visible on the wall. The scars of the coup d'état, from the day when tanks rolled on this city and young soldiers bombed their own national landmarks, closed the streets with guns drawn, shot tear gas at protestors, journalists, and people going home from work, and eventually stormed the offices where President Allende stood, where he had delivered his last broadcast to the people of a free nation, hours before he would be killed. We couldn't stand there long, the energy emanating from that spot was alive and hard, brutally painful. I wouldn't have believed that one could feel things like this if I'd been told, but there it was, enveloping our hearts until we walked away.

On my fourth day in Chile I went to my old neighborhood. June accompanied me, and I know I was brimming over with anxiety about what I would find. She had heard me describe the place, my memories of home and school, and she knew how thrilling the prospect of returning was. She shared in the excitement, bouncing the camera, watching my face for signs of recognition. We walked to my old street, I touched my old door and ran my hands along the weathered walls where I used to play. June took a photograph of me on the sidewalk where I used to roller-skate, drawing sparks with the metal wheels. Everything seemed smaller, narrower. The distance to my friends' house down the street was amazingly shorter than I remembered. I spoke with an older woman who knew everything about the place, even though she'd only been living there three years. She had been the owner of the stationery store where my mother would take me every fall to buy school supplies. I realized that she probably sold us my first fountain pen, my first bottle of ink.

Following a route that was a sort of mental map, we walked to the store where my mother and I had bought bread every day; I found it only by accident, because I had memorized the black and white tile floors. They were an Escher-like design of stair-step cubes. I used to pretend to climb them, endlessly fascinated by the optical illusion they offered. The establishment had become a hardware store, a fact that seems incongruous to me now.

And then we walked to my old school. I was anxious, afraid I would find it hopelessly changed. I didn't even want to think about whether I'd be allowed in or not, since it was the middle of summer. But my old school was the same, undergoing repairs before the new year, but basically the same building, the same iron gate. I stood before it, musing again over the fact that the walk there from my house had seemed so brief. "Ring the doorbell," said June.

Inside, the flood of images I thought were lost was almost overwhelming. The yellow tiled hallways, the windows, the yard with the same old trees, the yellow pillars now painted brown halfway up. I looked in the auditorium where I'd recited a poem once, shaking like a leaf. I found the second-grade classroom where I met my teacher for the first time, touched the chalkboard, the chalk, the desks, and the little chairs. In the third-grade classroom, images met memories and finally became three-dimensional. I was seven. My teacher passed back our poems written in pencil. Mine was corrected in red and had earned the equivalent of a C+, but I no longer understood what I had written. I didn't see my friend's paper, but she didn't seem interested in the writing or the entire incident, for that matter. My teacher was kind, and she had words of encouragement for everyone. Sitting at my desk, my heart beat with shame. I knew I would tell my teacher, I had to tell her, even if every fiber told me that the courageous thing to do would be to keep quiet and let my friend keep the poem. She deserved it; I had given it to her.

"You'd better tell her," she told me later at recess. We were sitting by the trees, eating avocado sandwiches.

I've searched my memory for years, trying to remember my friend's name, her face. I only know she was one of a group of friends, that's all. But I remember my teacher's face. She was rarely stern with us, but that day she was. She spoke quietly to the two of us, and then to me alone. "It is wrong to do someone else's work," she said. "You took away her chance to try by herself."

I think I was lost for a few minutes, as I tried to take the impression of everything with me: the trees in the yard where several hundred little girls played, the yellow tiles where we lined up grade by grade and waited to go back to our classrooms after recess. I wanted to take it all with me because now that the past was real and tangible, I had to give up my memory of it, allow it to move into the future without me. Hadn't I always known this—that there is a time when the memories of childhood are forever severed from who we are in the present—or is this only true when that childhood home is very far away? The place where my first friendships were formed, the girls I loved, the teacher I adored—these remembrances were the canvasses of an artist painting from memory, always more beautiful than in real life.

And then, in that way that amazing things happen when we don't expect them or can't possibly believe them, the director of the school came to speak with us. She was a woman about sixty years old, maybe a little older, who kept her hair dark brown and wore just a trace of lipstick. And I recognized her—she was the teacher who had selected the poems to print in the school newspaper and who presented the green scholarship ribbons to us when we earned them. She must have pinned a few of those ribbons on my school uniform, but she was also the teacher who watched the punished girls standing by the flagpole when we were bad. She must have seen me standing there many a time.

We talked for a time, Señorita Magdalena and June and I. I don't remember what we talked about, but I remember my cheeks ached from smiling. And I remember, too, how aware I was of being lesbians, of my return to this all girls' school that continues to be a haven for girlhood and learning. As we left I had the most tenuous sense that I might recover something, something that I wouldn't lose again.

My memories of Chile often seemed fantastic to me. They seemed unreal, intangible, because they came from so far away. And they had seemed frail, too, in danger of fading, of changing, very much the way my own identity has changed over the years as I've become a writer, a person. My voice, my accent and intonation, the way I move and the way I relate to people are the parts of me that are untranslatable, I have decided, and for many years, there were times I gave up being myself.

At the same time, these memories, and tales of memories, have stubbornly defined who I really was under all that I have become here, under the label of activist, of woman and feminist, of leftist and lesbian, of lesbian mother, or of radical and generic Latina lesbian writer, useful for any gathering or conference, a must-have for any panel on politics, multicultural awareness, or foods from around the world.

Yet there, walking on a street that would take us to the museum of indigenous culture, I was an unformed child, moving among my people once again in a grown woman's body with a whole history I could not explain. I couldn't explain there what I was here, nor here what I had been there. This was a journey to see what I was made of, and the only thing I had time to do was see the country. No time to think, to process anything—just to feel.

When I was a child my family went to the beach in the summer, always in groups with uncles, aunts, and cousins. There was always someone with whom I could play the game of finding the sea. As the bus descended the hills from the capital to the coast, the road turned, the woods on either side changed, the pine trees and the eucalyptus became greener, darker, more fragrant.

Even though I was a child, I knew how to feel the proximity of the sea. I enjoyed half-closing my eyes and trying to decipher the clues in the air. It is something I do even now, on other shores with other oceans. In Provincetown, as the dunes get closer, the evergreens become gray-green and thorny. Or in Rhode Island, somewhere in the heat of the summer when the road becomes bright with sun, I know I can smell the Atlantic in the breeze.

Now I know that this desire to feel the ocean comes from those days of my childhood, jumping in my seat, peering out the window of the bus to be the first one to catch a glimpse of that blue, the Pacific in the afternoon of a faded dream. Whoever said it first won, "I see it, I see it, it's there, right there!" And though I don't know why it was so important to see it first, to smell it first and breathe in the salt air like balm for the spirit, I do know that this was when I first felt I belonged to the sea, and the sea belonged to me.

When we finally got to the beaches on this trip, I drank in the sun on the sand, ran along the edges of the pines, and tried to identify every smell that enveloped me. I poked around the beach, trying to find the exact pool of crystalline water where I played when I was six. The water was cold; no one else wanted to get their feet wet, but I had to wade in right away and gaze at the sea urchins and starfish among the rocks. It was a magical beach, one of the few where the water is calm, for the Pacific, despite its name, is anything but serene—the waves are usually high and the riptide dangerous.

In Algarrobo there is everything a beach town should have. Ice cream stands where the cones are blackberry, chirimoya, and coconut. The pastry shops have fresh sweet bread every day, and my favorite summer indulgence, a sort of tart filled with butterscotch and topped with powdered sugar that inevitably gave me a stomachache when I was a kid. There is a main street where the teenagers stroll endlessly, flirting, girls walking arm in arm and boys blaring radios by the game arcade. There are shops and art fairs that sell folk art and indigenous crafts, and a cultural center where we heard a folk group composed of teachers from a neighboring town performing traditional Chilean songs from north to south. The rhythms and the melodies varied widely, spanning the culture of colonial times to the era before the dictatorship, before the advent of the protest songs of the Nueva Canción. Yet it was clear that these musicologists were politically sophisticated and that their work was committed to trying to preserve an important piece of history of the country, before that piece is lost.

After the music and as the air grew chilly, dinner by the darkened beach beckoned. We followed our noses and found a restaurant where the seafood topped the menu, and ordered *chupé de mariscos,* a sort of seafood étouffée; *caldillo de congrio,* a bouillabaisse made with the biggest fish on Chilean shores; and whatever pastry we could still manage to sink our teeth into.

Back in Santiago, we set off by train with tickets for the southern city of Concepción. Waiting in the huge old hangar of the station, I felt very young. It was as if we were still living in 1958, my family and I, with me lost in the haze of summer in Santiago, my mother a young woman wearing a pale yellow dress, carrying wicker baskets and suitcases with rounded metal reinforcement on the corners. We would board the train and wait for the lumbering engine to move with the rhythm of movie trains, the only ones I had ever seen before, huge, in black and white, full of unsuspected events trailing their departure along with the smoke that made our eyes water.

But aboard this train there were just June and me and the other passengers headed south. There were few wicker baskets, and the suitcases had been replaced by black and turquoise nylon duffel bags, the passengers wearing headphones and mirrored sunglasses. Still, the gentle rocking ride was exciting. As we left the city, I made sure to take in how it faded from view and gave way to country pastures, since this is something I would surely have missed when I was six. But I hadn't imagined the vineyards that appeared among the foothills of the Andes, the endless fields, each one swathed in myriad greens, framed by rows of poplars and pines. The little rambling houses were crowned by fences with purple bougainvillea and more grape arbors than I could possibly savor with my eyes, and here and there a fat brown horse grazed alone.

When we got hungry and the train porters walked by in their white jackets offering ready-made sandwiches and beverages, we unwrapped the provisions my cousin had packed for us, just the way our mothers had always done: hard-boiled eggs, a salt shaker, fresh bread and meat for sandwiches, ripe peaches and apricots guaranteed to make juice run down our arms. We ate everything in the golden afternoon as the train sped through the vineyards, fields of corn, farms, mountains, rivers. Other Chileans looked politely at our tea and smiled. They were now too sophisticated to eat food from home on the train, buying theirs in the bar car.

I'd fallen asleep before we got to Chillán, the little town where my grandmother was born and where the earthquake happened in 1936. I hadn't heard the announcement that we wouldn't be stopping there long. The train pulled in for just five minutes, not enough time for me to run out and try to recognize the station where I'd seen the bread vendors coming up to the windows of the train, fresh loaves wrapped in cloth, small baskets filled with freshly baked empanadas, the aroma intoxicating the children and the parents of so long ago. I still saw them there as we pulled away.

Because of what my mother told me, I own the memory of the earthquake in Chillán in 1936. In the south of Chile, my grandmother is living with her three older children—my mother, my uncle Chacho, and my aunt Lorena. The youngest is three, and my mother is about seven. My grandfather is far away, in Santiago, and my grandmother is working hard during the day, exhausted at nights. The tremor begins suddenly, in the dark; it rises to a crescendo, a disaster devastating Chillán and towns for kilometers around. My grandmother awakens and thinks of the children sleeping in the bed next to hers. Before she can move, a beam crushes her, burying her in the debris of walls and roof. She gets up though, tearing a gash in her back as she lifts the beam off herself, and she reaches the children's bed. She pulls my mother out, and the little girl pulls her brother and sister out through the tumbling house. My aunt Lorena shouts in her three-year-old voice, *Who the fuck is throwing rocks at my house!* The four make it to safety, and they wait for dawn under the standing door frame. My mother remembers the smoke, the ruins, and as day approached, the door frames standing like skeletons in the twilight, the only part of a house that never falls down in an earthquake.

When my grandfather eventually locates his family, they move to Santiago to a quiet house, big enough for the children and for a garden. One central garden wall is built of thick, sturdy adobe, meant to last. A trellis bearing purple bougainvillea is attached to it, and my grandmother knows it will never fall down. My uncle Chacho will remember this all his life, telling his children that it will never fall, even in an earthquake. The bougainvillea is my grandmother's pride; it blooms luxurious every spring, and by the time I am the first grandchild playing in the garden, I too know that this is the safest spot in the world.

I still cannot describe all I saw, all that was given back to me on this trip. But I can rattle off the thousands of impressions that tumbled onto me, which I attached carefully to every part of my being—they would not all have fit if I'd tried to absorb them only with my mind. I tasted blackberry jam in my aunt's kitchen and wept, not because of the riotous taste of the blackberries exploding in my mouth but because she had shown me the door she had kept after the house fell down in the earthquake of 1985. In Santiago's central market I feasted on seafood and fruit, and when I finally sat down to have tea with my favorite bread, I made everyone laugh by asking for a moment of silence before I tasted it. I met cousins and their children for the first time. I was embraced by people whose entire life spanned the thirty years I'd been gone. In the plaza, I sat quietly counting the members of a new generation who'd been born during a dictatorship. I saw the scars in the buildings that were bombed during the coup d'état. I averted my eyes whenever I saw a police officer.

I never asked my cousins how they survived in a country at war. They never asked how one survives without a country. We looked at each other a great deal, searching for ourselves, I realize. Two of my women cousins sat with me with their children in the neighborhood park. Their brothers, my cousins, stood by, listening. We were telling stories. My uncle Chacho took a photo of all of us. My younger cousins had never heard the story of our grandmother in the earthquake of 1936, and asked me to tell it. The story was all the more important now, since our grandparents are dead and Aunt Lorena also died two years ago. Her daughter received this story as a gift. "The wall with the bougainvillea never did fall down in the earthquake of 1985," said Tío Chacho. "It was torn down to build the new house."

His daughter nodded. "It was the safest place in the house," she said. "I always played there, trying to climb up the trellis."

"And I, too," said our other cousin. "I ran there with my little brother in '85 and sat under the bougainvillea, holding onto the tree and the wall."

"We were scared," said her brother, now a young man of nineteen.

I stood silent for what seemed an eternity, and another moment lingered, unhinged from time as it had in my former classroom. Today, I feel as though I'm still there, though I'm here. Somehow, I feel parts of myself that I thought were lost coming back to me. I began to feel this as I traveled, my voice returning, the tone of my voice, my movements, the way I ask questions, the way I give things. One night, driving down a dirt road as the sun lingered in the summer sky, I felt the certain knowledge that the heavens are closer to the earth in the south of Chile. I don't know where I heard this, perhaps in a song, but as we covered the terrain, the wide expanse of yellow fields darkening in the night, the gigantic pines reaching solidly up into the evening sky, I felt I had every right to claim that this was so. The heavens were right there above our heads, touching my heart. And I was so glad to be home.

I woke up each day of our seventeen days there with another certainty: that I belonged somewhere, that I would be understood when I spoke, that I moved and talked and sang like many people around me. I felt as though my human envelope, encasing my features, had been returned to me; it was one that was uniquely mine, one that fit my temperament and the way I moved in the world.

There aren't many things we can bring with us from our journeys, especially knowledge. Most of the knowledge we carry about us like a bunch of fragrances tied together with memory. It gets stirred up now and then, and the distances of time become meaningless, the same way physical distances become meaningless in a journey. Or perhaps not like that at all. What I think I know is that a journey can help us to learn the things we should have known by standing still.

As we flew back east over the Andes, the sun was going in the opposite direction; everything is relative. I was so tired, I forgot to have my usual moment of sheer fright when I realize that we're a bunch of helpless people sardined together in a flying vessel with very thin metal walls. I had my face pressed against the window, trying to see every snowy peak and every blue lake hidden in the mountain ranges. The view is astonishing—almost enough to cure any neurosis about leaving or staying and the impossibility of living in two places at once, of living two lifetimes at once.

But that is what I'd wanted from this journey when I started. To find that my leaving never happened. To see that I had never lost any part of myself. But the only things I have kept with me from this trip are those that have probably accompanied me through all the years of absence. The light on the mountains, the sun setting on the vineyards as the train speeds by. The knowledge that there are people who sound like me, who sing and laugh like me, and that in that faraway south, the earth really is closer to the sky.

LUCY JANE BLEDSOE is the author of the novel *Working Parts*, winner of the 1998 American Library Association Gay/Lesbian/Bisexual Award for Literature, and of *Sweat: Stories and a Novella*, a Lambda Literary Award Finalist. Her work has appeared in *Fiction International, New York Newsday, Ms.* magazine, *Aethlon, Northwest Literary Forum*, and in many anthologies.

REBECCA BROWN is the author of seven books of fiction, most recently, *The Dogs: A Modern Bestiary* (City Lights, 1998). Her work has been awarded the Boston Book Review Award, the Lambda Literary Award, the Pacific Northwest Booksellers Award, and a Washington State Governors Award. Her writing has been widely anthologized in both the United States and Great Britain and translated into Danish, Norweigian, German, Japanese, and Dutch. She has lived in Spain, England, and Italy, and now makes her home in Seattle.

DONNA ALLEGRA writes fiction, essays, and poetry. Her writing has been included in *Hers: Brilliant New Fiction by Lesbians, Queer View Mirror 2, Queerly Classed—Gay Men & Lesbians Write about Class, Does Your Mama Know?—An Anthology of Black Lesbian Coming-Out Stories, Girls: An Anthology, Mom,* and *Hot and Bothered—Short Short Fiction of Lesbian Desire.*

JUDITH BARRINGTON lives in Portland and is the director of the Flight of the Mind Writing Workshops for Women. Her most recent book is *Writing the Memoir: From Truth to Art* (Eighth Mountain Press, Portland).

TERRI DE LA PEÑA has been publishing her work since 1988. She has written the novels *Margins*, *Latin Satins*, and the forthcoming *Faults*. Her fiction and nonfiction is regularly taught in Chicana/o Studies, women's studies, and lesbian and gay studies college courses. She lives in Santa Monica, California.

NISA DONNELLY is the author of *The Bar Stories: A Novel After All* (1989), which won the 1990 Lambda Award for Lesbian Literature, and *The Love Songs of Phoenix Bay* (1994), both from St. Martin's Press, and the editor of *Mom* (1998), an anthology from Alyson Publications. She lives in northern California.

MARIANNE DRESSER has published stories and essays in several anthologies including *Tomboys!*, *Queer View Mirror*, *Portraits of Love: Lesbians Writing about Love*, *Food: A Taste of the Road*, and *The Road Within: True Stories of Transformation*. She is the editor of *Buddhist Women on the Edge: Contemporary Perspectives from the Western Frontier*. She lives in Oakland, California, with her canine companion and fellow road-tripper, Bodhi.

MARGARET ERHART is the author of three novels: *Unusual Company*, *Augusta Cotton*, and *Old Love*. Her essays have appeared in the *New York Times*, the *Christian Science Monitor*, and in several anthologies. She lives in Truro, Massachusetts, and teaches creative writing in the Truro elementary school.

SONJA FRANETA works as a Russian translator and English as a Second Language instructor. She coordinated the first Siberian Queer Film Festival in 1996 in Tomsk. She has published in the *Harvard Gay and Lesbian Review*, *Lambda Book Report*, the *Advocate*, and the *Moscow Guardian*. She lives on a boat in the San Francisco Bay Area.

SARAH GROSSMAN has been published in the anthology, *Beginnings*, edited by Lindsey Elder, and in the *NW Gay & Lesbian Reader*. She has traveled extensively throughout South and North America, and as of late has been traveling to early days of the American West through the stories of the elderly patients she cares for as a physical therapist. She is appreciative of the supportive literary community in Seattle where she lives.

SARAH JACOBUS's essays and short stories have appeared in *Sojourner, Sinister Wisdom, Bridges,* and anthologies including *Hers: Contemporary Fiction by Lesbian Writers.* She is Coordinator of Literary Programs at PEN Center USA West in Los Angeles and a longtime activist in the movement for a just peace between Israel and the Palestinians.

AUDRE LORDE (1934–1992)—writer, activist, and educator—authored many books of fiction, essays, and poetry, most notably *From a Land Where Other People Live,* nominated for the National Book Award (1974), *Zami: A New Spelling of My Name,* from which the piece included in this collection was selected, and *Coal,* a collection of poetry published in 1976. In 1991 she was bestowed the Walt Whitman Citation of Merit for her poetry.

CAROLE MASO's works include *Ghost Dance* (1986), *The Art Lover* (1990), *Ava* (1993), *The American Woman in the Chinese Hat* (1994) —from which the piece in this collection was taken—*Aureole* (1996), and *Defiance* (1998). Currently she is a professor of English at Brown University.

GERRY GOMEZ PEARLBERG's new book of poems is titled *Marianne Faithfull's Cigarette* (Cleis, 1998). Her anthology *Queer Dog: Homo/Pup/Poetry* (Cleis, 1997) received a 1998 Firecracker Award for Poetry. Her travel writing recently appeared in *Travelers' Tales: A Dog's World.*

SUSAN FOX ROGERS is the editor of several anthologies including *Another Wilderness: Notes from the New Outdoorswoman, Solo: On Her Own Adventure,* and *Alaska Passages: Twenty Voices from above the 54th Parallel.*

MARIANA ROMO-CARMONA is the author of *Living at Night,* a lesbian novel set in the late 1970s. Her work has appeared in *Compañeras: Latina Lesbians, Beyond Gender and Geography, Mom, Pil-*

low Talk, and *Queer 13.* In 1991, she received the Astraea Foundation's Lesbian Writers Award. She was coeditor of *Colorlife!* magazine, *Queer City, Cuentos: Stories by Latinas,* and *Conditions.* She now teaches in the MFA program at Goddard College.

REBECCA SHINE lives in Portland, Oregon. This is her first publication.

LINDA SMUKLER is the author of two collections of poetry: *Normal Sex* (Firebrand Books) and *Home in Three Days: Don't Wash,* a multimedia project with accompanying CD-ROM (Hard Press). She won the 1997 Firecracker Alternative Book Award in Poetry and has been a finalist for the Lambda Book Awards. She has received fellowships in poetry from the New York Foundation for the Arts and the Astraea Foundation and has also won the Katherine Anne Porter Prize in Short Fiction from *Nimrod* magazine. She is coeditor, with Susan Fox Rogers, of *Portraits of Love.*

EVELYN C. WHITE is a visiting scholar in Women's Studies at Mills College in Oakland, California. She is editor of *The Black Women's Health Book* and author of *Chain Chain Change: For Black Women in Abusive Relationships.* Her official biography of Alice Walker is under contract with W.W. Norton.

BARBARA WILSON's books include the novel *If You Had a Family* and the memoir *Blue Windows: A Christian Science Childhood,* winner of the 1998 Lambda Literary Award for Best Lesbian Autobiography and nominated for the PEN Center USA West Creative Nonfiction award. She lives in Seattle.